Her quest can end in longing
. . . or in fulfilled ecstasy.

Anne Sinclair has been haunted by visions of a handsome black-haired warrior all her life. His face invades her dreams and fills her days with passionate longing. So the beautiful laird's daughter leaves her remote Scottish castle, telling no one, to search for the man called Stephen—a man she does not know but who fights in war-torn England, a place she has never seen.

Stephen Harrington, Earl of Langlinais, never expected to rescue this unexplained beauty from the hands of his enemy. And yet, when their eyes first meet, he feels from the depths of his soul that he should know her . . . that he needs to touch her, and to keep her by his side forever. For unknown to both, they are in the center of a centuries-old love . . . a love that is about to surpass their wildest dreams.

Avon Romantic Treasures by
Karen Ranney

My Beloved
My Wicked Fantasy
Upon a Wicked Time

If You've Enjoyed This Book,
Be Sure to Read These Other
AVON ROMANTIC TREASURES

The Bride of Johnny McAllister *by Lori Copeland*
The Duke and I *by Julia Quinn*
Happily Ever After *by Tanya Anne Crosby*
To Tempt a Rogue *by Connie Mason*
The Wedding Bargain *by Victoria Alexander*

Coming Soon

The Dangerous Lord *by Sabrina Jeffries*

KAREN RANNEY

My True Love

An Avon Romantic Treasure

AVON BOOKS ◆ NEW YORK

AVON BOOKS, INC.
An Imprint of HarperCollins*Publishers*
10 East 53rd Street
New York, New York 10022-5299

Copyright © 2000 by Karen Ranney
Inside cover author photo by Susan Riley Photography
Published by arrangement with the author
Library of Congress Catalog Card Number: 99-95332
ISBN: 0-380-80591-X
www.harpercollins.com

First Avon Books Printing: February 2000

AVON TRADEMARK REG. U.S. PAT. OFF. AND IN OTHER COUNTRIES, MARCA REGISTRADA, HECHO EN U.S.A.

Printed in the U.S.A.

WCD   10   9   8   7   6   5   4   3   2   1

To Eura West

*A woman of great moral courage
who taught me to love learning
and how to be brave*

My True Love

Prologue

Dunniwerth Castle, Scotland
January, 1629

Is she going to die, Betty?"
The child, Anne, stirred in her bed. The low murmurs summoned her from sleep. At first she thought it was the distant rumble of thunder. But it wasn't an oncoming storm, only a soft impassioned whisper that seemed to brush against her cheek. She turned and cuddled into the soft down pillow. There was warmth beneath the covers and safety within this room. But outside the chamber, the world was a bitterly cold place as Dunniwerth shivered beneath a mantle of snow. The moon waned, the chill air frosted the lips and made painful the breath.

"Oh, my little love, I do not know. But I must go and be with her now. You must be strong and brave, Stephen." A faint scream punctuated the words.

"I will, Betty."

Anne was enticed into awareness by the sound

1

of a boy's voice. Young, still, with a hint of what it might be when he grew to manhood. She rubbed her fists against her eyes, then blinked them open and yawned. It was dark, perhaps even midnight, when the world should be shadowed and still. Instead, there were people in her room.

Anne sat up and peered through the opening of the bed hangings at the foot of the bed. There was no one there. Her parents slept on the other side of the castle, their chamber reached through a long and wide hallway that loomed with shadows and drafts.

It was only the edge of a dream, she told herself, and lay back against her pillow, wrapping her arms around it.

"Please. Do not let her die."

She blinked and sat up again. A frown marred her eight-year-old forehead as she scrambled to the side of the bed. She pulled open the hangings but there was no one there. She slipped from the bed, made a face as her bare feet touched the cold wooden floor, then pulled the extra wool blanket from the foot of the bed. Wrapping herself in it, she scurried to the window.

She had to stand on tiptoe in order to open the latch. The shutter opened silently on oiled hinges. From here she could see the moonlit outline of a sentry on Dunniwerth's square tower, his breath a whisper of white against the dark sky. But no one stood on the walk outside her window. She closed the shutter and darted to her chamber door.

She drew it open, peered outside. The hallway was empty, save for a sentry seated on a stool near her parents' door. She lifted her hand in a wave, but he did not respond. Hamish was asleep again.

It was only a dream.

She was Anne Sinclair, the only child of Robert Sinclair, laird of Dunniwerth. She was very much her father's daughter, and he highly prized courage. For that reason, she always pretended not to be afraid of storms, and dared herself to touch bugs. Now she pushed aside the bed hangings and slipped into her bed again, huddling beneath the covers. But instead of laying down and pulling the blanket over her head, which was what she dearly longed to do, she scooted along the soft feather mattress until her back was against the carved headboard. Her arms went around her blanketed knees as she stared into the chilled darkness.

It was only a dream. Just like a storm, it had passed. *There is nothing to be afraid of, Anne.*

"I will be very good if you let her live. I'll not go to Langlinais, and I'll be more diligent with my Latin. I'll try to like my father. Only, please, let her live."

A voice, not her own. The sound of a young boy's entreaty to God.

She knelt up on the bed and clenched her fists together, hid them beneath her arms.

Ian told her that ghosts liked to frighten young girls. But Ian was a ten-year-old bully who liked to frighten her.

They wait until you're asleep, Anne, and then creep up to the side of your bed, all soft and silent-like. If your foot falls over the edge, they gnaw on it.

They know if you've disobeyed and come to punish you.

Ghosts would like you, Anne. You've eyes like a puppy.

She should waken her mother. She would come into the bed with her, reassure her with a soft voice. But Anne was eight, not a bairn.

Was it Ian, come to play a trick on her? Her eyes darted around the room. Her father would not take kindly to anyone invading the sleeping chambers of Dunniwerth, let alone a boy who had made her life miserable ever since she could remember. He was a bully, was Ian, and she tried to ignore him when she could.

"Please, God. Do not let her die."

Anne clenched a fist tight against her mouth until her teeth bit against her knuckles. There, in front of her, at the end of the bed, the air seemed to waver, turning silvery along the curved edges. It looked not unlike one of the bubbles escaping from the laundry tubs on wash day, gliding on the air and rising as high as the treetops around Dunniwerth.

But it wasn't wash day. She was at Dunniwerth on a Monday night in January. All these things she repeated to herself even as the bubble expanded.

A boy sat on the edge of a bed.

Suddenly it was silent in the room. The faint screaming had stopped. The boy brushed the backs of both hands against his cheeks as the door opened and a tall woman entered. Her apron was spotted with blood, her brown hair damp from sweat.

"There, now, I knew I'd find you still here," she said gently.

The boy looked up at her, a look of concern on

his face. "Is Mother all right, Betty?" There was a quaver to his voice.

"Have you seen nothing of your father, then?" the woman asked.

He shook his head.

"It's all well and good then," she said, wiping her hands on her apron, "that he's stayed in London."

Betty knelt on the floor before the boy, reached out with large, red-knuckled hands to touch his shoulder.

"Your mother's gone to God, Stephen, just as we all must one day. She's taken your baby brother with her."

She brushed back his black hair when he said nothing. "Such things sometimes happen, my dear boy. Women do not always survive childbirth. It is the way of the world."

Betty cupped his cheek, smiled gently into his face. He only bent his head, but Anne could see that his hands were clasped into fists on either side of him. A moment later, the woman left the room.

"I don't want her to be with God," Stephen whispered. "I want her to stay with me."

Tears fell down his face, unchecked. As she watched, Anne felt a tear slide down her own cheek.

What would she do if her mother died? Even the thought of it made her hurt.

Anne could not bear to see the boy's silent grief. It seemed so much worse because he was alone. She stretched out her arms to him, as if she could pierce the bubble that separated the two of them. If she could be with him it would be better.

"Don't cry, Stephen," she said, her voice a chilled whisper in the wintry night. "Please, don't cry."

Her hands stretched out imploringly, palms up. As if she expected him to put his hand on hers and pull her through the silvery mist. She wanted to touch him, to help him.

Nothing happened, even as she wished it with all her heart. She could hear the sounds of his tears, felt them on her own cheeks. Felt, too, the horrible gray pain surrounding him.

It hurt, this grief. More than anything she'd ever felt. As if she cried inside, too, but those tears were hot.

One moment he was there, the next he was gone. The bed hangings were simply bed hangings, not a giant bubble. The ceiling was straight and flat, not curved. The only silvery shimmer was the moonlight filtering into the room from between the shutters.

Anne sat back against the headboard and studied the shadows around her. There was nothing there, nothing but soft silence. Even the sentries outside on the walls seemed to be mindful of the sleeping occupants of Dunniwerth.

Her hands clenched on the edge of the sheet as she brought it up to her face.

She stared into the darkness, certain of only one thing. It had not been a dream. Her tears were proof enough. That, and the aching emptiness she felt inside.

The loch bordering Dunniwerth land was not large; Anne could see its dimensions clearly from her chamber window. The island in the middle of it was mostly overgrown, a place of trees and green shrubbery.

The island had always been forbidden to her. Up until this moment she'd never questioned such a dictate. Nor had she dreamed of disobeying it. This morning, however, she sat in the flat-bottom boat and pushed herself away from the small dock. It took her some time to figure out how to use the oars, but finally she did.

This is wrong, Anne. You should not do this. Father will be angry. The admonitions accompanied the journey, but they made no difference. She had to see the wise woman. She had to know.

She reached the island finally just as her palms, reddened and sore, began to hurt. Placing the oars in the bottom of the boat, she jumped onto the shore at a place that looked to be well trod. There was no dock as at Dunniwerth, only another small boat tied to a post embedded in the earth. She tied the rope of hers to the same stake and followed a path that led away from the shoreline.

A few moments later Anne came to a clearing. In the middle of it was a tidy cottage. The thatch was so thick upon the roof that it draped down the walls, shading the small structure before touching the ground and blending into the grass. It was as if the cottage were part of the earth itself. A meandering path set in a necklace of smooth stones led the way to the front door, now ajar.

The old wise woman was said to be privy to all manner of knowledge. She could reduce a boil simply by looking at it. Or ease an aching limb by the touch of her hand. Too, she was known for the mixtures that eased a winter's cough and the bitter tea that soothed a bellyache. But most of all, she could see inside a person's heart and divine the future. Anne had heard some girls whispering about having their fortunes told.

This pleasant-looking, mushroom-shaped cottage did not appear to be a place of mystery but one, rather, of laughter. From somewhere came the sound of singing, a tune so light that it urged her closer.

As Anne neared the door, the song ceased. Inside, a shadow turned, came toward the door, was bathed in a shaft of sunlight.

Hannah, the wise woman, was neither old nor frightening. Her face bore a type of sweetness not unlike that of Anne's mother. Her smile was coaxing, gentle, her eyes the color of a summer sky. Her blond hair was wound into braids and sat upon her head like a crown. She'd adorned the coronet with tiny blue and white flowers. The dress she wore was a simple one, flowing to her ankles and topped with a spotless apron.

She stood quiet and still with her hands folded together at her waist, a tall, slender woman who bore Anne's wondering inspection with a simple grace.

"Did your father send you?" Even her voice was different from what Anne had expected. It seemed crafted of small bits of melody.

Anne shook her head and dared a word. "No." She looked away, then back at the woman, who stood motionless before her.

"Then why have you come? To have your future told?"

Anne could not frame the answer. It was something more important than the future that she wished to learn.

"Give me your hand, then," Hannah said kindly.

Anne slowly extended her hand and placed it in the wise woman's. Hannah looked down at the palm. Her smile never faltered as she studied it.

"You will have a long and prosperous life. You will be happy all your days."

The words tumbled from Anne's lips before she could catch them. "Am I a witch?"

The smile disappeared from Hannah's face, and once again there was the impression of stillness.

"Why would you think that?"

"I see things," Anne whispered. Visions that made her hurt, they were so real.

Hannah stepped aside, a wordless invitation, and Anne slowly entered the shadowy cottage. It was small and tidy, with a scent of spice in the air. A rack of hardening candles sat near the lone window. From somewhere came the chirp of a bird, and she finally located the sound coming from a wicker cage along the far wall. A sparrow sat at the bottom, his wing wrapped with a length of cloth.

"He'll be fine in a week or two. He flew into my door. Didn't you, little one? I think he was trying to impress a lady bird."

Hannah reached out and placed her hand upon Anne's head, the fingers warm against her scalp. The other hand tipped up Anne's chin. Her blue eyes softened with some emotion Anne could not discern. It was not anger, nor was it pity. It looked not unlike her mother's glance when she'd done something well, pride mixed with love.

"What sort of things do you see, Anne Sinclair?"

"How do you know my name?" Fear sat like a cold and solid thing in her stomach.

Hannah's smile broadened. "You have your father's eyes and the color of his hair."

"Will you tell my parents that I've come here?" She stepped away from the wise woman, trying to hide her fear.

"If you do not wish me to, I shall not."

"They would not understand." Silence, while she met the woman's gaze. "Please do not tell them. My mother would cry and my father think me evil."

"Evil?" The word seemed to hang in the air between them, drifting there in the silence. Hannah's hand felt cool as she reached out and cupped Anne's cheek.

"I must be," she said softly. To want to be at a place she had never seen, with a boy she did not know. But when the visions came, they seemed to take her from Dunniwerth, and make her wish with all her heart not to be here. To be, instead, with him. Wasn't that evil?

"Then tell me, Anne. Tell me what you see and why you think yourself evil."

Silence while Anne wondered how to frame the words. Then she realized it did not matter how she spoke them. The wise woman would either believe her or she wouldn't.

Twice more she'd seen pictures of the boy, Stephen, in her mind. Just before sleep he came, until she could almost believe it was a dream.

"I see a boy," she said, reaching into the wicker cage with one finger. The bird uttered a sharp little chirp of alarm, then subsided. He did not flee from her gentle touch upon his head, but instead seemed almost to lean into it. "A boy named Stephen."

She turned and looked at Hannah. "I feel like I know him." *As if he was my very best friend.*

Hannah went to a jar, filled two tumblers from it, then placed them on the table. Sitting on one chair, she smiled and gestured to the other.

"Come," she said, "share some cider with me. It comes from Dunniwerth fruit."

Anne pulled her fingers free of the cage, held them out as if they belonged to someone else. They still trembled, and she curled them close to her palms.

She sat opposite the wise woman, taking a piece of warm bread when the plate was held out to her.

"I am a witch, aren't I?" she asked. The words were whispered, as if she could not bear to speak them aloud. She did not look at Hannah. If she did, the wise woman would see tears in her eyes, and a Sinclair did not weep in front of a stranger. "I cannot be a good one. I can't see the future like you. I know no spells." She traced a finger along the scarred wooden tabletop. "Is there no tea I could drink, no herbs I might take? Are there no words you could say over me to take this away?"

"I am no witch, Anne," Hannah said, her voice kind.

Anne glanced up at her, blinking rapidly.

"Young women come to me to have their futures told, and I speak the words they want to hear. In truth, their destinies are their own. But I cannot tell the future and I have no potions."

Hannah placed her hand on Anne's. "I don't

think you're a witch, Anne Sinclair. If you were a witch, there would be other signs. What have you done that harmed another?"

"I lost the brooch my mother gave me," Anne confessed, staring down at the table.

"That is carelessness, not rancor," Hannah said with a kind smile. "Who have you bedeviled?"

Anne thought of Ian and his taunts. If she were truly a witch, she might have silenced him. Turned him into a spider, just like the ones he liked to throw at her.

She shook her head. "But Ian says there are witch finders about," Anne whispered.

"Not at Dunniwerth, Anne Sinclair."

She nodded. That much was true.

Hannah reached out and tipped her chin up. She blinked, but then forced herself to meet the wise woman's eyes. "You are not a witch, Anne. Do you believe me?"

She wasn't completely sure that she did. But she'd been raised to respect her elders, to listen to their words and heed their instructions. So she nodded her head and made herself smile.

Chapter 1

Dunniwerth Castle, Scotland
March, 1644

Anne tied the rope to the post erected for just such a purpose, then reached into the bottom of the boat for her basket.

She and Hannah had become friends in the fifteen years since a frightened child had gathered her courage and ignored myth, legend and the dictates of a father she adored.

As Anne had feared, her original journey across the loch had been discovered. Her father had, surprisingly, not prevented her visits to the wise woman. However, he had insisted that she learn to swim the loch, and be taught in the proper manner of rowing the small skiff.

Anne took her short cut through the trees, glancing at the odd circular building in the clearing as she did so. She'd discovered it on her third visit to the island. Once a year she and Hannah tended to this place, removing the weeds, straightening the stones that lay in front of the building. It seemed

13

the proper thing to do. The small structure with its arched doorway and elaborately carved keystone looked to have once been a chapel. And the gravestones were sad markers that turned the clearing into a place of reverence.

Anne stepped through the opening in the scraggly bushes, past the large stone in the shape of a boot. Still further up a small incline, and she was there, the path to Hannah's door more worn but just as inviting as it had been all those many years before.

"You are late," Hannah said as she entered, her smile taking the sting from her words.

"You say that every time I come," Anne said, placing her basket on the table. "Just as I refute it."

"I am older than you. You are supposed to give me respect, not arguments."

Anne smiled at her friend. This, too, was a constant complaint. "You would dislike it if I conceded every point to you, Hannah. You would then have no one with whom to debate."

Hannah laughed, the gentle sound of it cascading through the cottage.

"You know me too well, Anne."

Anne smiled, placed her basket on the table. "I have the flour you wished, Hannah, and a bit of honey from the cook. She says that she will take a few of your candles in trade."

"Will she?" A raised eyebrow accompanied the remark.

"You know, of course, that she sells them," Anne said, glancing at her friend. The years had been kind to Hannah. There were few white strands among her blond hair, and her face showed its lines only in the bright sunlight. At this moment, however, there was a furrow on her forehead. A precursor to irritation. She'd been the brunt of it too many times as a child not to know the sign.

Hannah nodded. "I've heard as much."

"Why, then, do you not confront her?"

"There are some situations that are better left alone, Anne."

"Because you never come to Dunniwerth?"

Hannah glanced at her. It was a subject rarely raised between them. Anne's curiosity occasionally bubbled beneath good manners and the empathy she felt for the older woman. Even as a child she'd known that there were some topics that made Hannah uncomfortable. Today, however, the answer was important. Not solely because of a cook with trickery on her mind.

"Your loyalty to me is admirable, Anne. But it is a trifling matter." Hannah turned away, busied herself with checking the rising of her dough.

Anne said nothing, only stared down at the surface of the table. The wood was scarred, and a few marks had been caused by her own youthful exuberance.

She walked to the lone window in the cottage, looked out over the clearing. It was a peaceful place, this glade. A friendly place to spend a life. Still, she could not help but wonder if it had been enough. But that was not a question she could ask. Instead, she spoke of other things, circling the true reason for this visit for a few moments.

"I saw him again last night," she said. Her voice did not betray how deeply the vision had moved her. She stood still and waited, however, for Hannah's words.

"Your Stephen?"

Anne nodded.

"It has been a while since the last time. I had hoped he would be gone for good."

Anne glanced over her shoulder. Hannah was looking at her, the frown hinted at now fixed in place.

"I remember when you were a child and terrified of him. When did it change?"

"I was never terrified of Stephen, Hannah," she said with a smile. "Only of what was happening to me." She'd seen him often enough over the years, a friend who'd visited her in the moment just before sleep.

Anne stared out at the view before her. A clearing, a small knoll of land surrounded by large trees. The day was chilly, spring was on the horizon but not yet here. There had been fog upon the loch this morning. Some days it wreathed the small cottage in a cloudlike miasma. She held her hands tight at her waist.

It might have been easier to have been granted the ability to hear thoughts or predict the future. She might have turned her skills to warning people of their fate, to issuing cautions. A child birth could be predicted, a marriage foretold, a crop saved. But what she saw was of no use to anyone.

Her visions were like looking through a window just as she did now. Only this view was of Stephen living his life. She could not choose what scenes she might see. Nor had she any knowledge of when the window might open. At times she yearned to see him. But the visions came when they willed, not when she wished.

She'd been captivated by the small glimpses into a life so alien from her own. He lived in a castle so unlike Dunniwerth that it had enchanted her. Langlinais. Even the sound of it seemed exotic. She had watched him racing over the hills on his black stallion and seen him in quiet times when he sat and sketched the castle. She had even seen London through his eyes and felt his wonder at seeing the port so filled with ships.

Hannah spoke from behind her. "Pay attention to those men who pay court to you, Anne, not someone in your mind."

The words were like small pinpricks. Little wounds that Anne ignored. They had been said too many times.

"Sentiments that echo my mother's words, Hannah. Is this mania to get me wed because my birthday will be soon?"

"You are three and twenty. It is time."

Anne nodded. Another statement she'd heard often in the last few months. Not one of the various suitors her parents had suggested to her was without charm. Each was possessed of some attribute, some quality that made him acceptable. None of them drank to excess. Each came from good family. They were all able to provide for her and any children who would be born to them. But they did not have eyes the shade of midnight. Or a face so strong and vital that she recalled it even in her dreams.

"Have you ever wanted something so much,

Hannah, that you would have given everything you owned for it?"

"What would you wish for, Anne Sinclair, that you are not provided?"

To touch him.

Last night's vision had been the strongest of all. Stephen had stood in a tunnel of darkness, shadows of gray and black swirling around him. His hand had been outstretched as if, after all these years, he could finally see her. He seemed to implore her. He spoke, but his words were snatched away by gusts of angry wind. She had stretched out her own hand until she thought their fingers might touch. But instead of coming closer, Anne felt as if she were moving farther and farther away from him. He then looked beyond her and she became frightened by the look in his eyes. She did not have the courage to turn and look at what was behind her. Disaster? Death itself? Anne only knew that she had stood between Stephen and this terrible thing. But whatever it had been, it frightened her and made her fear for him.

Instead of answering her, Anne asked her own question. "Have you never wanted to leave the island, Hannah?"

The silence in the small cottage had a sound all its own. Not unlike a bell whose peal deadened all other noise.

"I leave it often enough."

"Once or twice a year. No more."

"Why do you ask that of me, Anne?"

She turned, faced Hannah resolutely. "Because I want you to come with me."

"Where?" Hannah came and stood beside Anne.

The question was spoken, but the knowledge was already there on the older woman's face. An odd destination, one of heart more than of place.

"You do not even know if he's real," she said incredulously.

"He is real, Hannah."

"Because you wish him to be? The world would be a fine place if all our wishes would come true, Anne. But it does not happen." Hannah's face seemed to change. The anger vanished and in its place was a look of sadness before it, too, was gone.

"Have you not the sense God gave a gnat? A journey with no destination? Instead of being afraid you were a witch, you should have feared becoming a fool."

"Would you have me remain here all the rest of my life, Hannah? Without knowing if he was real or not?"

"Yes," Hannah said bluntly.

Anne smiled. "Give me a week, Hannah. That is all I ask. One week from my life. If I do not find him, then I'll return to Dunniwerth and be the meek woman you wish of me."

"You've never been meek a day of your life, Anne Sinclair," Hannah said wryly. "The idea is madness, Anne."

"No," Anne said softly. "The madness would be in not heeding this feeling." She turned away, faced the window again. "I can feel him, Hannah." She placed her clenched fist in the middle of her chest. "As if the spirit of him lives in me as well as in his soul. Don't tell me he's not real. Or that this longing I feel is only a dream."

He calls to me. Even now, as she stood in Hannah's cottage, it was as if she could hear him. A voice without sound. Words without speech. A longing so strong that she could not deny it. It was instinct and craving and something even more earthy and elemental. How did she explain it? Perhaps she could not.

She could not tell anyone what she felt at this moment. Not even Hannah. Perhaps she didn't know the right words. Or they'd never been crafted. She was afraid and confident. Confused and certain. Extremes. That's how she measured this feeling.

She turned. "Come with me, Hannah."

"Or else you will do this thing alone?"

"I am not that foolish, Hannah."

"But you will convince someone else," she said dryly. "Who will explain this idiocy to your parents?"

"What could I say, Hannah? That I've held this from them all my life? Their hurt would vie with their disbelief."

"Where will you go? How would you find this man who does not exist?"

"He exists," Anne said, closing her eyes as if she saw the route in her mind. "Three days ride due south. A road veers beside a deserted abbey, and there we need to head west."

"A vision, Anne?"

She blinked open her eyes. "Directions, Hannah."

By the look on her face, it was clear that she had startled the older woman. "There are not that many places named Langlinais. One of the peddlers I spoke to thinks he knows it."

Hannah pursed her lips, frowned again. Then she nodded once, a sharp jab of chin. Concession, then, in a gesture.

Chapter 2

Anne thought that the only jarring note to their journey was the ease with which it was accomplished. Her parents had departed two days earlier for Edinburgh. It was a coincidence of timing due more to her father's wish to sign the Solemn League and Covenant than to happenstance. But to Anne it was as unexpected as it was blessed. It made their own departure from Dunniwerth one performed without explanations.

They wound their way south from Dunniwerth. A strange procession comprised of herself, Hannah and Ian, the tormenter of her childhood now grown and one of her father's most trusted soldiers. Douglas, a sweet young man of slow wits and amiable disposition, made the fourth.

Hannah lost no opportunity to voice her displeasure of this quest. Ian seconded each complaint. He'd refused to accompany her at first, had agreed to do so only afer she'd made it clear that she would continue her journey with or without him.

"Tell me why you're set to go to England, at least," he'd said.

She'd studied him for a long moment, wondering if he would understand something so fey as her visions, her dreams of Stephen. Or would he ridicule her just as he had when they were children? She'd said nothing, remaining silent even in the face of his obvious disapproval.

Anne felt suspended in time as the days passed, neither wishing to go back, but almost afraid to reach their destination.

What would she say to Stephen when she found him? *I have seen you since you were a boy. Do you remember the time you raced over the meadow? Your horse threw you, and you lay there for the longest time. I was afraid you were dead. But then you began to laugh, arms and legs flung out on the grass, your face lifted to the sun.*

A hundred memories. She'd become accustomed to his presence in her life. A nightly ritual. Washing her face and hands, kneeling for her prayers, scrambling in between the sheets and waiting until sleep came. At that moment before dreams, murmuring his name. A blessing or perhaps a summons. It did not often happen, but when the visions came, when she saw him, she smiled her way into her dreams.

She was a Sinclair, and Sinclairs were always brave. A family motto if not a clan's. She would need her courage. Not only if she did find him, but more importantly if she did not.

You do not even know if he's real. Hannah's words. The only rebuttal? The image of Stephen laughing at something hidden from her. The sight of him standing so straight and tall atop the tower, staring into the distance as if he could see his future there and anticipated it. A hidden fist clenched as he endured his father's harsh words. She'd watched as he sat intent upon his studies and other times when he'd laughed with abandon.

Could she have simply wanted him to be real so much that she had imagined him? No.

As an only child, sometimes she had been lonely. Her free hours had been spent in drawing and imagining. She was, upon occasion, even known to talk to Stephen as if he were a playmate she'd devised for herself. There were nights when she'd begged for another story from Gordon, who was talented in such things. She had sat there captivated by heroes and mystics, curses and prophecies.

She could not deny that she had been a child immersed, sometimes, in a world of her own creating. Even her sketches mirrored her love of fantasy.

But she had not imagined Stephen. Not a boy with midnight blue eyes and a dimple on his left cheek. Not a man with a tiny scar near his right eye.

If she had dreamed him, she would have made him less sober these last years. Given him a smile that came more often. She would have given him back the laughter he seemed to have lost in his childhood.

He was real. He had to be. And somehow she needed to find him.

It was not fancy that sent her on this journey. Nor boredom. She had been to Edinburgh twice, and the discomfort of the journey had not endeared travel to her. The feeling she experienced now was something she did not quite understand. It was as if she were being driven to do it and had no choice. The yearning within her was so strong that it felt elemental. As natural as birds flying south or the first flowers of spring popping up beneath the icy crust of earth. A quest that she could not help but perform.

Even Hannah had understood how important this journey was to her. She would have, if she had not found someone to accompany her, traveled on her own. An act of madness, perhaps.

Was she mad? Or simply in the thrall of something she didn't understand? She would know the answer to that question when she found him. And if she didn't.

There were fifty of them. All united under one goal, to move and protect the artillery that lumbered behind the Parliamentarian army commanded by General Thomas Penroth.

Their posts of guarding the six cannon had been awarded to them for the reason that they were exemplary soldiers. Not one of them had ever been disciplined. They obeyed orders to the letter. But more importantly, they believed in their cause. They were dedicated to the goal of removing the king from power.

The army was five days' ride away, but the cannon traveled slower due both to their size and weight and the care that had to be taken with them. Several outriders had been posted to guard the roads both ahead of the artillery and behind it. Capture of the cannon royale could very well determine the outcome of the war, turn the tide in the Royalists' favor.

One of his men rode up to David Newbury, the lieutenant in charge of the cannon. "There are riders approaching, sir."

"How many?"

"Not a large group, sir. Two men and two women."

"Too many to be spies, Samuel. Too few to be of any danger. Still, it's rumored to be Royalist territory."

"Should we intercept them, sir?"

"Do so," he said, frowning.

"They may be nothing more than innocent travelers, sir."

"I'm aware of that, Samuel," he said, allowing the barest trace of irritation to color his voice.

It was Ian who saw them first. A party of about twenty men riding toward them from the base of the hill. They were soberly dressed in black garments covered with dust. Well-worn crows.

"I don't like the odds," Ian said, his face grim. He glanced at Anne and then at Hannah. "They may be friendly or not. If I give the word, I want you to ride as fast as you can for the other side of the hill. Try to find cover."

"What will you do, Ian?" Anne asked, glancing at him quickly.

"I'll be right behind you," he said with a smile. "I've no wish to be a hero on English soil."

It was not hard to guess Hannah's thoughts from the look on her face. *This is what I feared all along.* Hannah, however, chose this moment to remain silent, a restraint for which Anne silently thanked her.

She only wished her friend rode with more competence. The past six days had not been easy on Hannah, but fulminating looks had been the only complaint she'd offered. She commanded her horse with tentativeness. If they were forced to flee, speed would be necessary, and that was only accomplished if a rider had control of his mount.

Anne glanced at the route Ian had indicated. There was a narrow track that cut across the hill, a crossing evidently used by farmers to drive cattle or sheep. The problem with taking that path was their ignorance as to what lay on the other side of the hill. Was it meadow or river or impassible terrain?

Such caution might not be necessary. The men who approached them might well be no more than travelers. But as they rode closer, the men at either end edged forward until the line of riders curved toward them. Not unlike a trap.

Anne moved her horse further from Ian, then reached down and gripped Hannah's reins. The three of them exchanged a look. Douglas, behind and to the left, was in blissful ignorance of what was transpiring.

Ian sat silent until the riders came closer. A man, evidently their leader, separated himself from the group. His glance swept over them, dismissed Anne and Hannah. Anne had received such looks before from men who'd come to Dunniwerth and were ignorant of the fact that she was Robert Sinclair's daughter. The same men, when introduced to her, fawned all over her in an effort to please. A lesson that had not gone unlearned. Rudeness was a weapon often used against the poor and the defenseless.

Anne gripped the reins tighter and clamped her teeth over words she ached to say. But she was no fool. She'd grown up with warriors. Even now, amidst smiles and bland words, Ian and the man who faced him vied for dominance. One did not get between two men taking each other's measure. It was a subtle posturing, one she'd watched a thousand times before. At Dunniwerth, however, the prize had been a woman's favor or a tankard of whiskey. Not the right to travel a road unimpeded.

"We've no political leanings," Ian was saying. "We're only simple travelers."

"Scots," the man said, the inflection in his voice giving the impression that he thought little of their nationality.

"Yes."

"Your business?"

"Why would you wish to know? Are the roads guarded now?"

"For your purposes, yes." The look on the other man's face could only be called a smirk. It did nothing to mitigate the angry red flush on her clansman's face.

"We are simple travelers," Ian said again.

"An odd time to be taking a journey. In the midst of war."

"Aye, that I would agree," Ian said. The look he shot Anne was as fierce as those he'd given her as a child.

"Perhaps it might be possible to convince you to speak with more candor," the man said, smiling.

"I've nothing to say."

"Then you've nothing to fear. You will not object to coming with us, will you? My commander wishes to meet with you."

"And if I decline?"

"It would not be prudent to do so."

Ian glanced over at Anne. She straightened in the saddle. For long minutes she seemed to remain breathless, waiting. This journey, so fervently wished for, had not been undertaken without thought. She'd suspected they might encounter a robber, a traveler with ill intent, even an inn keeper who would try to cheat them. Perhaps even a few soldiers.

But she'd not thought to face an army.

Ian glanced at her and winked. A mere blink of an eye. It was enough to make her lean forward, press her heels into the sides of her sturdy little mare, and fly.

She loved to ride, had done so ever since she was a child of six and mounted on her first pony. This mad dash across the sloping ground was filled with its own exhilaration, but coupled with that was a pounding fear. Behind her she could hear shouts. A quick glance told her that Hannah was still astride. Her face was pale white, the grip on her saddle convulsive, but she still sat her horse.

They rounded the curve of the hill. From here Anne could see a river in the distance, the silvery gleam of it undulating like a snake through the bowl of valley below. The grassy slope gave way to shale and loose rock, which made passage difficult, if not dangerous. The sloping descent was going to be even more difficult for Hannah.

The angle of the hill was steep. In places she slid down a foot or two on the rocks before her horse gained its balance again. Anne slowed her speed, glanced behind her. Ian was still with the men, Douglas at his side. He broke free, the two of them closing the distance between them quickly, the black-garbed Parliamentarians not far behind.

Finally, the slope turned grassy, close cropped as if sheep grazed here. The sound of a gunshot was not unexpected. She prayed they were out of range. Pistols were good for close fighting but poor for distance. One of a hundred such bits of knowledge she'd learned from growing up the only child of the laird of Dunniwerth. She leaned over her horse's neck and prayed they would escape.

Stephen Harrington, Earl of Langlinais, sat at his desk, his wounded left arm balanced carefully on its surface. He'd discovered that if he elevated his wrist, the pain was not so fierce.

He stared down at two letters he'd composed. The first was to the king, explaining his continued absence from the Royalist forces. Too many of his men had died, men of the Langlinais regiment. He'd brought them home to bury them. To honor the men he'd known since they had been boys together. His wording was too harsh. Almost demanding. He should rip it up and begin again. He doubted, however, that the meaning would be any less terse with a second attempt.

The second letter was as difficult to write. A

summons to his side of a friend he'd not seen for a few years. Stephen needed his expertise, his skill.

His thoughts, however, were becoming increasingly muddled. St. Francis said that all men mean well, that the road to hell is made smooth with their good intentions. Where had that thought come from? The same place, no doubt, that a hundred such odd thoughts had originated in the past hours.

He rang the bell, and when it was answered by Betty, he managed a smile and a request, both lucid, he believed. He saw the light of relief shine in his housekeeper's eyes as he gave her the letter. There, he had pleased one person. It was little enough of late.

Betty had been his second mother, sliding into that position when his own had died when he was a boy. She'd wiped his tears and kept his mother's memory alive with stories of her. He'd gone to her for advice and had his ears boxed when he was impudent. When he'd become earl, he'd made her his housekeeper, the only elevation she would accept.

He had attended the funerals of each of his men this last week, had stood beside grieving widows and silent children as they had been laid to their rest. The words he'd spoken had been as difficult as he'd feared.

He had been present not only because they were his men, but because it was expected of him. He was a man of Langlinais, and for generations those who'd depended upon Langlinais Castle had looked to the earls for protection in life and benediction in death. And although the castle was no longer occupied, the bond between townsman and earl was still firmly in place.

When a flood had rendered Langlinais uninhabitable two hundred years earlier, a new home had been built. One that had been constructed to proclaim the family's wealth. It sat perched on the highest knoll overlooking the river Terne.

Harrington Court's three floors were impressive, as were all of its seventy rooms. The Tudor east wing had been added on by the earl who'd served Queen Elizabeth as advisor. An admirer of the classical movement had altered the west wing, adding pillars and cornices to the exterior of the house.

Most of the cavalry officers who formed the Langlinais regiment had come from Lange on Terne, the town surrounding Harrington Court. A few of them were experienced and seasoned, having seen service in Europe and Ireland. They were probably more skilled and certainly better equipped than most of the Royalist troops. They were hardened by training, inspired by loyalty, ready and eager to follow their lord, whatever side of this strife he chose to serve.

A loyalty he was grateful for, even as the burden of it weighed heavily on his shoulders.

He leaned back against the chair. His eyes felt watery, and his skin dry. No doubt a result of the festering wound.

He closed his eyes, traced the fingers of his right hand over one of the absurd lions' heads that finished off the chair's arms. When he was a boy, he could place his fingers inside the lion's mouth. Now his fingers were too large even if he wished to duplicate a childish act. He did not.

Was that the gauge of wisdom, then? Our wishes or our deeds?

He smiled at himself. Another oddity of thought. Perhaps it was not so bad to be fevered. It left him with a depth of understanding he'd never had before, but then, that might be a delusion, too. He might be tossing in his bed now instead of sitting upright at his desk. He opened his eyes as if to test his location. Yes, he was here, just as he'd thought he was.

Laughter sounded odd in an otherwise silent room.

He reached out with his right hand and gripped the sketch he'd made. If nothing else, he could finish the details of the north wall while he waited. Complete the drawing to scale. But his fingers fumbled with the charcoal, and his attention was drawn to the window.

The afternoon was bright and sunny, a rare enough event in this wet spring. The view was of the east meadow, green and lush, shadowed here and there by a passing cloud. An alluring sight.

A movement to the right caught his attention. Two riders being chased by two more. No, the four of them being chased by a coven of crows. Parliamentarians? On his land? Men who chose to dress as soberly as himself. But not twenty of them, surely. He was tempted to dismiss the sight, turn away, and allow them passage over his meadow but for the plume of gray smoke. A pistol?

He stood, went to the door, braced himself against it, and called for Ned.

When he arrived, Stephen issued his orders.

"Have Faeren saddled," he said, "and summon the regiment to me."

"My lord, should you be riding?"

He would have dismissed any other man's concerns, but because it was Ned, he spared him a smile. It served both as an answer and a dismissal.

Ned simply nodded, his lips clamped over words he might have uttered. It amused Stephen that his old servant refrained from comment. There had been a time when Ned wouldn't have been so restrained. Why was he now? Because Stephen was ill? Or because he was now earl?

He walked back to his chest where his pistols were stored. For more than a year they'd been constant companions, but he'd not thought to use them on his own land.

He wasn't at his best, that he would agree. But it simply didn't matter. What happened here was his concern. Distilled to its simplest form, it was his duty. A motto. A family's creed. Duty, honor, loyalty.

In a matter of moments, he was mounted on Faeren and leading the charge across the meadow.

He led his men across the lowest point of the Terne river, up the embankment, and through the tip of the valley, where the meadow sharply rose again.

Stephen.

His name lingered on the air, a breath of sound, a whisper that sang in his ears. A trait of his fever, then. A sign that he was mortal, after all. The Earl of Langlinais, the leader of the Blessed Regiment, was not so blessed. Instead, he was hallucinating.

He spurred Faeren on over the undulating ground, heard the steady drumbeat of hooves as his men followed him. His face was stiff with tension.

Stephen.

He heard it again, a long, keening recitation of his name, the whistle of it tied, somehow, to a base part of him. An ancient, pagan place, one that recognized instinct and intuition and terror.

He felt a chill overcome him, something icy that seeped into his entire body, from mind to toes. He was more ill than he'd realized.

Just before they reached the river, Anne heard a sound behind her. A stifled note of surprise that had more effect on her than the report of the guns. She glanced beside her, found to her horror that her worst fear had been realized.

Hannah had fallen.

Anne reined in her horse, slipped out of the saddle and raced to where Hannah lay. The older woman's face was too pale, her breaths too labored. Anne knelt on the ground beside her, the sounds of the soldiers arriving muted beneath a greater terror.

"Hannah." A soft murmur of her name did nothing to rouse her. For a long, horrified moment, Anne thought her dead. But the pulse beat strongly in her neck.

Ian reached her side, dismounted. He stood in front of her, pistol drawn. A gesture of defense against the men who surrounded them only moments later.

When she heard the sound, she thought he'd shot at someone.

Pistols fired at close quarters had the ability to deaden the ears. In the open meadow the sound echoed and was repeated back to her. It was only after glancing up that she realized the sound hadn't come from Ian's gun. But from behind her.

She turned her head. Mounted on a large black horse was a man attired in as somber a uniform as the men who'd chased them. He was hatless; the sun gleamed on his black hair and the silver buttons that adorned his jacket. The silver handle of the pistol he brandished was likewise as bright, so much so that it shimmered in the sun's glare.

Behind him were six men, all with pistols drawn. Their uniforms declared them united in purpose. Their studied glare at the Parliamentarians guaranteed it.

But her gaze returned to their leader. The image of him held her spellbound. Bewitched in truth, just as she'd thought herself to be as a child.

The world hushed, stood silent. Her heart beat heavily in her chest; her breath came too fast and too tight. The sun's glare was too hot and too harsh for this moment. It should have been muted by an otherworldly haze. Or encompassed by the silvery bubble she'd seen as a child.

The men drew closer behind him. He did not look in her direction, but she could not tear her gaze from him.

Once she'd drawn a portrait of him, the better to keep his image close to her. She'd sketched him looking at her, his face turned as if startled in his discovery. His lips were half smiling, an expression that appeared natural, if rare these past years. The amused look in his eyes had warmed her. His face was sharply chiseled, as if God had hewn this image from stone. His jaw was defined, his cheekbones high, his nose was proud with just a touch of arrogance. His chin was squared, his hair thick and black. His eyes were a blue that was almost black, a midnight hue. There was a small scar at his chin and a tiny one at his temple.

It was a face too strong to be considered simply handsome. Still, it was a face not easily forgotten. But nothing she'd ever drawn or envisioned could equal the reality of him.

There was a presence to him. A power she felt even though she was several feet removed. It had nothing to do with his height or the breadth of his shoulders. It was as if he filled the space around him, dominated it.

He was not smiling now. His face was still, set in lines that mimicked stone. Power radiated from him as strongly as the sun's rays.

The look in his eyes dared the men in front of him to challenge him. Stephen and his men were outnumbered but not outmatched. She had no doubt that he would win if it came to a fight.

Stephen.

He flinched. The hand that held the pistol wavered, then steadied.

As if to counter his sudden inattention, he spoke. "You are on my land, gentlemen. Without my permission."

Their leader, the same man who had confronted Ian, answered him. "You would harbor spies, sir?"

He glanced down at Ian, who remained in a protective stance in front of her. "Are you a spy?"

"No," Ian said, not turning. His attention was still directed at the men in front of him, the muzzle of his pistol still pointed at their leader.

"And those with you?"

"We are no spies," Ian said stonily.

"There," Stephen said, speaking to the leader once more, "you have his answer."

"General Penroth will not be pleased with your interference, sir," the soldier said, his face tightening in anger.

Stephen's slowly dawning smile had a dark edge to it. "Penroth is not pleased by much," he said.

"And who might you be, sir?" the leader asked, surprised that Stephen seemed to know Penroth.

"The Earl of Langlinais. Give my regards to the good general," he said, his voice sharpening. "Now get off my land."

He didn't move until they'd reluctantly turned and cantered off. His men remained mounted and watchful even as Stephen slowly dismounted and walked to where Anne knelt on the ground.

He stood looking down at the three of them, his glance focusing upon Hannah's still paleness.

"Has she been wounded?" he asked, his voice pitched low. Anne shook her head.

The sun was behind him, his features obscured by shadow. Such a pose should have diminished him. But oddly it did not. She recalled the last vision she'd had of him, in which he'd been cloaked in darkness. An image not too dissimilar to this moment. A chill skittered over her skin and lodged near her heart.

He stood before her, a man of some power. An earl, he'd said.

She could hear him breathe. Not a vision. A person and not a myth. Nor a dream.

"Stephen," she said softly in amazement.

He made no move toward her.

She had stood at her window at Dunniwerth and longed to be at his side. She'd fervently prayed for one opportunity, just one, to touch him, to see if he breathed and was real, or only a creature she'd imagined.

She stretched out her fingers now.

Her hand wavered in the air between them. It felt as heavy as an anvil. He frowned, then stretched out his hand. Their fingertips touched. Just that. A brush of naked fingers. A tentative touch between strangers. One certainly allowed.

But voices entered her mind. Those of caution and prudence and sense. His men stood behind them, watching. Hannah lay senseless at her feet. Not a time to become bemused.

The silence between them was complete. She trapped in her wonder. He, in restraint.

She pulled back her hand. It trembled even as she brushed Hannah's hair back from her forehead.

He spoke first. "I will send for a wagon," he said. He bowed to her, and she in turn nodded. A gracious greeting. An expression of kindness. An act of protection.

When he walked away, she raised her head and looked after him. Ian frowned at her. No doubt as fiercely as Hannah would have frowned had she not been senseless. She did not doubt her heart was in her gaze. She was a laird's daughter, a woman of

Dunniwerth. A Sinclair. Brave, fearless. Proud. But pride had no place in these moments.

When the wagon arrived, two of the soldiers gently picked Hannah up and placed her in the bed. Anne scrambled in beside her. Ian led the horses. She looked around for Douglas, but didn't see him. Was he with the mounted men? A thought before she was distracted by Hannah's low moan of pain.

Anne didn't ask their destination, bemused in a way she'd never before felt. She placed her hands beneath Hannah's head to act as a cushion against the jarring of the rough planks beneath her as the wagon began to move. Her regret and guilt was balanced against a feeling of wonder. That he might be real, and she had touched him. Heard his voice. But coupled with that was an odd and profound sadness. One that confused her even as it kept her silent. She should have been suffused with joy.

Instead, she felt like weeping.

Chapter 3

"**W**hy in hell did you not get treatment for this, Stephen?" Richard asked angrily, glaring down at his arm.

He had ripped the sleeve from Stephen's shirt. A necessity, for the simple reason that his arm refused to work. Stephen had no experience with suppurating wounds. Richard's horrified look, however, conveyed the fact that it was as bad as he'd feared.

How did he tell him that there had been other things occupying his mind? Greater concerns than pain had intruded, such as getting sixty of his regiment through enemy lines and burying five of his men. By that time, nothing had cured it, not Betty's treatments or Ned's commonsense approach.

He leveled a look at Richard. "My duty," he said flatly.

Richard only frowned at him.

"So you would die for your duty."

"Has it come to that, then?" He hoped to God he would not die for so silly a reason. Defending his country? An acceptable demise. In the cause of

the king? Less acceptable, but he had been prepared to do so. Guarding his home? An act of
which he might, conceivably, be proud. But not a
rotting arm.

"I've never seen a wound so far gone. Are you
fevered, too?"

"I know better than to lie to you, my friend. My
thoughts are increasingly not my own." He allowed
his eyes to close. The light from the candles
seemed almost glittery. As if he viewed them from
beneath water.

"You damn fool."

The knock on the door halted the remainder of
his diatribe. Richard began to give orders with the
briskness of a battlefield commander. Stephen
opened his eyes. In the doorway stood Betty nodding at each command from Richard. Behind her
stood the woman from the meadow.

Richard had asked for more candles, and the
room was ablaze with light. The glow followed her,
swathed her in radiance. She sparkled as an angel
might, the luster gifting her dark hair with a radiance that brown hair did not ordinarily have. Was
it the heat that caused her cheeks to be tinted a
lovely rose, or were heavenly spirits equipped with
such earthly beauty? He was indeed beset with fever, he thought, as she came closer. No angel,
merely a stranger.

"I came to thank you," she said, stepping forward. The second time he'd heard her speak. The
first time she'd said his name. Just that. One word.
A lovely voice, one that held in it the sound of
bells. He smiled at the whimsy of that thought.

The rest of her words faded away as she glimpsed

his arm. Did she pale? He wanted to ask Richard to cover it up. Or her to turn away. He did not speak, to demand either would have been to reveal his shame. He had not neglected his arm intentionally, but it seemed, in hindsight, an act of such rampant stupidity that it now embarrassed him.

He was grateful when she fixed her gaze on his face instead.

"Have you any experience in caring for wounds?" Richard asked her.

The woman nodded. "But none as bad as this."

"I doubt you'll see as bad again," Richard said.

He disliked being talked about as if he wasn't present. Protest, however, was easier with a thought than an action. Men are measured not only by their actions but by their thoughts. He had a penchant, evidently, for remembering odd scraps of knowledge when he was fevered. An altogether idiotic ability.

Betty stood there looking horrified, her fists clenched in her impeccable apron. She had known he was ill, but he'd concealed the degree of it. To spare her the anguish she was obviously experiencing now.

"What is your name?" he asked the woman from the meadow. It was somehow important that he know. So much that he formed the words with great precision and uttered them carefully, strung together with the tail of one gripping the front of the other.

Another oddity of fever that he could so clearly see things that were not there. Like dancing words and angels' wings.

She came around the desk and stood at his right

side. His fingers wiggled in the air, the tips of them brushed against the fabric of her serviceable brown dress. A soft wool that echoed the color of her eyes.

"Anne," she said. "Anne Sinclair."

Not bells in her voice, but the barest trace of accent.

"You're a Scot." There, another sentence of some sense. He was absurdly proud of himself. His smile spread across his lips and was answered by hers. As if she had caught the idiocy of it. Or had great empathy for his simplemindedness.

He was Stephen Harrington. He'd spoken with impassioned zeal to Parliament. He had shouted commands in front of armed troops and motivated men whose only wish had been to turn and run from war. Yet lucid speech was absurdly difficult at the moment. He had uttered a tiny intelligible sentence and felt as if he should be knighted for it.

"I was knighted once," he told her. A confession uttered before he could think it. But the announcement of it hadn't reached him in time, so he was fined. A way for the king to fill his coffers. To be so honored in absentia had cost him a great deal of money.

She smiled then. He was grateful to her for her kindness, for the sweetness of her smile. So much that he wanted to thank her for it. He started to speak again, but she bent down and pressed her fingers against his lips. The gesture silenced him in its impudence.

Did she often get her way? She did not look stubborn so much as confident. Perhaps strong-willed. Today in the meadow, she'd looked angry with the soldiers who'd waylaid her. Not fearful.

Not one tear, one sob, had marred her face. Instead, her eyes had changed, been filled with wonder. What would cause such a look?

Why did her eyes seem so deep now?

"You should not be here," he said. The treatment of his wound would not be pleasant. He knew that only too well, having been versed on it a few minutes earlier.

"Do you wish me to leave?"

He should. He should smile and banish her with a look. Even stubborn, she would not be able to mistake it. She would leave the room with the same grace as she'd entered it. Perhaps even apologize for witnessing the nakedness of his vulnerability. But he remained silent, instead, for one reason. She was lovely, a powerful distraction, and she made him think of things other than the pain to come.

"Do you think you will faint?" she asked him. A profound question and an earnest one. But an inquiry, nonetheless, that few people would have dared to ask. He rewarded her courage with bravery of his own. An answer steeped in honesty. He was a man beset by that characteristic. If he had not been, his life would have been much easier to bear.

"I may," he admitted. "I've never been wounded before."

"Or known how to treat it," she said, glancing over at his bared arm.

His startled laughter came from deep inside him. Yet another oddity of this experience. Laughter eased the pain.

"Is it true that your regiment is called the Blesseds?" Richard asked, laying his instruments upon the desk one by one. Stephen glanced away from the preparations, kept his attention on the night-darkened window.

"It's a regrettable name," Stephen said.

"Why so?"

"It gave my men a feeling of invincibility. Until Seddonby. Then too many of them died."

He glanced at Anne. She was wide-eyed, her gaze fixed on Richard's preparations. He wanted her attention on him, not on those instruments of torture. A petulant thought, one entirely in keeping with his sudden wish to pretend he was somewhere else. Not here in this room of glittering light and stifling heat.

"Will he lose his arm?"

"I am rumored to be favored by good fortune," Stephen said, before Richard could reply. "He will not cut off my arm," he said. A comment that was reinforced with a look toward Richard. His friend frowned but nodded all the same.

Richard turned to Betty. "Stand behind him," he told the housekeeper, "and wrap this strip of cloth around his chest. Bind him tightly to the chair. He must not move. If you need more help, then call for it now."

"I will not move," Stephen said.

Betty stood before him, the strip of cloth in her hand, the look on her face one of pained indecision.

"It's all right, Betty," he said wearily. He dropped his head against the tall back of the chair. What words would reassure her? He did not wish to be bound in place like a trussed fowl. His word should be enough. Even weakened and fevered as he was, his vow meant something.

"He won't move," Anne said, as if she'd heard

his thoughts. She knelt beside him, braced herself against the side of the chair. Both her forearms bracketed his right arm, her fingers linked together behind his elbow. She moved closer, her body pressed against his knuckles. Distraction. A welcome one.

Their faces were only inches apart. He kept his attention on her eyes. He didn't think he'd seen such a shade before. A deep, dark brown, but in their centers a tiny gold circle. A coronet? Regal eyes, perhaps, to better suit the nature of their owner. *He won't move.* How certain she had been. How trapped he felt now in her confidence.

The first cut was unexpected. The pain was not.

"I come from Dunniwerth," she softly said. He stared at her lips. They parted for words. Sometimes a breath. Or a half-hidden gasp. They were, these lips, the most fascinating shade of pink. "My home is a huge, sprawling place of red brick, aged over the years until it is almost black. Nothing as lovely as this place."

"It was built nearly two hundred years ago," he said, congratulating himself on the placid nature of his speech. Not a hint of the fiery agony of his left arm.

"Dunniwerth is much older," she said, smiling as if she'd won the point.

He should show her Langlinais, and then she'd concede to age. The castle was nearly six hundred years old.

"My father loves its idiosyncrasies. My mother grumbles at its tiny rooms."

Such a lovely smile she had. He wondered if she knew it, practiced it as some of the women at court were wont to do. He'd caught a courtesan doing so one day in a part of the palace not swarming with people. She'd made faces at the mirror—delighted, surprised, suffused with joy. Her expression when she'd turned slightly and seen his reflection had been nowhere near as charming.

Another cut. This was the best of it, he suspected. From this moment on it would be worse.

She barely held him, yet he felt as bound as if she had linked chains about him. The tyranny of womanhood? Or his own masculine pride being held up to scrutiny? He would not scream, even as Richard scraped and prodded.

She had such lovely skin, unmarked by scars or the unhealthy pallor caused by the ceruse so often used at court. She had no need of artifice. Her cheeks were dusted with color. Her nose had a proud tilt to it.

"When you speak of your home," he said, "there's more Scots in your voice." Each word seemed chiseled from his throat for the effort it had taken.

Please, do not let me scream in front of her.

He opened his eyes fully and looked into hers, using that odd gold ring in them as a point of reference. His fever must be mounting that he would think himself lost in the warmth and the welcome of her eyes.

He felt, somehow, as if he knew her, and that he should give her some greeting to acknowledge that fact. Her look was compassionate, but there was something else about it. An understanding, as if she could peer inside his soul and see all the holes there. All the worthwhile things he'd done, and all the lacks and omissions of his life. With that look, she forgave him in an instant, offered absolution and forgetfulness.

He closed his eyes, willed himself away from the temptation of senselessness. It was too easy to drift into idiocy. He did not know this woman. Until today had never seen her.

He felt her cheek against the back of his hand. The softness of her skin lured him to think of the last opened petals of a rose in summer. How eloquent his thoughts when paired with pain. At least he was not so foolish as to utter the words aloud. He was no poet.

Upon his knuckles the faintest brush of her lashes. One side of his body too alert. The other adrift in searing agony.

He opened his eyes, studied her. Her eyes were closed, the look on her face one a madonna might wear, peace and comfort and effortless ease. He wanted her to take him to that place where she dwelled.

"Are you a student of poetry?" he asked, the words no more than a rasp of sound. Would she know how much they cost him?

She looked up then, her eyes warm with empathy. He wanted to tell her that such a look would not make him braver or urge him to silence. He was at that mark now. A line, perhaps, scratched in the dirt with his sword. Beyond this point he could not go. But it appeared as if he could, after all.

"No," she said, "Not truly. The only words I know are those of Alexander Scott, and they are not appropriate for this moment."

"Tell me anyway," he said.

Her cheeks grew a deeper rose as he watched. He smiled, charmed by it. So she was not as filled with confidence as he'd thought. It equalized them—he, with his wish to scream, and her with her embarrassment.

"I came to thank you for your kindness," Anne said. Did she understand his sudden wish for any diversion? A conversation about rabbits would not be amiss at this moment. "And for intervening this afternoon. I do not know what would have become of us."

Psalm singer or Royalist, either side in this war was capable of atrocities. Two women in a sea of men were not safe. But surely she knew that.

"Has your friend awakened?" Richard asked.

"A while ago," she said, looking up at him. Stephen noted that she kept her gaze carefully averted from what Richard was doing. If he could have distanced himself from the preparations, from this very moment, he would have. "She is in some pain, but I think she is more irritated with her horse than she is with her injuries."

"A good horse is a good thing," Stephen said. His ramblings were those of a schoolboy conjugating his Latin verbs. The trunk of my sister. The book of my father. A good horse is a good thing. He closed his eyes in disgust.

"I have a good horse," he said. An expression of speech not appreciably better, but at least it would lead to another topic. "Faeren," he said. "All the horses belonging to the earls of Langlinais are named Faeren." There, an entire sentence. One with some lucidity. "A legend, perhaps. One that stretches back so far no one knows its origin."

He opened his eyes again. Her face was truly
lovely in candlelight. All shadows and cream. Her
hair, curled about her shoulders and tied back with
a crimson ribbon, was the deep brown shade of her
eyes. Were they a matched pair, requested at the
moment of birth? *Chestnut eyes, please. And hair
to match. Here, then, an infant of promise. She will
be a beauty when she grows. Is that what you wish?
Yes, please.*

"Do you favor your mother?" Another whole
sentence. He caught Richard's compassionate
glance out of the corner of his eye. The worst, then,
was to come shortly.

"Is she the woman I treated?" Richard asked.
"There is some resemblance between the two of
you. Something about the chin and mouth."

Anne blinked at him. Stephen thought she
looked startled by the question. She shook her head
as if to negate it.

"My father," she said, but he'd lost the thought
as Richard moved to the fireplace.

"I think you might be wise to bind me," he said,
a confession more onerous than any he'd ever
made. It shamed him, even as it swam in truth.
Another image then of rum in a keg and the tiny
part that was his courage bobbing like a cork.

She did not bind him. Instead, she shook her
head when Betty would have moved closer. Such
faith in him. He did not know if it was misplaced.
He closed his eyes again. There was some security
in not knowing when it would come.

She drew closer until he could feel her breath
upon his cheek. His knuckles were against her

breast. He wished he might lay his head against her there, extend his arms around her. A bit of weakness that he'd never confess aloud. Not yet, anyway.

She spoke in Gaelic to him. A harsh, guttural language that she made lyrical. Her lips were close to his ear. Richard was using a brush inside the wound. More than that he didn't wish to know. His mind was capable of furnishing his closed eyes with enough images.

He clung to each word she spoke, as if they strung together a net to hold him. The smell of the poker was a warning. So, too, her startled gasp. Didn't she know that it was the treatment for wounds such as his? Her hand pressed flat against his cheek. Her fingers were cool; he curved his face toward her touch.

"Talk to me," he said, when she was rendered silent. She began to speak again, nonsensical words in a language he'd never known.

It became a cradlesong, the sound of her voice. A calmative that held him sane as Richard laid the poker against his open wound. He walked through the blood-red landscape with her as his companion. Her voice was a thread he somehow followed, a blessed sound, far more welcome than his silent, muted screams.

Until even those faded away, and he knew nothing else.

Dunniwerth, Scotland

Robert Sinclair, Laird of Dunniwerth, was furious. "What do you mean, she's not here?" he roared.

"Did I not set a guard in place?" This question was asked of the most senior of his troops left at Dunniwerth. Alex nodded but did not move his gaze from the floor.

"Do you not understand what it means to guard Dunniwerth, Alex? It is not to watch the bricks, man, but to protect the people!" This was said in an earsplitting roar. It had the effect of making the man wince, but it did not furnish Robert with any more of an explanation.

"Where did she go?"

Alex looked up then. There was petition in his look and a sorrowful lack of pride mixed with fear. He could almost be forgiven for that. Robert wanted to pull the head off his shoulders.

"All we know is that Hannah went with her, Robert. And Douglas. Ian, too."

"Should I be grateful, then, that there is anyone left at Dunniwerth? Was it a migration?"

Not one person in the hall could answer him. Or chose to. And Hannah? Leaving the island after all this time?

He looked over at Maggie.

His wife stood before a fire, intent on the blaze. She turned then, as if sensing his gaze. She still wore her traveling cloak, a long cape with a hood of soft red wool. The color accentuated her green eyes and auburn hair. She was still beautiful, even after all these years. A thought that did nothing to lessen the leaden feeling in his chest.

They had been married when they were both very young, a union of land and clan more than inclination. He'd seen her once from a distance, and she'd seen him not at all before they'd wed. It had not been love at first sight, and they'd only tolerated each other for years. But time had a way of gathering up respect, and somehow, respect had turned to love.

He turned back to the men arrayed in front of him. Once more he prayed for patience, and once more he listened to the story again. Told a hundred times, it would be the same. The four of them had ridden out of Dunniwerth's gates more than a week ago. No one knew where they went. Or why.

Maggie came and stood beside him, her face a study in calm acceptance. He knew that anyone looking at her would think her unmoved by the tale. In actuality, she did not easily show her feelings, being more stoic than even he upon occasion. Later, perhaps, she would come to him and lay her head upon his chest and allow him to comfort her. But for now her misery was complete and personal and solitary.

Their daughter was missing.

"Go," he said, waving a hand to the men in front of him. Outside, people were congregating in patches, conversation muted. The men who'd accompanied him home would be speaking in low tones to their wives. Children would be shushed, and mothers would be weeping sympathetic tears.

Where was his daughter?

He rubbed his hand over his eyes, pressed against them with thumb and forefinger, willing himself to cease thinking the worst.

"Has Hannah taken her, Robbie?"

He turned. Maggie stood watching him. The question had been his, too.

"Anne is a grown woman, Maggie. It's a bit late to be stealing her away."

"Then she would have wanted to go. Why?"

He studied her face. There was love between them. Hard won but there, nonetheless. A question lingered in the air between them. One she had never asked. Had she thought it all this time?

"I never went to the island, Maggie."

She moved toward him, smiling. She reached up her hand and cupped his face. "I know, Robbie. I know."

He extended his arms around her, and she sighed against him. It was a moment for fear and worry and questions. But it was also, Robert Sinclair thought, a time of forgiveness. There was no way to wipe away the past, but Maggie had eased it a bit with her simple gesture and her smile.

Chapter 4

Harrington Court, England

Her laughter was full and rich, coaxing forth his own. His hands at her waist were her only support as they twirled in a circle, her arms thrown out, the cloud of her hair shining in the sun. An angel flying in the air.

He had never known such joy. Such utter freedom of the senses and the soul. Would that this moment were his forever. To feel again and again. To pluck from his memory and recall when he grew old.

In the way of fevered dreams, she grew closer and then further apart. Finally, she walked away from him for the last time. He called to her, stretched out his hand, but she continued to walk away. At the edge of the horizon, where the sea met the sky, she turned and blew a kiss to him. A smile was his last link to her as she became no more than mist. There had been tears on her cheeks. And in his heart.

My beloved. My own true love.

A voice came to him, one rough and impatient. A band of something cold and wet bound his forehead, cooled his skin. He wanted to thank the hand that placed it there but was cast into another dream before he could frame the words.

He made a sound in his sleep, a cry of terror, as his world became black again. The voice above him eased him. The hand upon his forehead was cool.

An angel, then. The voice of an angel commanded that he rest or he would never heal. And so he tried. One did not gainsay God.

Someone pressed something to his lips. A bit of cheese, some wine? Only water. The sound of a lute seemed oddly familiar. There, her laughter again.

Come with me, love. A voice that sang with the sound of bells. *He turned and she was there, holding her hand out to him. Her hair was black as night. No, brown as a chestnut. A sweet face. A lovely one. Eyes a shade of green. No, deep, dark, with gold at their centers. Eyes to lure and warm.*

I am so very tired. A thought. Into it came her voice. Or his. God's again?

I am here. Sweet love, remember me.

The dream shifted again. A woman's face again. A smile, a beauty patch, a cloud of scent. A laugh, his own.

Home. Sleep.

Rest now. It's the only way you'll heal. I'll be here.

Voices in his head. He gave himself up to the angel's voice, and fell into a deep and dreamless sleep.

*　*　*

"You still have not found him?" Anne asked.

"Do you think the soldiers took him?" She looked up at him, horrified.

They stood in the garden. Ian had asked to speak to her, so she'd walked here with him. She'd never imagined, however, that his news would be so terrible.

He nodded. "It is the likeliest possibility."

"What will they do to him, Ian?"

"Shouldn't you have worried about that earlier, Anne?" Ian asked, his voice tight with anger. "Before we left Scotland?"

She looked down at clasped hands.

"The earl's men and I have scoured the countryside, Anne. There's no sign of him."

Douglas was a sweet boy. But just as humor was something oddly missing in his nature, so was initiative. He would not know where to hide. Or where to come, if he managed to escape the soldiers.

Shame sat on her like a wet woolen cloak. He was a member of her clan, and she was the daughter of Dunniwerth. Therefore it had been her responsibility to assure his safety. She had not. The condemnation was there in her thoughts as well as in Ian's words.

"Are you never going to tell me why we left Scotland?"

He'd agreed to accompany her only because he'd been given the responsibility for her safety. And, he'd told her that he wasn't at all sure she would remain at Dunniwerth if he'd refused to come to England with her. In that, he was correct.

Ian had not approved of the journey, nor of his traveling companions. He had said that Hannah was too old, a remark that caused Hannah to cease talking to him for one whole day. His comments about Douglas were even less charitable.

"If you treat him as if he can do nothing," she had told him, "then that's exactly what he will do. Give him an opportunity, Ian. Let him show you how helpful he can be."

Unfortunately, Douglas had vanished. Not very helpful.

Ian frowned down at her, his stance watchful. As if he were on sentry duty and she was an approaching shadow.

"Was it worth Hannah being injured and Douglas lost?" he asked, when she said nothing.

He was not, in that moment, unlike the boy who'd taunted her. He did not spare his words in case he might cause her hurt.

If he'd asked her the moment they'd arrived at Harrington Court, she might have confessed to her confusion. There was no castle, and the man who'd come to their rescue in the meadow was a forbidding stranger.

It was only later, when she'd held Stephen, that she'd felt that sense of connection to him. That man, adrift in pain and fevered, had been more like the one she'd known. As if illness had stripped him of a shell he had worn, revealing the true man beneath.

"Does it have anything to do with him?" A glance back at the house made Ian's meaning clear enough. Anne was surprised at the question, at the insight it revealed. "You haunt the hallway outside his door, Anne, as if you cannot bear to be away from him even in sleep. Even when Hannah sends you from her room, you do not stray far from the house."

She could feel her cheeks warm.

"Do you think yourself invisible? I am not the first who has noticed it."

"But you are the only one who finds it necessary to comment upon it."

She frowned up at him, willing him to go away. It was not in her nature to be rude, but at that moment she wished to be. She wanted to silence him. He spoke of things he did not understand. But she would not make it more clear to him.

"The sooner we are gone from here, the better, Anne," Ian said curtly.

She watched him as he walked away. And felt a guilty pleasure in his departure.

Chapter 5

⟨⟨⟨◦◦◦⟩⟩⟩

Hannah sat in a chair beside her, eyes closed. But when a knock sounded on the door, she readily answered it. She feigned sleep, but was as alert as a magpie. Anne didn't bother hiding her smile.

The maid bustled into the room with Hannah's morning tray. Something Hannah heartily disliked, being waited on with such assiduousness. But in this she was a captive. She could barely move due to the soreness of her ribs. Rest was the very best thing for her. A fact that even she recognized, although she would have denied it had she been asked.

"Place the tray on the table first, Muriel." Betty stood in the doorway, hands folded at her waist. She looked around the room with the proprietary air of any goodwife. Did the windows need washing, the pewter polishing, the brass shining? She frowned at the fireplace, looked swiftly at the floor. Anne knew that as soon as Muriel left the room, she would be given orders to sweep both.

Anne looked up at Betty's entrance and returned

61

the housekeeper's smile. Her first sight of Betty had been when she was eight. Back then, she'd appeared a tall woman with large hands. But to a child all adults are tall. Now she appeared only of average height.

She felt a fondness for the housekeeper and thought that it might be reciprocated. A bond had been forged between them the night she'd knelt at Stephen's side. A conspiracy of care.

Amidst the clink of china and Hannah's and Muriel's voices, she asked the question she had asked every morning for a week.

"The earl? He is well?"

Every day Betty brought her word of his progress. "The physician says he is healing and such sleep is good for him" had been the message for three agonizingly long days. The news had gradually improved. Two days ago his fever had broken. Yesterday he had insisted upon getting out of bed.

Today, however, she answered Anne's question with a smile. "He is up and dressed. Insisted upon it," she said. "He looks much his usual self," Betty said. "Although a little more pale and somewhat thinner."

Relief flooded through Anne so quickly and fiercely that she felt almost lightheaded from it.

"I feel it is a bad sign, indeed, Muriel, when your mistress and Anne are deep in conversation," Hannah said, eyeing them both with some disfavor. "Either you are to be punished, or I am to be starved." She poked at the toast on her tray. "A plan that looks to have already begun."

"You will frighten Muriel, Hannah," Anne said, looking over at her. She smiled at the maid. "I can tell you that she does not mean half of what she says."

"I do not?" There was a frown on Hannah's face.

"No," Anne said. "I think you are being quarrelsome simply to see what kind of reaction you can get."

"I am not," Hannah protested. "I am simply tired of this room and tired of remaining in it."

"Then I will ask the physician to see if you cannot at least begin to walk tomorrow. Would you like that?"

She slitted her eyes at Anne. "I am not a cat to be coaxed to purr, Anne. And I am capable of asking him questions on my own."

"If you were a cat," Anne said, feeling absurdly cheerful, "then I would simply rub you between the ears." Hannah's lips twitched. "He has promised to pay you a visit this afternoon. Ask him then," Anne said, daring her.

"He is a pompous know-it-all," Hannah said.

Anne said nothing, but her smile broadened. Prior to every visit from Richard Maning, Hannah had insisted her hair be brushed and her face washed.

Hannah eyed her as if she'd heard her thoughts or could divine them in her smile. "Go away, Anne. Go for a walk. Take the air."

Betty caught her look and smiled. "I'll ask my husband to set up a stool and a table in the garden. You might wish to sit and draw there."

Anne looked over at Hannah, torn. She would have dearly loved to spend a few hours outside, instead of the few minutes she allotted herself each morning.

Betty's hands were folded at her waist, her head tilted, a bit like an inquisitive bird. "I'll be within hearing distance of the bell," she said.

It was, in the end, too tempting to be gone from this room, to sit in the garden for a little while. Anne nodded, capitulating.

"See? We all agree," Hannah said. "It is your mood that needs improving. Not my own. I am a thoroughly pleasant individual. A truly amiable soul," she said, turning to Muriel. The young maid looked somewhat stunned by such sweet-tempered attention, Anne thought, as she left the room.

The knot garden was imposing from above, but almost overpowering up close. Instead of the intricate designs cut into the hedges, all that was truly visible was their size. She felt as if she were trapped in a maze, one created for giants. With relief, Anne found herself in a smaller place, a garden with its beds mulched and readied for the first blossoms of spring.

Betty's husband turned out to be a short, wizened man with a face filled with wrinkles and the most charming smile she'd ever seen. He reminded her of what a gnome might look like if he'd been transported to the surface of the earth and instructed to marry and live among humans.

"Did Betty send you out, then?" His blue eyes twinkled at her. "I'm Ned," he said, nodding back at her. "Been married to the woman since Adam was a boy. Know her right enough I do. She's a great one for the freshness of the air." He smiled once again, then turned his attention to placing the table where she wished. With a wave he disappeared behind the knot garden, gnomelike.

She sat on the stool Ned had provided and laid the drawing board down on the table. The board had been a present from her father on her eleventh birthday. Its surface was only about a foot square, making it easy to carry. It had been constructed to act primarily as a slate. The wood had been bleached until it was nearly white, then oiled until it shined. Such a surface allowed her to practice a sketch with charcoal. When she was finished, she needed only to wipe it clean. Two knobs at the top held paper when she was ready to render her sketches onto a more permanent surface.

She removed the drawings she'd started from the pocket of her cape. Unlike her father's mapmaker, she didn't so much as draw what she saw as much as feel it. An explanation that might have amused the man.

People rarely sat still long enough for her to sketch them. Dunniwerth was a busy place, with most of its inhabitants given duties to perform. Therefore, a glimpse might be all she had of a face or a smile. She learned to store an expression away in her memory, to be unearthed when there was time. The emotion a smile carried or a laughing pair of eyes was more important to her than color.

Perhaps it was because her work was done in monochrome. Shades of gray and white and black. One day she hoped to work in colors, to take the knowledge of what she'd learned from shadow and transform it into a painting that might last for a hundred years. Instead of a sketch that lasted only a few.

She began to work on her drawing. Such occupation eased her, hid all of her worries and fears. The past week had been an unbearable one. Constrained by propriety, by the cordon of servants that stood between them, and perhaps his own wishes, she'd been unable to help nurse Stephen. But the wish was there, and the wanting, too.

She'd had to be content with hearing of his recovery from Betty's daily reports.

Would she see him soon? Another concern that was supplanted by her work. Too many questions, not enough answers. But then, Stephen had always been a mystery. At least now, she knew he was real.

"What do you think you're doing?" Richard scowled at him from the doorway.

Stephen handed the two lists to William.

"My duty," he said shortly. "Give the list of foodstuffs to Betty," he told William, his young aide. "Tell her I understand that we are short on supplies. What she needs can be obtained from the village."

He had already sent out scouts to find General Penroth's location. The general's proximity concerned him. He disliked the idea of the Parliamentarians being this close to his home. Should Penroth wish to fight him, he was woefully unprepared. Sixty men against six thousand were not odds he would choose.

William nodded. He was the son of the mayor of Langlinais, had been with Stephen since Edgehill. He had been, like so many of the regiment, untried in war. But unlike most, William was suited for it. It was rumored that Oliver Cromwell possessed the same type of instinctive military nature.

"You've barely recovered."

"But I have," Stephen said, standing. His left arm was bent and bound to his chest, a position it would retain until his wound healed.

"You would coddle me, Richard."

His suite of rooms occupied the whole of the east wing. A commodious series of chambers. Enough space to raise a family if the rest of the house disintegrated around him.

He'd discovered in the last days, however, that it was not altogether a comfortable place. The bed was soft, the furnishings as elaborate as any in the house. The windows let in a soft light. The wall-coverings were in a soft hue, unlike the garish green parlor. There were enough touches to remind him that it was his chamber and therefore home. But it was too quiet and left too much time for thoughts he'd rather not have had.

In his study, he could at least be of some use. Time was fleeting, and he'd lost too much of it in illness.

"I want you well," Richard argued.

Stephen smiled. "I am as well as I can be. The king will expect me."

"Must you return? The war will get on well enough without you."

"I'm not sure the king will. His commanders are quarrelling, and his advisors are idiots."

"You sound more like a Parliamentarian than a Royalist," Richard said. His look seemed to measure the effect of his words.

"You are not the first to have made that pronouncement."

"Then why fight on the side of the king?"

"I am the Earl of Langlinais," he said simply. "My home is six hundred years old. A kingdom at least as venerable as the king's, if not divinely acquired. I can understand his wish to keep his intact."

"So it is empathy that makes you fight?" Richard's look was one of skepticism.

"Perhaps," Stephen said.

"I've not your compassion," Richard said. "But I can admire your loyalty, even though I think it misplaced."

"A great many Englishmen feel as you do."

"Why do I think you are one of them?"

Stephen said nothing. There was, after all, nothing he could say.

Richard studied him intently. "Have you grown that cautious in the past years?"

"It is better to remain silent at court, Richard. Words are often twisted, while silence can never be misinterpreted."

"Then I do not envy the role you've chosen," Richard said. An expression of emotion that surprised Stephen. "If you cannot put faith in your companions," Richard said, "perhaps it is time to trust your enemies."

He left the room before Stephen could answer. Another dilemma. What could he have said? There was too much truth to Richard's words.

Stephen walked to the window, stood staring out at the panorama.

This morning an encroaching storm cast dismal colors over the landscape. The lowering clouds were dark, almost black, swept across the sky by winds that bowed the branches of tall trees and fluttered through the thick grass. A monochromatic array of black and gray tinted the hills.

He loved his home. Loved it almost as much as he hated war. Yet its very existence would be threatened if he did not leave to fight for the king. A paradox he accepted even as he wished it were different.

The house echoed with life around him. Six men of his regiment were at Harrington Court. They were soldiers who had not come from Lange on Terne or the neighboring villages, or they had no place to stay with relatives.

It was an odd billet, his ancestral home. The floorboards creaked overhead, boots tapped against wooden floors in a strange tattoo. Water gurgled in the pipes from the cistern on the roof.

He'd learned from Betty that the supply of ale had been replenished twice. Plus two of the maids fancied themselves in love. He only hoped that the sentiments were returned and his men had not taken advantage of the young women employed at Harrington Court.

A motion caught his eye. He glanced below. Anne Sinclair sat in the garden, her head bent over her task, her cape fluttering in the breeze. What did she labor on so diligently? Why was she here? Where had she been going when the soldiers had waylaid her?

Who are you?

Questions he should have asked her, instead of simply pondering the nature of them alone.

Chapter 6

─────∽◯◯◯◯∽─────

She was capable of sitting for hours focused upon a drawing and did so on this occasion. She found herself distracted, however, by the increasingly brisk wind. Finally, she surrendered. The sketch she was working on did not interest her as much as a playful breeze. It tossed her hair about and furled the edges of the paper. As if it dared her to follow where it led.

Standing, she placed the board carefully atop her sketches and pulled her cape around her shoulders. She walked through the garden gate and let the wind take her where it would.

The breeze caught her cape and whirled it around her ankles. A last breath of winter or a puff of spring come to tantalize and tease. Above, the sky boiled with gray clouds, lending a somberness to the scene.

Anne frowned as she caught a glimpse of something in the distance. A spire, perhaps, or an outcropping of rock. But it seemed to be something more. A line of thick trees flirted with the view.

The air, hazed by the brisk wind, added to the mystery.

It appeared almost like a tower. Not a square tower, as Dunniwerth boasted, but a round and elegant structure topped with crenellated teeth of stone. There was something familiar about it, something haunting and mystical that lured her to walk across the expanse of green and see it more closely. A few minutes later she was out of breath and transfixed.

It was her castle.

A pair of birds sat close together on a branch nearby, their heads still and almost touching. Their tail feathers were in perfect alignment, pointing to the ground, identical white spots upon their tips like tiny arrow points. They looked to be discussing the climate or the other birds or something that only birds would know, a discourse held in a secret language undecipherable by mere mortals. The call of a crow, raucous and demanding, dislodged them from their comfortable perch, led them into being birds again and not companions.

A squirrel chattered at her, clung upside down onto the broad trunk of a venerable tree. His face lifted, and he frowned at her, as if questioning her presence, so silent and still in this place of enchantment.

For that was what it was. A time out of time, held frozen for that moment or however many moments she stood there.

The last time she'd seen it had been in her mind. Nestled beside a boiling river, haughty and aloof in its befogged majesty. The bailey had been green with growth. The air had been perfumed with scents of flowers, and from the embrasures had come the petulant warble of newly hatched baby birds.

She could almost feel the grass of the bailey beneath her feet, knew where it grew bare in places like a bald man's pate. She could point out how high the river swept to the side of the wall. Below the buttery was a stairway that led to the riverbank, and it was here supplies were brought into the castle. There was a chamber that contained an odd oblong basin, and the oddest room of all, empty except for a tall wooden structure that fanned out like a broody hen and was filled with quills and glass bottles and stacks of parchment.

Time had changed the place she'd seen in her vision. Time and the hand of nature, if not man's. The castle rose up before her, no longer haughty. A stone maiden, perhaps, her dignity still intact, but her face wrinkled and worn. Even the sky, dismal and gray, seemed to mourn the change. One of the three towers was no more than rubble, another leaned perilously to the side. Only a third still stood proud and resolute. Memories furnished her eyes with details missing in actuality. The gate was no longer there, the broad front door had been taken down.

A river stretched between her and the castle. The only way across was a brick bridge that spanned the expanse. Time had not treated it well. It looked to be almost fragile, imperiously so. Anne walked slowly over the bridge, gauging her safety by the groan and creak of hidden timbers. A stone crumbled and fell to the ground, and for a moment, her imagination sent her following it, turning head over feet, toward the frothy water. She looked over the side, surprised to find that the river was placid beneath her.

At the other side of the bridge, the ground rose upward slightly to the middle bailey. There the grass was thick and green and as tall as her knees.

Once it had been a place where people congregated. Laughter and jests, gossip and news, they had all been exchanged upon this broad rise of earth. There to the right was the upper bailey, where the entrance to the great hall lay. She walked a few dozen feet beyond, stopped, and looked around her. A gate should be here. One constructed of iron and stone and fitted with a small guardhouse.

A feeling of almost unbearable sadness rose within her. She turned slowly, measuring the destruction around her. Hearing in her mind the echoes of voices and long-ago laughter.

She was not there when Stephen entered the knot garden. The wind gusted around the topiaries in mad delight, flapped the edges of papers on the table as if summoning his attention. He removed the board she'd placed there and studied her drawings.

An artist, then. He'd not known she had such talent. But then, he knew few things about her. Only that she'd spoken his name in his fever and lured him close, eased him when he was in pain.

The first drawing was a caricature of a young maid, but where cruelty might have accentuated her prominent ears and made even more pronounced the shape of her large teeth, she'd been rendered lovely. At her feet, obviously groveling, was William, his aide. The second sketch was of Richard. He was standing at a bedside, a cup in his hand and a medicine chest tucked beneath his arm. There was a look of fondness on Richard's face and an exasperated look on his patient's. Stephen suspected the patient was Anne's companion and that the drawing was less caricature than truth.

It was something they shared in a way. His drawings were limited to structures, buildings that fascinated him and stirred his imagination. His fingers dealt in sharp angles and lines that followed a mathematical precision. He saw the world as it had been and wished to bring it back to life. She saw the world as it was and parodied it. He could delineate brick and stone and indicate where mortar was chipping, but he did not have the power to summon forth a smile.

He came to the third drawing. His fingers held it steady against a growing wind. It was Langlinais. Not as it was, but as it might have been. The river acted as a mirror for the towers, the arches of bridge, and the crenellated roofs. A growth of willows, their branches heavy and trailing, marked the path close to the river, the sturdy wooden dock, and the retaining wall. She was not only capable of summoning forth amusement, but of creating pictures of great beauty.

She'd evidently studied the ruins well, just as she had some grasp of history. Another mystery to layer upon the first. Identity and intent.

He replaced the drawings where he'd found them, then glanced behind him. He looked up at the window on the second floor. His study summoned him; his work was not yet done. There were other duties he must perform, provisions he must order, letters to send. Instead, he stepped away from the hedges that lined the garden.

The hill upon which Harrington Court was perched was higher than the rest of the land around it. From here he could see the ruins of Langlinais. And walking in front of the east tower the figure of a woman.

Unwisely, perhaps, he followed her.

A doorway led to darkened steps, the interior of the tower made even more dim by the overcast sky. Anne braced her hand against the curved wall as she began her ascent. It seemed as if her feet knew the way, as if she'd seen these sloping steps before, could count their number in her mind. One hundred twenty-eight.

A handhold was there, finally, and she placed her fingers within its worn groove and wondered how many hands besides hers had sought its safety. It was easy to pull herself up through the opening. Less so to stand upon the windswept tip of the tower and feel part of the oncoming storm.

She had seen this place before. Had watched that view through Stephen's eyes.

She saw now the scene of so many of her visions. Not Harrington Court but this castle. Here he had stood as a boy, as a youth, as a man, looking out over his domain, feeling a pride of place and destiny and heritage. He had planned here, had sat against the curved wall with his legs drawn up and sketched the castle as it should be. She'd wanted to learn to draw the day she'd seen him doing so.

And found a love in it. Did he feel the same?

His life had not been as serene as she would have wished for him. Another vision had placed him within reach of his father's fists. She had cried aloud that day and wished him far from there and to safety.

She knelt on the floor, her hands tracing the line of bricks. He'd hidden his sketches here so that they would not be destroyed. A hidey-hole to protect what was most precious to him. She'd created one for herself, too, although she'd no need. But she'd searched through the clearing on the island for the perfect tree and hidden her best drawings in the knot created by a fallen branch. In prior years it might have been used as a nest, but from that moment on, she'd placed her treasures there, feeling a kinship with the boy she'd seen all her life.

Her fingers trembled as she found the brick, coaxed it out bit by bit. Behind it was a rectangular space where, as a boy, Stephen had kept his drawings. She reached inside and found it empty. She hadn't expect it to be otherwise, but she smiled at her optimism.

The wind was rising, soughing around the curve of the tower, keening like a piper's lament. She glanced up. The sky was black and angry, the storm no longer approaching but directly above her. A spear of lightning darted from one cloud to another, followed by a rumble of thunder that seemed to praise the show of light.

Her hand trembled around the brick even as her stomach clenched. A child's fear. One the woman had not quite outgrown.

It is God's way of talking, Anne.

A giant lives in the clouds, Anne, and his breath is the wind.

Don't be afraid, my child. It is but the rain come to nourish the flowers.

Somehow those kind words had not eased her terror. Not then. Not now.

She should not have been here, but she was.

He stood disbelieving, half in and half out of the opening to the roof.

Finally, he pulled himself up, stood defiant against the growing storm.

She looked up at him. Her skin was tinted by a rosy blush, her brown hair blown by the wind. Her eyes were made almost black by the encroaching darkness.

She knelt before the hiding place he'd made for himself as a boy. He'd laboriously removed a brick from the inner wall and hollowed out the space behind it. A place to store his most precious things, his treasures. No one knew of it. How had she known?

Her lips appeared tremulous, as if they captured a sound and hid it trapped inside. His name again? Or had that been merely a fevered dream? This might be one. But he felt the wind blowing against his face, could feel the sudden chill of it. From somewhere close he heard thunder.

She stretched out her trembling hand, the second time she'd done so. Just as before, he held out his own, touched her fingertips.

The moment was important, portentous. He did not speak, could barely breathe in the spell of it. Once again, he felt as if he should know her, should say something to her, but the words escaped him. The moments stretched between them so strong and real that he might have reached out with his hands and touched them. Wrung them into tiny seconds. But instead, his fingers barely touched hers.

Impatient to end his confusion, he reached out and gripped her wrist so tight that he could feel the blood pound there, could measure the warming of her hands.

He took one step toward her. Then another. She closed her eyes as a rumble of thunder overhead shook the tower. Her fingers trembled against his wrist. Fear of storms? Or of him? He let loose her hand, stepped back.

She stood, faced him. The wind pressed her skirts against the long line of her legs, blew her hair behind her so that there was no subterfuge, no shadow to his study of her. Only the line of cheek and chin, the sweep of a throat and a pulsing beat there.

She came too close, her hand once again breaching the distance between them. A look of compassion flickered over her face even as her fingers brushed tenderly against his folded arm.

The thunder sounded like cannon fire. Her eyes closed; her fingers curved against his shirt. It was not him she feared, then, but the storm. The wrath of nature itself.

She took one step closer. Propriety did not halt her. It was as if her greater fear silenced any thought of it. Or perhaps they had already vaulted over those gates the moment she'd whispered in his ear and kept him silent in his pain.

"How did you know about this place?" One of

a hundred questions he had for her. He was not as much enraged as he was confused. He told himself she would say something that would easily explain. Except that she said nothing. Instead, she trembled and her face paled.

An arc of lightning flashed above them, a vein of light that surged across the black sky. The storm was above them, so loud that he would not have been able to hear her answer had she given him one.

The clouds, tired of their show of bravado, opened up, showering them with heavy drops. In only seconds they were drenched. Her eyes were closed, her face as pale as death. But she made no move to escape the rain. It was as if she were frozen in that moment, held stiff and taut. A streak of silver lightning plunged into the ground, followed almost instantly by a hollow clap of thunder. It felt as if the air had been split in two.

Her eyes opened wide, the look in them stark and wild. She pulled away, escaping into the darkness of the stairway.

He followed her down the spiral steps. Halfway down another burst of thunder halted her. Her back flattened against the curving wall, her eyes clenched shut. Just before he reached her, she moved again, descending the remaining steps slowly, as if she finally realized her danger in taking the slippery steps too fast.

As she reached the stone floor, the lightning struck again. The glare of it illuminated the interior of the tower. His foot touched the last step as the world seemed to shatter around them. She ran toward him, her figure made white by the unremitting glare. Her face was ashen, her hands clenched into the fabric of her skirt. Her arms pressed around him, her cheek lay flat against his chest. Her trembling vied with the shuddering earth.

He held her with his uninjured arm, the two of them encapsulated in darkness. Another flash. He looked up. The sky sizzled. Then the world became white fire, his hearing deadened by the eruption of sound. He was pressed against the curving wall of the tower, his arms holding tight to Anne, as the ground shuddered, helpless, beneath them. The wind blew the dust around the inside of the tower in a whirlwind; the rain entered from the stairwell opening and dampened the air. It was an otherworldly scene, one that he could have easily imagined in one of his fevered dreams.

When it was over, he pulled away from her, pressed his fingers against her cheek. She tilted her head just so, as if she leaned into his touch, fitted herself to it. His fingers trailed to the base of her throat, his thumb extended upward beneath her chin.

She glanced up at him then. A look not unlike the one she'd given him in the meadow. His fingers halted their exploration. He dropped his hand. The storm raged around them, and his thoughts were as chaotic.

The storm, instead of abating, seemed to hover overhead. The sound of it increased, the tower magnifying the deep rumble of the thunder until it sounded as if God himself snarled.

Perhaps it was because their clothing was sodden

or because he'd spent the last week dreaming of her, but he was suddenly acutely aware of each curve of her. His hand trailed around her waist, feeling the suppleness of it, the gentle taper of her hips beneath the material of her skirt.

In that instant, he envisioned her naked against him, standing on tiptoe in order to fit her body more perfectly to his. He would hold her there, bend his head in order to rain kisses on her shoulders, press his face against her breasts, touch her softly and sweetly and with the greatest care. He could almost feel her bare skin beneath his fingertips. Could taste the texture of her lips, feel the warmth of her breath on his flesh. He wanted, suddenly, to press his lips against her throat. Just that. A kiss to measure the pounding of her blood, the heat of her skin.

She placed her hand on his chest, and he felt the texture and heat of her palm against his skin, as if his wet shirt were not there at all. He did not wish to touch her, because he knew, with an odd sense, that if he did, he would draw her closer until there was nothing between them at all. He would remove her wet clothes from her and offer her veneration for the beauty of her rain-drenched body. There would be nothing to guide him but this confusion that had ruled his life from the moment he'd seen her.

She looked almost fragile with her head bent before him, her hand upon his chest. A bridge of flesh. A woman of stubbornness, talent, mystery.

The boyish Stephen peered out behind responsibility and authority and wanted to demand of her why he felt as if he knew her. Pugnacious and stubborn, his childish self would remain until granted the answer. Then, after she'd told him, maybe he would know why he thought too much about her, not enough about those things listed on a scroll in his mind. All the various tasks that remained for him to perform were somehow made unimportant beside the enigma she offered.

She startled him then by standing on tiptoe and placing a sweet and simple kiss upon the corner of his mouth. Here, it seemed to say, I have marked the spot, and this will be where my lips rest. Then she fingered the line of his jaw with her thumb, as if she tested the angle of it.

He had never been a man of touch. He had about him, he believed, an almost iced reserve that warned others against coming too close or venturing too near. Even as men clapped each other on the shoulder or clasped a hand, they rarely did so with him. Yet he remained silent and still beneath her explorations.

He disliked feeling helpless, wound together by the knots of all his wants and desires. But he was, unbelievably. There were men who were frightened of him, who saw his raised sword and blanched. Others knew of his reputation for good fortune and battle prowess and fled before they met.

She simply stood and kissed him.

She pulled back her hand and stepped away. He wanted to ask her to keep it there. Perhaps to kiss him again. But he was a man of sense and a fearsome strength of will. Duty. Honor. Loyalty. The doctrines of his life. He stepped back, away, a safe distance from her touch. But he was not protected from her smile, so sweet that it seemed to take the place of the absent sun.

The wind had risen, and she was soaked clear to the skin, her trembling not strictly from the storm but from the cold. It kept her safe, that small shiver. Rendered her helpless and therefore someone to be sheltered, cared for, and defended. At that instant, he had fewer thoughts of seduction than of protection. He would see her back to her chamber, give Betty orders to cosset her if need be. Keep her safe and away from him until he left. For her sake, if not for his.

His better impulses had him walking to the door at the base of the tower. Once there, he turned and looked at her. The storm had not abated, but it was as dangerous here. This place offered shelter, but with temptation.

But because she was a woman under his protection and because she trembled from the storm and because a part of him still wished to remain with her, he turned to her and extended his hand.

Silently, she walked to him, placed her hand against his. Palm to palm, the link they shared seemed an acceptance of another bond between them. One he could not decipher and did not truly wish to.

He'd killed his share of men, because it was war and someone had decreed that they were his enemies. He was prepared to face death for his country, to give his life if that were necessary. A courage that came from necessity and in a sense from honor. But he suddenly found himself afraid in a way that labeled him coward and knave and fool. This woman with her small smile and her flushed cheeks was a greater danger to his peace than the chaos of war itself.

Chapter 7

❧❧❧

Anne held tight to his hand, wished that she were not so cowardly. *A Sinclair is brave. Fearless.* An incantation that had been repeated to her and by her since she was a child. A recitation to balance the terror that storms induced.

They were nearly to the bridge when the lightning struck again, a sword of light that brought with it a stench of fiery air. As if God himself lived in the clouds and was annoyed by their show of defiance. The earth rumbled, lifted up beneath the pummeling. She fell to her hands and knees just as the thunder roared.

It was as if the earth had ended. The world stilled horribly for a second and then exploded. The ground shuddered. Boulders fell around them. Dust rose, was dampened, enshrouded them in a cloud, as if Langlinais was disintegrating around them.

Stephen pressed his hand to the back of her head. She needed no further urging to press her face against his chest, grip his shirt, and murmur a silent prayer. She closed her eyes, more than frightened.

All of her childhood terrors were being realized in this moment. And all of its wishes.

Just the day before, Anne had worried for him. Had lain in her borrowed bed and stared at the ceiling, fervent prayers easing her to sleep. Now he knelt with her and held her to him. A dream? Another vision? No. There was too much will in this man, too much power.

His injured arm was protected by being bound to his body. Her lips rested against his fingers, breathed against his skin.

An eternity later the sound gradually faded, the storm appeased. Her grip on his shirt eased. She pulled back. Not far, but enough to glance up at him.

He was looking down at her.

Anne reached out her hand and brushed her fingers over his cheek, feeling the warmth of his skin and the softness of it newly shaven. His unsmiling lips were full and almost hot beneath her fingers.

She'd expected to see him pale. Wan, perhaps, from the sick room. But this man bore no signs of illness.

Beneath his restraint, just beneath the somberness of his look, was another man, one who looked out at her from flashing eyes. One she might have feared had she not been so fascinated. There was a look in his eyes she'd never seen, not in all her visions. As if he saw her as a woman and had his own thoughts about what he'd like to do with her. It was a look the men of Dunniwerth were always careful to mask. She was Anne Sinclair and, as such, almost inviolate.

But this man dared. A discovery, then. He could

silence her with a look and make her cheeks heat. Not from embarrassment, which might have been wiser. Instead, anticipation. Her blood rushed, hot, through her body. Her breath grew tight.

Stephen lowered his head slowly. She might have pulled back, but she didn't. Simply waited and sighed when she felt the texture of his lips, the heat of his mouth. She arched closer to him, her lips falling open beneath his. He coaxed her to him, the emotion hinted at in his gaze there in full measure in a kiss. He murmured something, a word, an enjoiner, an endearment, or a command, she wasn't sure. His hand came up and flattened gently against her cheek, tilted her head. She moaned, a simple sound that echoed her body's enchantment with such a thing.

She wanted to be inhaled by him.

Her helpless murmur connected them, a breath passed from one to the other. The kiss grew deeper until there was only darkness in her mind. The sweeping majesty of a sky without stars.

A breath escaped her, one and then another. There were no thoughts in her mind, only an ache that brought no pain. It spread through her body, heated her breasts, raced to her toes. She was a secret becoming unveiled, a rumor being shouted, a girl changing to woman.

Her fingers dug into the linen of his shirt, pressing against the texture in frustration. His skin was shielded and covered and barred from her, and she could not touch him, absorb the heat of him.

Long moments later, he lifted his head, ended the kiss. She blinked open her eyes, a sound of protest on her lips.

His face was burnished in the soft shadows of the morning storm, his breath as rapid as hers. Realization of where they were seeped into her passion-drugged mind. They knelt together on the sodden ground beneath a gentle rain. In the north the sky was clearing, and a patch of blue indicated that nature was done with its tantrum.

She should have stood and walked away. Or protested the kiss. Said a word that lightened the moment. Any one of several dozen things. Instead, she stared at him, her breath still caught in her chest, her blood racing hot through her body.

His fingers reached out and pressed against her bottom lip. The very tip of her tongue touched it.

"Who are you?" he asked, his voice hoarse with desire.

A dreamer. Words she didn't speak.

But he did not seem to expect her to answer. He stood and held out his hand. Anne rose reluctantly, placed her own atop it. *Kiss me again.* Not a maidenly thought. Yet she wanted another kiss or a hundred of them. She wanted him to lead her to that place his kiss had lured her, where all she could feel was the touch of his lips and her own response.

She arranged her sodden skirts around her, sluiced her hands over her face, drying it as well as she was able. Stephen did the same, the moment freed from its awkwardness by their similar gestures.

The sun began to shine as if in apology for what the storm had caused. Not brightly, but with a watery gleam that illuminated the scene of destruction. She looked around them. The lightning had come dangerously close. The tower that had stood there a moment ago was only a mounded pile of stone and brick now.

She was stunned at how close they had come to being killed.

"Too close," Stephen said from behind her. An echo of her thought.

She nodded.

A glint among the bricks caught her attention. Something glittered in the gray morning. She picked her way through the debris, reached down, and retrieved it from beneath a crumbled bit of stone. It was a coffer, its rounded wooden lid elaborately carved. A gold adornment in the center of it was what she'd seen shining.

"What is it?" she asked, holding it up for him to see. It was surprisingly heavy. She handed it to him when he joined her.

There was no lock, just a simple latch, which he pried up with his finger. Age had made it difficult to move, not intention. The leather hinges gave way and crumbled as Stephen raised the lid. Inside was a wooden block darkened with water and age. He lifted it up and out of the coffer. Not a wooden block at all, but two flat pieces of wood holding at least a hundred pages of parchment tightly pressed together.

The first page was brown and crumbled. The latter half of the book had suffered water damage a long time ago. It was no longer legible. The ink looked to have remained stable, but the parchment had hardened into a black sludge. The first page, however, was as white as the day it had been prepared.

"Do you read Latin?" he asked.

Anne shook her head.

He scanned to the bottom of the first page, then glanced at her, a half smile curving his lips. "It's a codex written by my ancestress. She was rumored to have been a scribe."

She watched as his hands closed the rounded top of the coffer. His fingers traced the intricate carvings of the wood, the detail of the gold medallion. Even the hinges, little more than crumbling leather, were touched gently.

"It must be more than four hundred years old."

She stretched out her fingers and touched the coffer in awe.

He frowned, studied the rubble, then bent and removed a few more stones. "It shouldn't have been here," he said. "Only armament was stored in the tower, but even so it hadn't been used for years."

"Unless it was placed there on purpose," she said.

He glanced at her, surprised.

"Perhaps it was meant to be kept hidden."

They retraced their steps, Anne's attention on her footing over the crumbled stone. When she was clear of the mounds of brick, she looked up. Stephen's gaze was on her, his look shuttered.

"Forgive me," he said. "I should not have kissed you."

Silence stretched between them. An apology. How strange that she'd never thought him to offer one. As if he was shamed by their kiss and wished to eradicate the memory of it. The idea robbed her of speech. She looked beyond him to where the bridge spanned the Terne.

"Circumstance has made you a guest of Harrington Court. As such, you are under my protection."

Anne nodded. It was a true enough statement. Did he wish her to also agree that it had been wrong to kiss him? She would not, nor could she believe it to be. Rash, perhaps. She might grant him that. Destined? That, too, if he only knew it. But she felt no remorse about it.

"Do you truly regret it?" There, words that were even more improvident than the kiss.

"My honor would suffer for it if I were not."

"If I did not feel the same? Would that excuse your honor?" Was there a spark in his eyes? A twinkling star in the heavens of them? Or only something she wished to see?

"Do you always say what you wish, Anne Sinclair?"

"I rarely do," she said, giving him the truth. Her visions had been kept a secret all her life. Her journey here had been cloaked in silence. Even this last week had been one of omission rather than speech. "But I cannot regret kissing you," she said, a declaration and a bit of honesty that made him frown.

She left him then before she could say more. But she felt his gaze on her all the way back to the great house on the hill.

Hannah sat up with difficulty, surprised at the sign of weakness. Every muscle in her body ached, and it felt as if all her bones creaked in protest of her inactivity.

The door opened slowly, but instead of Anne or one of the maids, the physician's face appeared, his shock of white hair topped with a small and delicate bald spot. *Like the opposite of a nest,* she thought, hiding her smile.

He should have looked incongruous, but instead, such oddity of appearance suited him. He was tall and angular, as if he'd taken too many of his own potions and not enough meat. His face was the opposite, round and florid, his eyebrows bushy and white, and there were tufts of facial hair dotting his skin like little islands. His narrow-eyed glare, however, warned the unwary not to be fooled by his genial appearance. There was a quick-witted mind and a will of iron behind that smile.

She sniffed the air.

"Not gruel. I shall not eat it."

"It's a nourishing soup. And you will have no choice," Richard said, his grin challenging. "If you do not eat it, I will simply feed it to you. It strengthens the blood."

"Did you cook it?"

He placed the tray on the bedside table. "Yes," he said, his grin bordering on the smug. "It's comprised of several delicious ingredients."

"Eye of newt."

"Dandelion leaves," he corrected.

"It will give me a rash."

"It will aid your digestion."

"I don't want a purge."

"I've missed my chance, then."

"You are a foul-minded man, sir."

"While you are a delightful patient, Hannah. Possessed of the most amiable disposition, the sweetest smile, the most dulcet of voices."

"I believe you think I'm a canker."

His grin broadened. "I'm sure you don't mean

to be," he said amicably, all the while holding out
the spoon. "You might as well eat it," he said.
"Else I just may drown you in it."

She eyed it with suspicion.

"I thought physicians were supposed to be gentle
and caring."

"I am," he said. "Most of my patients think
highly of me. But I might ask the same of you. I
thought women of your age were supposed to be
grandmotherly and gentle. Frail, perhaps."

She eyed him with great dislike. His smile grew
more sunny with every passing moment.

It was the oddest thing, but she'd grown to quite
like the man over the past few days. His order that
she remain in this room, however, was onerous.

"I am not that old."

"Hmm," he said, nudging her lips with the
spoon. "Most hags are difficult to get along with.
They're crotchety and generally make life miserable for everyone." She told herself he was teasing.
That there was no reason to feel hurt. But she was.
Enough that she opened her mouth and drank his
vile potion. It wasn't bad. It needed a few more
spices, but she would die before she criticized it.

Another spoonful was taken, then another. Finally, she reached for the spoon herself, not even
bothering to tell him that she could feed herself
very well on her own. She had done so all week.

"I've hurt you," he said.

"Don't be silly."

"You're as far from a hag as any woman I've
ever known."

"While you're a troll," she said, and felt a bit
better at his grin.

"There, I knew you would return. The temptation was too great."

"You could do with some spices in your soup," she said, forgetting her admonition to refrain from comment.

"Then I will confess. I didn't prepare it," he said, motioning with his hand for her to continue to eat. She did so. In fact, she was ravenous. A few vegetables would not be amiss in this broth. When she said as much, he only continued to grin.

"I suggest," he said finally, "that you gain your strength and go tell cook. She is a formidable woman, but then she needs to be to cook for a place this size. My own home is much more modest."

"All I've seen of Harrington Court has been this chamber," Hannah said, looking about her.

Besides the huge box of a bed there were two matching candlestands embellished with inlay. Between the two ceiling-to-floor windows dressed in green brocade stood a dressing table draped to the floor with a similar material. The top was covered with a linen kerchief and adorned with a large mirror, as well as several ornate bottles of a pale green hue. A tall cabinet with folding doors sat against the opposite wall. One closet held clothes while another hid the closestool. On one of the candlestands was a brass bell, a solid-looking thing of some distinction. The sound it gave off when she raised it was loud enough to summon angels. The two chairs arranged in front of the window were quite comfortable.

Altogether, the accommodations were lovely, the hospitality unexpected. Yet she'd still to meet her host.

Hannah leaned back against the chair once her meal was done. She frowned at Richard, then allowed him to take her hand and ease her to her feet.

She sat on the bed, not bothering to hide her distaste for what would come. It was time for Richard to tighten her bindings once again, a necessity but not unduly painful, although she felt shy and ill at ease.

Neither of them looked at each other when he acted as physician, as if to distance themselves further from the intimacy of his fingers on her bare flesh. No man had touched her since Robbie. It startled her to realize how pleasant it was and how very much she'd missed it.

"Have you finished torturing me?" she asked when he stepped away. Her side ached like blazes. She closed her eyes but allowed a small smile to appear on her face.

She didn't see him lean close, but she felt the whisper of his breath against her cheek.

"You're a fraud, Hannah," he said, the teasing humor in his voice warming her. "I think you're a kind and gentle creature."

"You've been taking too much of your own medicine, sir," she said.

"Would it be amiss to have you call me by my name?" he asked. "It has been a long time since a lovely woman spoke it."

She frowned at him. He was altogether too much at ease with blandishments.

"It is Richard, should you consider it."

Once installed in a heavily stuffed chair, she allowed him to tuck the coverlet around her legs, not once criticizing him for his efforts.

Instead, she thanked him softly. The word incited a smile and a twinkle in his eyes. He wiggled his eyebrows at her, and she laughed despite herself.

"Thank you," she said again, and touched his cheek with her fingertips. "Richard."

He looked as if he would say something. But he withdrew and straightened, his eyes growing warm and less filled with humor.

"Shall I stay and keep you company?"

When she said nothing, he only smiled at her. He left the room, closing the door softly behind him.

Hannah remained staring at it for a long time.

Silly man.

Chapter 8

~~~ ✦ ~~~

Anne answered the knock on her door to find Betty standing in the hall, her arms laden with material.

She softly smiled in greeting as she entered the room. The material turned out to be Anne's only spare dress.

"I've had it sponged," the housekeeper said, "since you were caught in the rain."

"Thank you," Anne said, touched by the gesture and grateful for the opportunity to change. She only wished she'd been able to save her sketches. They'd been half shielded by her drawing board, but even so, the rain had done enough damage for them to have to be drawn again.

"I've come with more than a dress," Betty said. "A message from the earl."

Anne waited, curious.

"If you would be interested, the earl would like to show you what he's discovered in that old book the two of you found."

It was anticipation Anne felt and something more. An awareness she'd never had before. But then she'd never kissed a man the way she'd kissed him. And wished more of it if the entire truth were divulged.

"Has he done something to offend you, miss?" A question uttered in an offhand tone. But Anne had seen Betty when she was a child, knew that her feelings for Stephen stemmed not from mere loyalty but also from affection.

"Did he say so?" she asked carefully.

Betty placed the dress in the armoire, fluffed the skirt before rolling up the hem. "He asked me to tell him how you accepted his invitation." She turned and studied Anne, then smiled. "I shall report that you did not appear angry."

Anne smiled back at the housekeeper.

He stood when she entered, an act of civility to which she was not accustomed. The men of Dunniwerth were not rude or uncouth. But she was one of them and did not expect the treatment they might accord a stranger.

It made her oddly awkward to be the subject of such undivided attention. He had the ability to render her not only mute, but nervous. Or perhaps only acutely aware of him.

She'd kissed him. Passionately. Fear of thunder and lightning had been supplanted by another emotion. One that had never been explained to her, but whose power was equal to a storm's fury. She clasped her hands in front of her and studied the top of his desk. Did passion show? Reveal itself in some way that he might discern the nature of her thoughts?

It would not disturb her if he knew. Another discovery, then.

The coffer was placed near the front of his desk, the codex spread out before him.

"You know Latin, then," she said to ease the silence.

"My old tutor would say not well."

"I speak only Gaelic and English," she admitted. "My kinsmen speak the one, and my father wished me to learn the other."

He came around the desk then and stood close to her. So close that surely he could hear the pounding of her heart. "I am glad he did so. Else we would never be able to converse. I know nothing of Gaelic."

She nodded, an absurd gesture, but one of nervousness more than assent.

"It was Gaelic you spoke to me that day," he said. "What did you say?"

Words she should not have said, mingled with the truth. A tale of her visions mixed with feelings, emotions too strong to be voiced in English. Words he would understand, sentiments he would not.

She walked to the window. It stretched from the ceiling to where the sill was placed a few feet above the floor. Had it been deeper, it would have been a perfect place upon which to sit. A strange thing, that the afternoon should be so bright and sunny when the morning had been so dark and brooding. The view was of the meadow and beyond, to the curve of the river Terne.

He had never asked her how she knew his name, and she had never asked how he had come to rescue her.

There were more secrets between them than there were revelations. As if each of them had a veneer that needed to be stripped away, the better to see the soul more clearly.

Who would be the first to lay bare hidden thoughts?

"Do you take refuge in silence, Anne, when you do not wish to answer a question?" She glanced back at him. There was a small smile on his lips.

"A habit of my childhood, perhaps. I found that if I remained quiet, people didn't notice I was there."

"I doubt it's possible to ignore you," he said dryly.

She wondered if it was a compliment he offered or an insult.

His slight smile both answered the question and warmed her.

"Adults have a habit of doing so around children," she said. "Children are often ignored, as if their small stature measures their minds. I confess to taking advantage of their inattention. I discovered that I could learn the most wonderful things by remaining quiet and still."

"Such as?"

So she was to be the first to reveal herself. It was a capitulation that made her smile. No one at Dunniwerth would have thought her so pliant. She was, perhaps, too headstrong. A bit of strength, however, was never amiss when dealing with all those Sinclair men.

"Impudent things. Gordon drank more than anyone knew. Agnes had a sweet spot in her heart for him and filled his cup the moment it became empty. Hamish had a way of charming all the women, and some charmed right back. I did not understand everything I saw at the time, but I soon learned that it was better to remain silent rather than to question anyone about it."

"What happened when you asked questions?" he said.

"Well, there was the time I asked my father if God only lived in the kirk or if he lived in Gordon's tankard like he said." She glanced over at him. "He just stared at me. Or when I asked my mother why men always try to look down Moira's bodice. My mother just made a choking sound and walked away."

He seemed surprised by the sound of his own laughter.

"What kind of child were you?" she asked.

He glanced at her quickly as if to divine the reason for her curiosity. What would he do if she were to tell him that she wanted to know everything about him? She wanted to learn those pieces of his life she hadn't seen, discover the emotions behind the glittering anger she'd witnessed and the smiles of happiness. She remained silent, instead, encouraging him to speak with a wish.

"A serious student, set to the task of learning more to keep my tutor employed than for the joy of it. I remember reciting Latin verbs only because my father was to be home the next day and was to test me on my knowledge. In my position of heir I was expected to excel."

"Did you?"

He smiled. "Yes."

She smiled at his confidence.

"It was the Sinclair prayer I spoke that day," she said suddenly, giving him half the truth.

"Will you translate it for me?"

She let her fingers trail over the edge of the mullion as she did so. "The might of the Father of Kings, with the wisdom of his glorious son, through the grace and the goodness of the Holy Ghost, be with us at our beginnings, and give us grace in our mortal life living."

"A beautiful sentiment."

Her amusement was real. "My father always adds one sentence to it." She looked up at him and smiled. "Grant us the power to prevail that we may not come too soon to your kingdom, and the wisdom to rule beside you when we do."

His laughter caught her off guard. Had it been possible to freeze time, she would have wished it done now. Him standing before her, his smile transformed into a lusty laugh. Despite his injury, or perhaps in counterpart to it, he looked fit and strong. A tall man with broad shoulders. He stood, sovereign over this room and any space he commanded. A man who any other man might wish to emulate. That the visions had promised, and that they had made true.

He'd asked if she was a poet, and she'd responded negatively. But from some place she remembered something uttered by a man of sweet words. *And he is half a god.*

"I saw your drawings," he said.

She turned away, focused on the view outside the window. No, in truth she didn't see it at all. It seemed that more revelation was in order. She was private about her sketches. Occasionally she gifted them to people. The sketch of the young maid was for William, in gratitude for his help in looking for Douglas. The picture of Richard and Hannah had amused her. And Langlinais? She'd done it because she often gained comfort from sketching the castle, as if it held some power over her moods.

"I envy your talent," he said.

She glanced over her shoulder.

"My father's mapmaker taught me. He is a truly gifted man. His maps are works of art, decorated with tiny birds and animals. His lochs are so skillfully drawn that they look as if you might be able to swim in them."

"You are as accomplished, Anne."

She shrugged, oddly embarrassed.

Flanking the windows were two bookcases stretching from floor to ceiling. She walked to one of them, surveyed the titles. Two languages she did not know.

"Your education was more complete than mine." She fingered the tooled leather spine of one of the books. "My father decreed that I was not to grow up unlearned. So anyone in the clan with something to teach me took their turn. From my mother there was needlework and patience. I'm horrible at both," she confessed with a smile. "But I do know how to mix chalk and vinegar to clean the silver and use a horsetail and rag for the pewter and brass. Old Peter taught me how to catch a fish. So I'll never go hungry," she added in an aside.

"As long as there are fish around," he said wryly.

She smiled. "Hamish instructed me on the pipes, but he laughed the one time I attempted to play them. I thought I would never get my breath back."

"What did your father contribute?"

"How to swim and ride, to tally the annual barley crop, to bargain with the peddlers who came to Dunniwerth."

"A woman of many talents."

"I was taught that a willing mind was a virtue," she explained. "But I confess to not wanting to know certain things."

"Such as?"

"Stitchery," she said. "As I said, I am woefully inadequate. And tanning leather, perhaps."

His smile was surprisingly warm.

"Diverse topics. I know nothing of needlework, but I agree with you about tanning. It is a necessary chore, but it has a powerful odor."

"I should never like to learn a stableboy's job."

His smile broadened. "There are worse occupations," he said.

"I hope you will not tell me," she said, and smiled.

"Poverty," he contributed. "I am very glad not to have had to learn about poverty."

She thought about it. Dunniwerth was not as large as Harrington Court, but it was still a prosperous holding. She'd lacked for nothing as a child, was considered an heiress by some. She nodded in agreement.

"Wounded," she softly said. "I have not asked about your arm. Is it truly better?"

"I am a paragon of healing, according to Richard."

She smiled. "While he does nothing but fuss at poor Hannah."

"He has a great respect for your friend."

"I suspect they are kindred spirits," she confessed. "He is forever grumbling at her, and she is constantly complaining about him. But her words are only a screen. She is excruciatingly polite to people she despises."

"So it is a mark of her favor if she is rude?"

She nodded. "She would hate to realize that she is so transparent, however," she said, looking about the room. She had been here before, but her attention had not been on her surroundings. Only Stephen.

The room was filled with objects that drew her eye. The walls were lined with leather imprinted with a detailed geometric pattern. The ceiling was as ornate as anything in the rest of the house, with huge swags touched with gold leaf.

But the objects that filled the room were of greater interest. There was a massive globe, which sat firmly on a three-legged stand, a graduated series of blue-patterned ceramic bowls arranged on a set of shelves. On the top of a tall chest was a bronze bust of an imperious-looking man, his head topped with short curls, deep lines framing an unsmiling mouth. He looked down on Stephen's desk as if he were judge. A gilt and enameled silver disk that depicted a battle scene lay propped against a high shelf, and a basin crafted from brass and inlaid with gold and silver, stood alone atop a low chest.

She turned, her mind filled with questions. As she did so, her glance happened on the mantel. A piece of embroidery caught her eye. The last thing she'd done with needlework had been a sampler decorated with huffing caterpillars and lazy bees. This was a work of art embroidered with tiny colored beads. She picked it up by its silvered frame, studied it in the sunlight.

It was only the size of her palm, but it depicted a beautiful girl with blond ringlets and a soft smile.

"This is lovely," she said.

Stephen walked to her side, looked down at the portrait. "It's Sarah," he said. "Richard's daughter. She is very talented. The miniature was a gift from her."

She replaced the portrait carefully where she'd found it.

Such gifts were personal, meant to be shared by dear friends or those with closer ties. The thoughts that swirled in her mind had their roots in a greater emotion than envy.

Her father had a sense of great fairness, and he had instilled it in his daughter. Lessons that had not been all that easy to learn.

If she was given two gifts, she was to offer one to another child. Before she received a new dress, the poorest member of the clan was outfitted. If she was offered a treat, such as a sweet or a piece of honeyed bread, it was only after those around her had been served first. It was difficult, sometimes, to be Robert Sinclair's daughter.

But she'd learned to share and learned, too, to be responsible for those who did not have as much as she.

This afternoon, however, those lessons dissipated into mist. All she felt was a possessiveness that nearly swamped her. An emotion that had been forbidden to her as a child was now so strong that it was almost savage.

Mine. All that she felt for Stephen could be distilled into one word. One word to account for all the prayers, all the dreams, all the wishes of a childhood. He was hers. Not for sharing, nor for granting to another. She had no wish to be unselfish and she was not capable of tolerance.

"She married last year," he said, his words settling on her like feathers. Or cold water on the fire of her sudden and surprising rage.

She turned away, pretended a study of a ewer encrusted with lapis lazuli until she calmed.

Finally, she glanced up at him. He was unsmiling, his glance somber. He looked as if he would investigate her soul, peer inside her eyes until he came to the core of her. What would he find? A woman with too many sins, one of which she'd not known she possessed in such a degree. Pride, stubbornness, and now envy. Or perhaps worse. Covetousness. This journey had illuminated all her faults.

She walked away from him, not trusting the sanctity of silence. She wanted to say too many things, and they were tamped down by only a thin layer of reserve. It was no more sturdy than a flaky pie crust bubbling up in places.

An odd structure in the corner of the room caught her eye. Her leather-soled shoes made a hollow sound as she walked across the wooden floor.

She'd seen it before. In a room devoid of all other furniture. Gently, she placed her hand on the nearly black wood, sensing that it was a very old object. Nearly as tall as she, it was a structure formed of three pieces, a center unit and two flanking areas of the same height. She went around to the back of it. One side was divided lengthwise, the other contained several pockets. The surface of the main unit was slanted and divided. Two holes were carved into the top, but only one was filled with a reservoir of greenish glass.

"It belonged to Juliana," Stephen said. "It's a scribe's desk and the only piece of furniture to have survived the flood at Langlinais."

Her fingers rested on the slanted top of the desk.

"I know nothing about the art of being a scribe."

He smiled. "You are right to call it an art. She was very talented in her glyphs. Almost as much as you are in your drawings."

She smiled. "Thank you," she said. "I'll confess to even more ignorance," she said. "I don't know what a glyph is either."

"Come over here and I'll show you."

She sat where he indicated at the side of his desk. This chair was not unlike the one in which he sat. But whereas his was elaborately carved with lions, this one was adorned with bears. Dozens of bears in various poses. "It's a very interesting chair, isn't it?"

"My father thought so. He had a dozen or so commissioned." He looked up. "Do you like it?"

She didn't want to offend him, but the words stuck in her mouth. His grin relieved her. "Each one is uglier than the next," he said, smiling. "The one with the snakes is particularly loathsome."

He handed her a sheet of parchment. The wooden bindings had been removed from the codex and set aside. The text that began the page began with the initial W. It was decorated in startlingly vivid reds and blues and green inks.

"See that figure?" he asked, pointing to the girl

resting at the point of the letter. "That's a glyph."

On the middle of the *W* was a delicate drawing of a young girl, her legs swinging over the edge of the letter. On her face was a smile, so real that Anne could feel her own lips curve in response. Everything was perfect about the sketch, from the tumbling golden hair to the diaphanous garment the girl wore.

"She was far more talented than I," she said, in genuine appreciation. She smiled up at Stephen. "Did she do them throughout the codex?"

He nodded. "She interspersed her text with drawings. One resembles Sebastian, her husband. She also drew another knight," he said, turning to a separate page.

Anne studied it with the same fascination as the first drawing. Juliana had depicted a man dressed in padded cap and armor of intricately drawn links of mail. His white tunic was emblazoned with a cross consisting of four arrows joined together at the points. The symbol was duplicated on the short triangular shield at his side. The look on his face was one of cunning. In his hands he held a cup, which he held aloft. Juliana had drawn small points emanating from the chalice as if light streamed through it.

Anne tilted her head and studied the drawing, wondering what it was about the picture of the knight that prompted such a sense of recognition. It was as if she knew him.

"She left several recipes for her inks," Stephen said, carefully turning the brittle pages. "I'm grateful that it's easier to simply purchase ink today."

"Would you like to have lived in Juliana's time?"

"Been a knight?" He smiled. "It's nice to consider such things, isn't it? The romance of an era filters through the years, but we do not realize what it might be like to live then. The inconveniences, the lack of amenities."

"Do you think they considered it? Or did they just do as we all do? Live our lives in the way they've been fashioned? Perhaps a woman of four hundred years ago would be amused that we think her life is considered fascinating."

"And perhaps one day people will think the same of us."

It was an odd thought, that someone might think of her in the distant future and wonder what she'd thought and felt and dreamed. "But for them to do so, I must leave something behind. Something to prove that I've been here, to mark my place."

"Perhaps people do, in the form of their children."

"Juliana did, didn't she? Else you would not be sitting here."

He looked surprised by the thought, then glanced down at the codex once more.

"I've translated her words. I haven't used my Latin for years, but I've become accustomed to the cadence of her writing."

"Cadence?"

He nodded, then smiled over at her. "She writes almost like poetry. It has a rhythm. Here, let me show you.

" 'I have been earnest in my attempts to transcribe these words and diligent in my efforts. May

God bless me for my attempt and forgive my omissions and errors. I have made no judgment of these pages, only a faithful rendition of them. My task is to impart the truth of these matters to all who come after us, who would know of the true story of Langlinais Castle and the threat that stands between us and lasting peace. Would it be that this chronicle were never needed. That all that is Langlinais will remain fast and without peril.' "

Her gaze never left his face as he read Juliana's words. His voice was low and resonant, enunciating the words slowly as he translated.

" 'Sebastian, Lord of Langlinais, and I married when we were children. I was sent at the age of five to live at the convent of the Sisters of Charity. It was almost within the shadow of Langlinais. It was there I was to be taught the skills of chatelaine of such a great castle. I dutifully learned those tasks I needed to know in order to fulfill my role as the Bride of Langlinais. I found my true joy within those convent walls, the skill of scribe that I use now to place these words upon parchment.

" 'I heard that Sebastian left Langlinais to go on crusade. I was content enough to remain at the convent and wait for him. But finally he returned, and I prepared myself to leave the convent. Such a summons never arrived. But years later I was sent for and arrived at Langlinais. It is at this moment that my chronicle begins.' "

Stephen was correct. There was a rhythm to Juliana's words. As if she sat before them now and told her story. Not unlike Gordon at Dunniwerth, with his warm voice and his way of changing the tempo to make the tale more dramatic.

"Was that normal, for wives to be sent to convents?"

He looked up. "Only the better born, I think. Langlinais was considered a major demesne in England at the time. To be its chatelaine would require a great deal of skill and work."

He returned to the translation.

" 'My first meeting with Sebastian frightened me. My lord husband wore a monk's robe and remained in the shadows. Sebastian wished a marriage that would never be one in truth. There was such an air of mystery and sadness about him that my heart was touched even as my mind was set to questioning. I did not know why he was so careful never to come close. Not then.' "

Anne leaned her arm on the desk, propped her chin in her hand. Not only was Stephen's voice alluring, but the story he read was fascinating. What must Juliana have felt? Why had her husband worn a monk's robe?

Stephen glanced over at her, smiled as he read.

" 'My lord knew that I was lonely and agreed to meet me for conversation. We sat upon the floor of the east tower in the darkness, speaking of our lives. Mine, having been relegated to the convent, was measured by the hours. Sebastian's had been marked by great deeds. I learned how he had become a knight, why he'd studied in Paris. We talked of my translations, of Ovid and Catullus and men whose words still sang with beauty over the years. But he would not speak of his time on crusade or those years when he did not summon me to his side.' "

"Who are Ovid and Catullus?" Anne asked.

Stephen leaned back in the chair, glanced away, then back at her. The look on his face, she suspected, was not unlike her own when she did not wish to answer a question directly. Or when the answer was something she was certain would not please. Her smile widened as she watched.

"My tutor would have said godless men, for all that they were learned in their time."

That did not explain the hesitation of his answer. She remained patient, her gaze never leaving his face.

" *'Amabo, mea dulcis Ipsithilla,*
meae deliciae, mei lepores,
iube ad te veniam meridiatum.' "

"What does it mean?" she asked softly.

He looked straight at her as he answered. "My sweet Ipsithilla, my delight, my darling, let me come to you at noon today."

"Is that all?"

"No," he said softly. "Catullus goes on for several lines, describing what, exactly, he will do to sweet Ipsitilla when he arrives at her house."

She felt the warmth rise to her face. She looked down at the desk. "Oh."

"His work held a great fascination for me when I was younger," he said wryly. "He was not forbidden, but his words led me to think of things not related to my studies."

"And now?" A dangerous question. Especially when the room had grown so still. As if even the gentle breeze dared not brush against the windowpanes.

He smiled and released her from suspense. "Now war takes precedence over individual wishes."

He bent to his task again.

" 'One day I happened upon Sebastian at his prayers. A faint light from a candle threw my thoughts into disarray. He was not wounded nor was he deformed by battle. My husband was blessed with a manly beauty that awed me. I did not understand why my lord had hid his appearance, but he would not discuss it. Nor why our marriage must remain one of such distance, and why he was so careful never to touch me—' "

A knock on the open door startled her. Stephen, however, merely looked up, his expression one of calm acceptance. But then, his thoughts were probably not as forbidden as hers.

It was William, and with him another of Stephen's regiment attired in the blue uniform that marked them as Langlinais men.

"What news, James?"

"We found Penroth, my lord. He is encamped two days away. But his force is not large. No more than fifty men."

"Outriders?" Steven asked.

James nodded. "But there are rumors of a large force to the north. At least twenty miles away."

Stephen glanced at Anne, then nodded to James. An effective dismissal, she thought. Done with the ease of a man accustomed to command. But he did not dismiss his men. Only her.

"Perhaps we should continue this another time," he said, rising.

She smiled, a cool, polite smile. One of understanding. Acceptance. It did not, she hoped, show one tinge of regret or one bit of fear. But she felt both at this moment.

In a move that would have pleased her mother and amused Hannah, she left the room silently. The questions she ached to ask were held tight behind smiling lips.

Ian stood in the shadows watching. He had protected Anne for so long that it was second nature to do so. Fool, he chided himself. That was not why he waited here. He wanted to know if his suspicions were correct.

She left the chamber, finally. Her dress was not askew, nor was her hair mussed. The Englishman had not dishonored her then. But there was a look on her face that displeased him.

It was obvious that she felt something for this Earl of Langlinais. Ian wished he'd never seen this place, or agreed to bring her here. Did she realize why he'd done so? Not because she was his laird's daughter. Not because she had asked him to, wording her request in such a way that it was near to a command. But because she was Anne.

His Anne.

From the beginning, he'd known something was wrong. There was more to this quest than she'd told him. The moment she'd seen the Earl, everything had begun to change. She'd had a look on her face he'd never before seen. As if this Englishman made her smile inside.

Ian's mouth twisted in a grimace. She'd been so enchanted with the man that she'd not noticed that the search for Douglas still continued and that Ian was gone most days from this English place. He'd not found his clansman. Only one reason to curse this journey.

The other soured in his stomach. She treated him as if he were her brother. Or worse. A servant hired for the day. She sent longing glances toward the Earl's chamber, and sought information as to his injuries, but not once asked how he fared.

He turned and walked away. He was determined to leave this place called Langlinais the moment Hannah was able to travel. Perhaps once she was home again, Anne would see what had been in front of her eyes all along. A man who loved her. A worthy man. A Scot.

Chapter 9

❝**I** knew I would find you here," Richard said, looking around him.

The castle of Langlinais was only a shell of what it had been once. "Don't you have something less strenuous to occupy you?"

"You're more solicitous than Betty," Stephen said, bending to retrieve another brick.

"And you more stubborn than your father," he said, frowning. "I used to wonder that you didn't sleep in this miserable place. "Why do you keep picking it up, Stephen? It will just keep falling down."

Stephen smiled at his friend.

"Because it does keep falling down, Richard." He bent and picked up a piece of stone and iron that had become dislodged from the upper wall, moved it to the side. Working with one arm kept the job small and the results infinitesimal.

He didn't bother trying to sort through the debris caused by the destruction of the north tower. It had only been a matter of time until it had fallen. Although Langlinais had been nearly submerged

when the Terne flooded two hundred years ago, the
north tower looked to have had extensive renova-
tions performed on it long before then. The intervening years had only made the damage worse. His
efforts now were directed at the ruins of the great
hall.

He looked around him, studying the further destruction that had occurred in the past two years
since he'd been home. It was not just the lightning
that had done damage. The back wall of the chapel
had crumbled, and the last of the retaining wall had
fallen into the river.

Unlike the old abbeys and monasteries that dotted the countryside, the stones and bricks of Langlinais were not taken to use as building materials
for new construction. The villagers of Lange on
Terne acceded to his wishes. Even if they had not,
the castle was rumored to be haunted. A notion that
made Stephen smile.

"At least your father didn't have a chance to destroy it," Richard said, looking around him.

"He would have, if he'd known it mattered to
me," Stephen said.

He had long since tired of trying to understand
his father's antipathy. It had existed for itself, in its
own right, separate and apart from anything Stephen might say or do. Perhaps it was based on
something tangible, or perhaps his father had simply been one of those people who are miserable
and wish the world to share their misery. Or perhaps he'd wished for more sons to follow him and
been discontented with the one he'd had. A thought
that had often led Stephen to wonder why his father
had not remarried.

Stephen had chosen to ignore Randall Harrington

with the same alacrity with which his father had
ignored him. It was not difficult after all; ten
months of the year his father lived in London.

His father would, on his rare visits, discharge
one of the servants because of some personal idi-
osyncrasy that annoyed him. He'd once dismissed
a footman because he hadn't liked the man's eyebrows. He'd decree that certain rooms were to be
redecorated or closed off and others used instead.
He would terrorize the servants with his shouts,
demand full meals for his many guests at any hour
of day or night, and be generally abusive to anyone
who questioned his many dictates.

Yet, for all his petty tyrannies, Randall Harrington had built a church for the town of Lange on
Terne and sponsored several boys as apprentices in
trade. He'd given dowries to more than twenty girls
whose families could not afford them, and endowed
at least that many boys with funds to begin their
own careers in the army. It was a lesson in life that
Stephen never forgot. Even a man filled with vices
has some virtues.

On the day he was informed of his father's death,
Stephen was fourteen years old. He'd brought his
father home to be buried in Lange on Terne. His
spirit had rebelled at placing him beside his mother,
but he'd done so for her sake. She had, after all,
loved the man.

He had become, when he was fourteen, the heir
to a notable fortune, immense property, enormous
responsibility, and a heritage that stretched behind
him for six hundred years. He'd rehired those people his father had discharged in the past year, fired
his steward, paid off his mistress, and proceeded to

behave in a manner not given to fourteen-year-old boys.

His childhood had left him on that day, and in its place a more somber man had been born. But there were times when a hint of his childish voice could still be heard from some place deep inside where memories dwelled.

"I wonder what he would think, Stephen, to know that you've prospered despite him," Richard said.

"He would, no doubt, claim it his influence, Richard."

The two men shared a look of unrepentant humor.

"I did not like the man, Stephen, but then, you knew that well."

"Everyone in the county knew you disliked him, Richard. I think he believed you and my mother were childhood sweethearts and that she'd never been reconciled to their marriage."

"What romantic tripe," Richard said, smiling. "Mary Lynn and I were friends, nothing more. She adored your father, was delighted to be a countess. If anything changed her mind about their marriage, it was him, Stephen, not me."

Stephen grinned, his mood lightened by Richard's blunt honesty. There was little hypocrisy to Richard. The more unpalatable truths he often delivered cloaked in humor. With his friends, however, he simply dispensed with the humor and said what he thought.

Richard moved from his position against the wall, idly brushing dust from his sleeve. "You love this place, don't you?"

Stephen looked around him as if viewing Langlinais for the first time.

His father had wanted to tear the castle down brick by brick, sell the stone. Had he never noticed the carved embrasures or the fact that the bridge resembled a Roman aqueduct?

Langlinais seemed more than brick and stone and crumbling mortar to him. There was something magical about this place, something that gripped his imagination and always had.

Over the years he'd examined the ruins of the chapel, studied the foundation, unearthed the stones and brick until he had begun to understand how Langlinais had been constructed six hundred years earlier. One day, he wanted to put the whole of it back together, to experiment with different types of clay and ash in order to duplicate the type of mortar originally used. A secret dream, precious now that there was little time to do so.

Did he love Langlinais?

"Yes," he said simply.

He smiled, picked up another brick, and placed it on the pile beside him.

"You should not tax your arm in that fashion," Richard said.

"I hope you're as solicitous of your other patient," Stephen said.

Richard made a noise that was a cross between a laugh and a grunt.

"She is not as well pleased with my skill, I'm afraid. She orders me about and has the oddest notions of medicine. She would have me believe she has more knowledge than I. I spent half the morning defending some of my practices."

There was a note in his voice that intrigued Stephen enough to comment upon it. "Why do I think you enjoyed every moment, Richard?"

"It would be impossible not to enjoy it," he confessed with a twinkle.

"When will she be well enough to travel?"

Richard eyed him. "You wish her gone before you leave? How long would that be?"

Stephen had been absent for nearly two weeks. The Royalists needed his regiment, their expertise with armament, even the fanatical enthusiasm that greeted their arrival on a battlefield.

"A few days, perhaps."

"It had better be longer than that, Stephen. I doubt you could sit your horse an hour right now."

Stephen smiled, genuinely amused. Richard had no idea what conditions they'd endured during the last eighteen months. "I would take that bet, my friend," he said.

"Then I'd better go and care for my other patient," Richard said, and left the ruins.

Stephen bade him farewell with a smile.

"General, sir." Thomas Penroth turned his head to watch as his aide cantered up to him. "General, the outriders have brought a prisoner."

He said nothing as one of his lieutenants, David Newbury, approached him. The man was as excited as if he brought him a prize, much like a cat would present a bird as a dubious gift.

Five hours later it was evident that the prisoner was either a great prevaricator or he was devoid of sense. And directions and knowledge, and the answers to the simple questions of his origin and destination. He pointed. First to the east, then at subsequent times to the west, north, and south.

"I ran," he said again when asked how he had come to be on the road. Once again he was threatened with being flogged.

He smiled instead of looking frightened.

For good measure, Penroth had had the man stripped to the waist and a few lashes applied to his back. He'd screamed, run into the corner, and had huddled there, weeping.

When he'd been thrown back in the chair it was with the same degree of force that might befall any other prisoner, but Thomas had felt the bite of shame. An absurd notion to feel in war.

They discovered, in the next three hours, that the man's name was Douglas. They'd no indication of surname or purpose in being in England. He was a Scot, but beyond that the man could furnish little information.

"Let him go," Penroth said, when it was obvious that they would get no more.

His aide turned to him, the surprise all too evident on his face. "General?"

"Let him go," he repeated. He looked over at the man with the child's mind. He sat upon a camp stool, his arms draped between his knees. He no longer looked up with an air of expectancy when someone entered the tent. Instead, he shivered. As if pain or fear had finally made him aware of his danger. It hadn't mattered. He'd told them nothing.

Penroth's men were regimented, strictly disciplined. There were fines and flogging for drunkenness, for taking the name of God in vain. For a hundred other infractions of a rigid set of rules. This was war and he had never swerved from his cause, thinking that it had been blessed. He could not, however, help but think that he had erred in this matter.

"Let him go," he said for the third time and left the tent.

He summoned Newbury to him, waited impatiently for the man to attend him. When the leader of the patrol entered his tent, Penroth did not greet him nor did he bother to upbraid the man on the condition of his uniform. Instead, he made him repeat every word that had transpired between him and the man claiming to be the Earl of Langlinais.

"Are you certain?" Penroth asked, even though he'd heard the tale more than a few times.

"Yes, sir."

"Go back to where you were," he said. "Look around. There must be a town nearby. See what you can discover and report back to me as soon as you can."

The man nodded and left.

He sat on the edge of his cot, an unwieldy affair made of a wooden frame and rope support. It made up in comfort what it cost his servants in time to break it down and set it up again.

The Earl of Langlinais and his Blessed Regiment. Indeed. If he never heard his name again it would be a blessing. The last time he'd faced the man it had been a rout. They should have won the battle. They'd outnumbered the Royalist troops nearly three to one. There was no doubt as to the outcome, but when he had been advised of the tide of the battle, Thomas had nearly had the messenger flogged for lying.

They had not encountered any other troops for over fifty miles. His orders were to proceed north and meet up with additional Parliamentarian forces.

Had it been coincidence that his men had met the earl? Or had they stumbled onto his home? If so, why was the Earl of Langlinais not with the king's troops? Or, even more important, were the king's troops waiting to ambush the Parliamentarian forces the further north Penroth traveled?

Questions General Penroth could not answer.

The inclusion of a Scot into the mix was troubling. Were the rumors true, then? They said the king was seeking a secret alliance with James Graham, the Earl of Montrose.

Parliament would hear of this, he vowed.

But Parliament rarely acted with any immediacy, preferring to govern by committee. If it could be lost, confused or misunderstood, Parliament would do so. Would he not be wiser to act against the earl himself?

General Penroth vowed that he would gather what information he could and then make a decision. To leave the Earl of Langlinais in peace? Or trap him when he least expected it?

Chapter 10

❦

Stephen sat against a backdrop of yellowing brick. His black hair was almost to his shoulders, blown back from a tanned face by a gentle, teasing wind. His gaze, midnight-blue eyes narrowed, was focused on a vista she could not see. The sunlight created a nimbus of light around him, created highlights in his black hair.

Anne looked about her, wondering why such a place had the power to both move her to tears and make her smile. It was only brick and mortar after all. Her own home was almost as old. But Dunniwerth teemed with life, while Langlinais seemed only to echo with it. Long-ago voices that sang in the wind.

When Stephen turned and glanced at her, she felt her breath still. He was not handsome. Instead, his was a virile face, one of strength and power. A silly woman would fear him. But she had whispered in his ear and felt his breath on her cheek. And kissed him until her heart had caught on fire.

"I wondered if you'd come," he said when she drew closer.

"Ned told me you would be here."

He smiled. "He is more taciturn than I would have wished. Did he say nothing else?"

"Only that I was to come if I wanted," she said, smiling. "You offered me a four-hundred-year-old story," she said. "How could I not?"

"Do you mind sitting here? The day is fair and bright."

"And it is much too lovely to be indoors," she finished.

They smiled at each other in perfect accord. Another bridge, another link.

He sat on the half wall and held out his hand for her. She placed her own on his. His palm felt strong and wide, a long strip of callus running from the tip of his index finger to the base of his thumb. She wondered if it was caused by days of holding the reins of a horse or wielding a sword for hours.

Even something so simple as touching his hand could make her breath feel tight in her chest.

She sat beside him, arranged her skirt. Her hands were folded in her lap. She looked at the stones beneath her feet, but her attention was directed toward Stephen.

He opened the codex and began to translate.

" 'Sebastian finally told me that he had been captured by the Saracen. It was Jerard, his squire and steward, who spoke to me of Sebastian's act of generosity in sparing him. It was for this reason that my lord could not pay his own ransom. The Templars, therefore, lent him the money to be released. But not until Sebastian had spent more than a year in a dark and dank cell.' "

"Who are the Templars?"

"The Poor Knights of the Temple of Solomon. They were a very powerful group of warrior knights formed about five hundred years ago. Their original mission was to escort pilgrims to the Holy Land, but they were disbanded there. There were those who considered them more powerful than the Pope."

"And Sebastian owed them money?"

He frowned and nodded. Then continued to read.

" 'The loan due the Templars weighed heavily on my husband in addition to the two secrets he held. It is my belief that they stripped him of any peace he might have felt at returning to Langlinais.' "

"Two secrets?"

He nodded, his attention seemingly as caught as hers by Juliana's words.

" 'Sebastian told me of Magdalene, his father's concubine and a woman who had been almost like a mother to my lord. At the death of Sebastian's father, she went to live in France, becoming a Cathar. It was at their fortress, Montvichet, that she died. Magdalene left with my lord the treasure of the Cathars, one of two secrets Sebastian kept hidden from me. Magdalene had summoned him to Montvichet, but he arrived too late to save her. I asked him once if he had gone on Crusade to find his faith, and he only smiled. I believe now that it was a great test he'd offered God. God does not like to be tested and granted Sebastian an answer. That answer was the second of his secrets.' "

As his lips framed the Latin words, the structure of them almost poetry, Anne recalled an image of him as a youth in almost the same posture. The setting had been different, but the intensity of his concentration had been the same. The love of language for the sake of it, the fascination with learning. He had sat, when she'd seen him then, with his hands upon his knees and his back swordstraight. His tutor had stood over him, a tall, fullbodied man with a look of geniality on his features. But his eyes had been narrowed, and occasionally he'd poked the air with his finger as if to emphasize a point or accentuate a passage. The voice of the young Stephen was neither timorous nor shy, but in it there was a hint of reticence.

The years had stripped that from him. Matured and hardened him. Perhaps it was court that had done so or perhaps war. How odd that she had never seen a vision of him in battle. And how blessed, too. She would not have been able to bear it.

" 'Sebastian sent word to the Templars, asking for an extension of time in which to pay the remaining sum. The letter he received in return was written by his brother, Gregory. He had left Langlinais to find his fortune and discovered the lure of the Templars, instead.' "

She wanted, suddenly, to understand the words he spoke so fluently as he translated Juliana's codex.

"Is it easier for you to do that?" she asked him. "To speak the Latin first and then the English?"

He glanced over at her. "It reminds me of my lessons," he said, smiling. "Perhaps that's why I do so. I had not noticed."

She would like to learn Latin, to have that connection with him. Many threads stretched between them, but he knew nothing of their origins. Her visions, her love of drawing, her absorption with Langlinais. She wanted some shared interest between them, something he might recognize, an association based on scholarship.

"How do you say secret in Latin?" she asked.

He glanced over at her.

"Or mystery?"

"The words are not dissimilar," he said, closing the codex. "*Secretum*, a secret, mystery. Or *aenigma* for mystery, riddle."

"Will you teach me Latin?"

His gaze was solemn, a natural expression for him. But she'd seen him laugh too often to believe him devoid of humor.

"There may not be time."

There, the first hint that he was to leave.

She stood and slowly walked to the other side of the great hall. Her footsteps echoed in the ruin. A whisper might have been heard like a shout.

There had been a fireplace in that wall, now fallen to the ground. The ceiling had soared upward nearly twenty feet. A set of stairs at the end of the hall had led to the sleeping quarters and odd rooms tucked into other rooms, such as the oriel converted to a bathing chamber and a room with louvered windows that had held Juliana's desk. Knowledge she'd gleaned through her visions.

If she whispered her secret, would he hear her? A perfect moment to say the words, to hear them ring in the resonant silence of this place. It was easy to command herself to say them. More difficult to do so. They would reverberate against the stones of Langlinais and fall loudly at his feet. Then he would be forced to examine them and her.

Declare her mad or witch. Refute them, repudiate her.

It was so much easier to pretend that the shadow was the substance. She was a traveler. They had been accosted. He was a stranger. She was a visitor.

Did he believe that?

There were only twenty feet that separated them, but it might as well have been measured in years and miles.

He remained in the same position, a half smile on his face. She'd drawn him that way once. The child had been fascinated with him, the young woman had wanted to emulate him. The woman? Had tasted passion in his kiss, was captivated by him.

His eyes darkened as she watched him. She looked away, finally. Too long for propriety's sake. Too long to dissipate the awkward silence.

She fisted her hands in her skirt and did not look at him. Instead, she looked down at the bricks of Langlinais. Over the years the corners had rounded from so many footsteps. But the same force that had eroded them also kept them banded tight together. A lesson, perhaps. One whose exact meaning escaped her.

"What is war like?" A question she could never have asked her father or the other men at Dunniwerth. They would have looked at her as if she were daft. Men spoke of war, and women were there when they wished their minds free of it. A masculine notion that had only amused the women of Dunniwerth.

"Noisy."

She looked up, startled.

His smile surprised her as much as his answer had. "As a boy I'd dreamed of being a great knight, like one of my ancestors. I envisioned myself cutting down hordes of Saracens with silent strokes of my battleaxe. In reality, battle is a strident thing. Not only the screams of the wounded and dying. Insults are traded before blows. The report of muskets, the boom of cannon, the shouts of commanders. Then, too, there are the prayers. Most men pray fervently both before and during a battle."

She tilted her head and looked at him.

"Then why do men fight?" she asked.

He frowned at her. "The easiest answer is because they are told to."

"But why is there war?"

He looked away. For a few moments he didn't speak. "Choose any answer," he said surprisingly. "It will apply to some confrontation."

"Greed."

He nodded. "A man often wants something that is not his. Territory. A common reason."

"Money."

He smiled. "A rich country has often been overwhelmed."

"Power?"

"The most common of all motives."

"Freedom," she suggested.

"A more complicated reason. A great ruler will couch all motives behind it. It speaks to the need within each man." He glanced at her. "Give a man the promise of being unchained, and he will fight for no other reason."

"God."

"The most complicated reason of all," he said.

"Countless wars have been fought with religion as the base. The Crusades were fought for it. Perhaps even this war. Some would say it's for freedom. Others would say the king's greed. It all depends which side is asked."

"The other side of the circle," she said, smiling.

"Circle?"

"Because I was an only child," she said, coming back and sitting on the half wall again, "there were those who thought my life to be one of great luxury. They didn't know that my father insisted that no hour be spent in sloth or that I had my own share of chores. I once complained to him that the children who envied me didn't know what it was like." She turned and smiled at him. "He took me into the courtyard and drew a huge circle on the ground around me. He told me to study where I was and what the circle looked like. Then he held my hand and led me out of the circle. Together we stood there looking down at the ground. 'Look at the circle again,' he said. 'It hasn't changed. But it no longer looks the same, does it?' It taught me that things are often seen different because of the way we view them."

"A wise man. How is it that he let his daughter enter England with barely an escort?"

"Ian would not consider that a compliment," she said. Not an answer, perhaps, but a portion of it. She was becoming too adept at prevarication. He was too riddled with honor and she too lacking. The thought should have shamed her. Instead, it angered her. This journey had been to find him, and all she had truly succeeded in was discovering her-

self. Not all the bits and pieces that had been revealed had been to her liking.

"Is he the man who guarded you so well?"

She nodded. A chore given to him by her father.
No doubt punishment for those years he'd made
her life miserable.

"Do you have some fondness for him?" His look
was solemn again. He had a way of doing that, of
hiding his thoughts and blanking his face.

"Ian?" She smiled. "He was my childhood tor-
mentor. He told me stories of witches and ghosts
and made me think that there were monsters at
Dunniwerth."

"Is he the reason you dislike storms so?"

His glance was quick, shuttered. Unbidden, the
memory of their kiss. It warmed her in ways she'd
not known a memory could.

"I wish I could blame him for that," she said.
"But they have always made me afraid. My earliest
memories are hiding beneath a blanket in terror."

"Sometimes it's good to fear something," he said
surprisingly. "If it prompts restraint and caution."

"Is there anything you fear?"

The question appeared to startle him. It stretched
beyond the carefully prescribed boundary between
host and unwitting guest. But the kiss they'd shared
had done so, too. The memory of it provided a
doorway between them.

"I fear a good many things," he admitted.

She remained silent.

A moment passed. Then another.

"It would be foolish not to."

She said nothing, but she began to feel a welcome amusement. It lightened the sadness that

threatened to overwhelm her and the anger that lay just beneath it. The first because he was leaving, and the second because she was too much the coward to tell him why she was here.

"Mice, perhaps?"

"Mice?" He frowned at her. "No."

"Spiders?"

He only shook his head.

"Parliamentarians, then."

His look of disgust amused her.

"People who are so wise about being brave are normally never afraid," she said.

"Perhaps they've conquered their fears."

"Have you?"

The look he gave her was tinged with irritation. "Are we to repeat the list?"

"No," she said amiably.

"I have some fears," he said. "Simply because I cannot immediately call them to mind means nothing."

She glanced away, hiding her smile.

"Perhaps you should begin to read again."

He studied her in silence. "Are you given often to orders, Anne Sinclair?"

She felt her face warming. "Yes," she confessed. She had a great many duties at Dunniwerth, one of which was supervising the women who carded the raw wool. Perhaps leadership came easily to her because of her father's position as lord. Or perhaps it was simply practice.

He picked up the codex again, but instead of opening it, he stood and extended his hand to help her down from the wall.

He was staring at her, his deep blue eyes narrowed. His face was not thin, but there was no spare flesh on it to hide the strong bones of cheek and jaw. His mouth was unsmiling, but the severity of it was marred by her memories of the kiss they'd shared. Too soft to look so firm. Too alluring for such a forbidding expression.

She knew him so well, had studied his face in the light of candles, in the harshness of a noonday sun, at gloaming. All his expressions seemed imprinted on her mind, so it surprised her that this one was difficult to decipher.

"Have I angered you?" she asked.

"In what way?"

"By saying what I did. I have found that it is easier to simply tell people what to do rather than to wait until it occurs to them. Most people do not mind direction if it is given fairly."

He smiled, and it seemed as if the smile held genuine amusement.

"You will find that I do not need much direction," he said. "As to my duties, they weigh only too heavily on my mind."

"I did not mean *you*, Stephen."

He chuckled.

"I didn't think you did. But it is unfortunately true that I have things to attend to."

His departure.

The sky was a clear blue, the air chilled with spring, the scent of it promising. Here and there were small puddles to give evidence of the storm they'd passed through only yesterday. The mound of rubble that had once been the north tower gave evidence of its fury and of the danger they'd escaped.

She wanted to stay right here, right now. Frozen

to this place and this time. Never to allow the time to tick one second past this moment.

Stephen, however, released her hand and stepped away.

Chapter 11

❧

A nne sat in her chamber and surveyed the night. She'd moved a chair to the window, sat with her bare feet upon the sill, her arms wrapped around her knees.

The darkness was total; even the stars were obscured. A three-quarters moon was tucked into a pocket of clouds and only made a rare appearance. She knew because she'd sat here for hours, hoping to lull herself to sleep. It hadn't worked.

She faced the reflection of herself in the night-shrouded glass of the window. There were other women at Dunniwerth who were more attractive. She'd never minded before that her chin was a bit too square or that she had broad shoulders. Nor did it seem to be a great burden that she was taller than many of the females she knew. Hannah was as tall, and perhaps that's why it hadn't struck her as odd. Her legs were long, her breasts perhaps too large.

One day, when she had just begun to grow from child to woman, she'd asked her mother why her chest seemed so much larger than before. Her mother had answered with a smile. "Because you

are being prepared for the children you may have,"
she said. But the men of Dunniwerth had looked at
her differently from that year on, and it did not
seem something entirely connected to her future
motherhood.

Her feet were large. The cobbler had always
made a comment when she'd gone to be fitted for
a new pair of shoes. It seemed the last was always
too small. Only during the last two years had her
feet stopped growing.

Ian had once called her a great hulking lass, and
it had made her cry, a fact that had made her even
angrier. It seemed that most of her life had been
spent being enraged by Ian. Even now. She asked
each day if he'd any sign of Douglas, and each day
he snarled at her. Today he'd done the same.

"Ask your precious earl, Anne. He's volunteered
his own men to help search."

The first she'd known of it. But the gesture had
not surprised her.

She wished, for the first time in her life, that she
was beautiful. Her mother was beautiful, with
lustrous green eyes and hair the shade of a fox's
tail. Hannah was less so, but there was character in
her face and more often than not humor in her eyes.

Was it a sin to wish for less character and more
allure? If so, she could not be the first woman to
have done so. In fact, she suspected that a great
number of her wishes were not at all uncommon.

She wanted Stephen to look at her and not be
able to look away. To be captivated by something
in her. Whether her wit or her eyes, she didn't care
which. She wanted to be kissed until she couldn't
breathe. Again. And to be touched, perhaps, on all

those various parts of her that had given her such grief. A stroke of fingers along her foot might make it feel more dainty. A kiss on her shoulders might applaud their width. A long, lingering look from toes to nose might very well excuse her height. A caress upon her breasts would venerate their size.

Wasted thoughts. He would not be here long enough to ever know of her secret wishes or forbidden ones.

From his words she could create a vision of war. Fill it in with what she'd overheard at Dunniwerth. Too easily, she could imagine him in the middle of it. With his sword raised high and his grin turned feral, he would be a formidable opponent. She knew only too well that he was mortal. She'd held him when he was in pain and witnessed the degree of it. Did he think himself immune from death?

He was a man chained by honor. She knew all about vows and promises and oaths. She was a Sinclair. A woman of Dunniwerth. Her clan was banded together by a sense of principle so thick it might be a rope. Or a noose.

Beó duine d'éis a anma, agus ni beó d'éis a einigh. Better a man lose his life than his honor. This proverb she didn't bother to repeat to a man who lived the meaning of it.

She would not beg. Sinclair women did not. It would be useless anyway.

She had watched as her mother had bade farewell to her father on numerous occasions, and each time he was out of sight, Maggie Sinclair had burst into tears. But she'd never collapsed in front of her husband, never begged him to stay or let him see her fear. The only words that had passed her lips

were admonitions for him to guard his back and
see to his own health. The harshness of her words
had effectively hidden a grieving heart.

"A Sinclair is always brave, lass." Words her
father had spoken too many times to count. For the
first time, Anne wondered if he'd thought of her
mother when he'd counseled her on courage. Could
she be that strong? Stand on the steps of Harrington
Court and watch Stephen ride away? She must be.

Had there been regret in his voice when he'd told
her he was leaving?

As much remorse for returning to war as for
kissing her?

It would be easier, perhaps, if he had remained
a vision. Only a caricature of who he truly was.
Only a shadow of the man. She'd wanted him to
be real, but he had become too much so. She
watched as the reflection in the window laughed at
herself and the tenor of her thoughts.

The night was a quiet one. Even the inhabitants
of Harrington Court were silent beneath the blus-
tery sky. She envied them their rest even as she
knew she would not share in it.

Chapter 12

Stephen rode Faeren hard, the straining muscles of the animal beneath him echoing his own need to outdistance his very thoughts.

He felt the blood pound in his veins, an elemental force of nature as primitive as the wind that blew or the orange and pink sky in the east.

He felt good, healthy, for the first time in days. Too soon he would be gone from here, and these moments would be savored in memories. Here there was no smell of burned powder or the stench of death. There was only the dawn of a spring day at Langlinais. A reward, then, for days spent in mire and muck and weeks of freezing nearly to death. Or perhaps it was something he earned by his wound.

Here, Stephen, a taste of something clean and fresh and sweet for all your days of pain.

He laughed aloud at the thought that God might deign to converse with him. He did not offer himself as saint, nor did he think himself that great a sinner to attract the attention of the Almighty.

He grinned into the wind and let his horse have his head.

The ground was a blur beneath Faeren's hooves, the flying clods of dirt behind them evidence of the wet spring. They marked the earth with their passing, but the crops would be planted soon, and the only indication that he had ridden a spring-fevered horse would be soon obscured.

What he left to history would be seen as bricks and stone and the reverence he felt for the legacy that was his. He doubted people would marvel at his life or his exploits as much as simply count him as one of many. A link in a chain that had never been broken.

Was there time to create a legacy? Something that might mark him as separate? A singular Earl of Langlinais? Were there enough years left to him? Or was he destined to die in battle? A question more properly asked of those who believed in predestination.

He rode to the top of the hill overlooking Langlinais. If he squinted, he could envision the castle as it might have looked six hundred years ago. A rambling place, whitewashed and glaring on a spring dawn. The three baileys would be green with lush grass, the garden would give off a heady scent of flowers. The river would be high because of the spring rains, the bank protected by a short wall built the length of the castle complex. Birds would nest in the embrasures as they did now, calling out a warning of an early-evening rain. Above all would be the sound of laughter.

Home. A longing for this place sliced through him like a sword. He could not retreat to the past.

He could not remain where he was. The only course was to go forward.

He turned, but before he could descend the hill, looked back at the castle. It had become what it was again. Simply ruins of a place he knew, had always known.

In the silence of the morning he could almost envision Juliana slipping into the north tower to hide her coffer and its tantalizing codex. Why had she done so? What were the secrets she alluded to so mysteriously?

A woman of mystery.

As if he'd summoned her with his thoughts, he saw Anne then. She stood beyond the gardens of Harrington Court. The dawn light blessed her with radiance, cast a gentle shadow over her form.

Was he a fool to think her not an enemy? They lived in perilous times, and she was from Scotland. That country was divided as to which English side to support.

A spy, Stephen? If so, she was a poor one. She'd held him when he was in pain, and her only act of secrecy was in drawing pictures of his castle. Betty liked her, as well as Ned.

As well as he.

She had not pulled away when he'd kissed her, had not repudiated him, only his apology. In fact, she'd looked irritated with him when he'd spoken it. Almost angered. A woman of some will. A terrible spy, if so. An intriguing woman.

He grinned and raced to meet her.

She didn't flinch as he reined Faeren up within inches of her. A test, then, if she'd known it. Or perhaps she did. There was something in her look

that said she did. A pride, if the flush on her cheeks
was any indication.

Or anger. She did not hide it from him. She was
no sweet miss with simpering manners. Nor was she
a courtesan used to men's fawning. She was
strangely both and neither.

A woman to be wary of, certainly. One who fascinated him too much. Hours had been spent with
thoughts of words he might teach her, Latin phrases
she could learn and in the recollection of them also
remember him.

The rising sun lit her face, as if nature itself recognized the delicacy of her profile. Her hair looked
as if it had recently been brushed, tied back as it
was with a scarlet ribbon. If he found one today or
five years hence, he would thread it through his
fingers and think of her.

He should not have studied her so intently, but
he found himself captivated. Her neck was slender,
leading to a chin and jaw that were finely carved.
Her lips were solemn in repose, the bottom one
more full than the top. The mouth of a lover. Not
a woman barely escaped from childhood, with the
glow of youth still upon her. The green dress she
wore hinted at a ripe figure; hips that curved and
breasts that thrust against her laces promised it.
Eyes as brown as the earth beneath his feet but
hinting at gold in their depths surveyed him with
the wise stare of an owl.

He had been wrong to compare her to a courtesan. He could not remember ever seeing a woman
at any court party who rivaled her in beauty. Not
that of paint and artifice, but natural and unre-

strained. A piece of gilt contrasted to the beauty of the sky. Nature won each time.

Her charm was more than her loveliness. It was the way she spoke of this place called Dunniwerth that was her home. The way she looked at Langlinais as if she felt the enchantment of it. And more. Something more that he could not explain, not even to himself.

He did not deal in imponderables, but only those things he might touch and feel. There were things in her eyes that lured him. She was a danger and a delight. She was frightened of storms and talked of circles, spoke in a burr of soft accent and enticed him to think of things he had not thought of for years. He found himself amused by her comments and cast into thought by her questions. Her presence at Harrington Court had never been totally explained, but he cared less for the reason for it than to understand the woman herself.

He'd known her for a week. Two, if one counted the time he was insensible. He'd talked with her on numerous occasions, been charmed by her wit, fascinated by the mystery of her, tempted by the woman.

He was at the king's mercy and subject to his will. As soon as her companion was ready to travel, she would be on her way, her destination and errand unknown to him. They would, in all certainty, never meet again.

It stunned him.

He raised his hand as if to summon her or place his palm upon the face of time itself. She glanced at him quizzically, a faint smile on her face.

"You are abroad early," he said, dismounting.

"I could not sleep," she said.

His night had been as restless. He wondered what had kept her awake. Thoughts, dreams, or fears?

"I did not think you could manage him one-handed," she said, nodding at Faeren.

He smiled, genuinely amused by her comment. "In battle I rarely use the reins at all. Otherwise," he said, "my sword would be useless." Faeren shook his head as if he knew he was being discussed. "He's trained to knee commands."

She reached out and rubbed Faeren's nose. He should have told her that he was a temperamental stallion renowned for his endurance and heart. Not a pretty pet. But he should have known his horse would be as easily charmed as his master. Faeren nearly preened beneath her attentions.

A wiser man would have parted from her then. Would have smiled and played the host with geniality and perhaps some fondness. He would have bowed and removed himself from her presence, attended to those myriad details that fell to him as a commander of men. Or even fled from her presence, prudence being wiser than regrets.

But he didn't. Perhaps he was fevered, not by a suppurating wound, but by spring. Perhaps he was lonely on this morning, and she'd stepped into the role of friend and confidante. Or perhaps he fooled himself that the mystery of Juliana's chronicles was the only thing that bound them.

"I've messages to send," he said. Words of apology to the king. But he did not tell her that. Instead, he offered her the only thing he had that was valuable. Time. It slipped through his fingers like ground diamonds. "Will you join me for the noon meal? There, where the trees border the river. We'll have our meal and a bit of Latin."

"And Juliana's chronicles?"

"Yes." There was little time to complete them. But he'd not hurried himself along, had taken each passage as if it had been delicious and to be savored. Juliana's words had served to join them together. He'd not wished the mystery too easily solved.

She nodded. Agreement without a word spoken. Effortless conspiracy. She was as unwise as he, then. Or as daring. She looked not at him but at his horse, and Faeren snorted. An equine laugh at human hesitation.

"What would you have done," she asked, turning to him, "if it had been your sword arm that was injured?"

"I would have practiced until I'd become proficient with my left," he said. A simple truth. One that did not seem to surprise her.

She looked as if she would have liked to say something, then had changed her mind. A small nod of either admonition to herself or warning to him not to ask.

He had the strange feeling that a fragile fence stretched between them, comprised of good manners and civility, honor and nobility, and virtue. He'd scaled it despite the fact that she was without protector and far from home.

She'd spoken his name and known of his childhood hiding place. But that was not the true depth of her mystery. It lay in the fact that she looked at him sometimes as if she knew his thoughts or could understand the words he did not speak. As if she was a friend who'd been away for a time and now stood waiting for him to recognize her. An odd sensation.

Nor was that the only one. Even with his amusement, even adrift in his confusion, in his wondering, he could not forget her touch. She'd placed her hands on him. Reached up to brush a kiss upon the corner of his lips, returned his improvident kiss with an ardor that had stunned him.

She'd asked him to name those things he feared. Afraid? Not of things he could conquer. Not of circumstances he could easily overcome. Not even of nature's fury. But of a woman who felt known to him, who smiled at him at this moment and urged him to think of warm beds and soft murmurs? Even a fool would be cautious, and he had never been a fool.

He stepped back, mounted Faeren again. He did not say farewell to her. It might have been good practice for the moment soon to come. Instead, he simply lifted his hand in a wave. Then left her.

Penroth's man walked along the cobbled streets of Lange on Terne and wondered at the neatness of the town. He was an Englishman but not a Royalist. It hardly seemed to matter in this small town. Not one person looked at his garments with anything like suspicion. Or wondered that his hair was cut shorter than most.

They were friendly in this place, a benefit to his mission. The only drawback to it was the fact that there were too many soldiers for his liking.

A little boy, no older than three, was being

hefted on the shoulders of one of those uniformed men. He pulled on his hair and bounced on his shoulders, for all the world as if the man were a horse.

"Your son?" he asked. A comment he'd half expected to be rebuffed, him a stranger and all. But the man stopped and smiled.

"He is," he said with pride.

"A great lad."

"He is that."

More conversation divulged that he hadn't seen the lad for two years. Duty had taken him from his home.

The earl's name was mentioned more than once in their talk. Again when he'd stopped for a tankard of ale.

"Oh, aye, we're all Langlinais men," one man said. "All born and bred in the town. And most of our men serve with the earl."

When he wished a good day to an old woman, she smiled back at him. A few moments of conversation gleaned him the information about Harrington Court and the Earl of Langlinais. More knowledge than he needed but given in exchange for a few words of kindness.

General Penroth would be pleased.

Chapter 13

~~~✧✧~~~

B etty sent one of the maids to the place Stephen had selected for their meal with a cloth, a bottle of ale, and a bowl of fruit. She filled a platter with cheeses and crusty bread, covered it with a napkin, and would have delivered it herself if Ned had not caught her hand as she walked through the kitchen.

"You can leave by that door when you're finished," he said, motioning over his shoulder to Anne. His blue eyes twinkled at her, even as he handed Anne the platter.

The wrinkles around his eyes spoke of years of labor in the sun. The hair on his head was graying and sparse. But it was his smile that lingered with her as she crossed the room and opened the door. That and Betty's laughter.

It was a soft sound, one that made her smile. Even during times of war, life went on. Smiles and laughter, joy, and hope. They were never completely extinguished.

Anne placed the platter on the cloth and looked at the scene below her. Langlinais was touched with the sun, the yellowing brick of it making it appear almost golden in the light.

Her legs curled to the side, her drawing board beside her. She was rarely without it. Her sketches were more than a way of occupying time. In her work she put all of the emotion she could not voice, all of the confusion of her life. She'd drawn pictures of Ian when she was a child and made him a grotesque monster. Or on his knees begging her forgiveness. She'd drawn Hannah in many guises, her father going off to war. A hundred pictures that held precious moments and scenes she always wished to remember.

Perhaps one day she would draw Harrington Court. Or Stephen mounted on Faeren. But for now, she held those sketches only in her mind.

The day was what her mother would have called soft. A haze seemed to settle over the landscape, one of heat rather than mist. She leaned back against the trunk of a venerable oak.

She closed her eyes, listened to the sound of the wind as it ruffled through the leaves. A bird called, and the River Terne gurgled a greeting.

An afternoon of peace. It was almost possible to believe that there was no war.

She was not anxiously awaiting him, nor impatient at his absence. Instead, she was asleep, an expression on her face of utter rest. Her cheek was pressed against the bark of the tree, a rough embrace he thought. He sat beside her as quietly as he could, gently pulled her toward him.

Her cheek would bear the imprint of his shirt, instead.

He should have awakened her, but she herself had said that she'd gotten no sleep the night before. What had kept her awake? Dreams? Wishes? He realized that he wanted very much to know.

Her hand brushed against his chest, and he held it tenderly there.

It was a fine hand with long fingers. No calluses marred her skin, no blisters. Yet it was not a delicate appendage. Her palm was almost square, the thumb long. It was a capable hand, one of sturdiness, of competence. One of talent. He could as easily see it controlling the reins of a horse as he could holding a piece of charcoal between thumb and forefinger.

She smelled of roses or some other flower that bloomed in spring. An errant beam of sunlight touched her hair and revealed the colors rampant in one lock. Red and chestnut and a shade almost blond. Strange that he'd never studied hair with such intensity before.

She was silent in sleep, her pose one of deep peace. Or like one enchanted. A small smile wreathed her lips, as if a dream gave her amusement. He wanted to touch her there with his fingertip. Measure the softness of a mouth that lured him to kiss it. Once he had done so, and she'd startled him by touching her tongue to him.

He sat with her, silent and charmed by the moment. The breeze blew more softly, as if it feared to wake her. Even the sound of the river was muted, cautioned by the wind.

A curious protectiveness invaded him. A feeling he'd never had for a woman. For his people and his land, yes. For a building, Langlinais. But never for one woman.

What would it be like to share his life with a woman? To shelter her and protect her? To take delight in doing so? To know that with her he might speak of things he feared with as much ease as he did those he enjoyed? He had felt that ease with few people in his life and never with a woman. Even his friendship with Sarah had been one of polite restraint. He had never stepped beyond the boundaries with her. Never wished to. She was a sweet and well-mannered girl who sparked his humor occasionally and his kindness always.

He had knelt with this woman in the midst of a dangerous storm and not known his peril. Instead, he'd been swept up into the passion of a kiss.

She'd been subjected not only to his lust, but to the absurdities of his thoughts. He'd wondered about her when he should have been making arrangements for Langlinais to be protected against the possibility of early summer floods. He'd thought about her when he'd been postponing his return to Oxford and to wherever the king would send him and his troops.

He could not stop thinking about that moment etched in elemental detail, when the bright blaze of lightning had illuminated her upturned face just at that moment he'd lowered his lips to hers.

How many nights had he lain awake, wondering what it might feel like to have her place this hand on him? To feel the strength of her fingers and the pads of her fingertips, the gentle line of nail on his skin? Too many nights to dismiss the memory of it lightly.

There, a confession that threatened the very essence of his honor.

He'd dreamed of her. Not only in his fever, but in his restless sleep. He'd pored through his books in Latin for phrases that she would wish to learn. Had found himself transfixed by the idea of reading to her from Catullus. The moment tempted him.

" '*Ille mi par esse deo videtur,*
ille, si fas est, superare divos,
qui sedens adversus identidem te
  spectat et audit
dulce ridentem, misero quod omnis
eripit sensus mihi.' "

Words he whispered as softly as the breeze around them.

"What does it mean?" she asked softly.

She sat up, pushed her hair away from her forehead. Her ribbon had become dislodged, and she looked around but could not find it. He did not offer to pull it from his pocket and give it to her.

He should have noted that her breathing had changed. Instead, he'd been captivated by a hand, the curve of her cheek, his errant thoughts.

Still, there was nothing to do but to tell her. "He is close to a god, he who sits and watches her. And listens to the sound of her laughter as he is seated there. A rival to a god with such delight."

"How beautiful."

"The poet was very ardent about the woman he loved."

He found himself oddly discomfited. Not because he'd been discovered quoting Latin. The poets at court had often waylaid a likely conquest to regale her with verses they'd toiled over. Poetry with more libidinous intent than his selection. His awkwardness came not from his words but his thoughts. For those alone he should probably have been slapped.

"*Ní hí an bhreáthacht a chuireann an crocán ag fiuchadh,*" she said with a smile.

"Gaelic again?"

She nodded. "Beauty will not make the pot boil."

He began to smile, eased from the moment by her teasing look.

"We Scots rarely talk about love," she said. "Most of our proverbs have to do with practical matters. *Fearr an mhaith atá ná an dá mhaith do bhí.*"

At his look, she smiled. "Better one good thing that is than two things that were."

"Latin scholars were the same. Most of them spoke of the great questions of life, mortality, and immortality. The nature of man."

"Are you certain?"

She tilted her head and looked at him. There was a mark on her cheek, a tiny scratch, and he pressed his thumb upon it. A gesture he did not know he was going to make until he did so.

He pulled his hand back, concentrated on her question, not on the fact that her cheeks now bloomed with color.

"Do you mean have I read all there is? No."

"Did you never think that certain thoughts were not deemed important enough to save?"

"A censor who decreed that certain words be considered sacrosanct and others discarded?"

"Or a great many, century after century," she

said, sitting up completely. There was a peace still on her features, as if she'd not wakened fully yet. But she debated with him. Yawns and riddles and the ability to kiss him until his blood burned. A unique woman.

She frowned at him as if she knew his thoughts had drifted. "Juliana's work might not have survived if it had been found two hundred years ago. Perhaps one of your ancestors would have decreed it a silly thing, a woman's thoughts unworthy to save. Or a man of the Church might have seen it as heretic and tossed it into a fire."

"If that were true, then Catullus and Ovid would not have survived."

"Perhaps," she said. The look on her face indicated her thoughts. A wall stopped her logic. He did not help her across it.

"You do not lose arguments easily, do you?"

She laughed. "What you see as stubbornness was only survival at Dunniwerth."

He smiled at her, charmed again.

She yawned and placed her hand over her mouth. She'd not been embarrassed to have found herself leaning against him. In fact, she'd not been shy about the fact that he'd discovered her asleep.

A fascinating woman. Another time, perhaps, he would have celebrated the fact that fate had put her in his life. Now he could only wish that circumstances were different.

Chapter 14

The ale was hearty, the cheese sour but balanced by the surprisingly sweet bread. She would have eaten rocks, Anne thought, if it meant sitting beneath a tree with him and enjoying these moments.

He opened the codex, found his place.

"Are we nearly finished?"

"There are about ten pages," he said. "But the writing is cramped."

He sat there, lit by the sunlight that filtered through the leaves.

She reached out one hand to forestall him before he began to read. "How do you say 'warrior' in Latin?"

"*Proeliator.*"

"Not a pretty word."

"Not a pretty occupation," he conceded.

"What will you do after the war?"

He smiled. "A question that is forbidden on the battlefield. Did you know?"

She shook her head.

"A superstition. Never question another soldier

as to his future plans. That way, fate is not challenged."

"Otherwise he may not survive?"

"So it is said. But we are not on the battlefield now, and I'll answer you," he said. He sat against the trunk of a tree, looked up at the canopy of branches above them. "I want to rebuild Langlinais," he said. "One day I'll replace the windows, erect walls where there are now only piles of bricks. I've plans to have the gates at both ends of the baileys restored."

"A monumental undertaking," she said.

"Perhaps a foolish one," he conceded. "As it is, Langlinais can barely withstand another disaster. But it seems a shame to let crumble into dust something that has stood for so long."

"It is your heritage."

He smiled. "My father used to say that nobility is my heritage."

"He sounds like a very wise man," she said.

He raised up one knee, placed his right arm upon it. He looked off into the distance. "I used to think him uncommonly so until I realized that he took credit for the thoughts of other men. He was fond of quoting historians and philosophers. Except, of course, he claimed their words as his own. It is easy for a rich man to give away a loaf of bread. But for a poor man to do the same is an act of true generosity. Give any man a country, and he can be a king. Narrow his kingdom to a hovel, and you'll discover the nature of the man. All repeated wisdom, borrowed words. I remember the first time I read something he was purported to have said. It was a great shock."

"How sad," she said, "that he did not trust his own thoughts."

He glanced over at her, the expression on his face one of surprise.

"There is a woman at Dunniwerth who does the same. If she hears a tale that sounds intriguing, then she retells the story as if it is her own. As if her life is not worthy enough without adventure and she must collect the experiences of others in order to enhance it. Perhaps she simply wishes for people to like her. Or admire her."

"I doubt my father cared about the opinions of others. Except for the king, perhaps. But he never understood that the king had little use for him. As long as Charles received Langlinais loans from time to time, he was content to have a fawning earl in attendance."

"Why do you fight for him when you so obviously dislike him?"

"My opinions do not matter," he said, smiling. "If all men refused to fight unless they admired their leader, there would be nothing but anarchy."

"Or peace, Stephen."

"I suspect this same argument has been made between men and women since before Juliana's time."

He opened the codex, effectively changing the subject.

" 'There were those who would judge Sebastian, although he was a force of goodness and kindness. Judgment is in itself a form of evil, that one would condemn without kindness, seek to destroy without understanding. But his horrible secret became the basis for the miracle of Langlinais. It is a sad thing

that no one will ever know it transpired or that
Sebastian of Langlinais was touched by God.' "

"A miracle?"

His frown echoed her confusion. "I've never
heard of a Langlinais miracle," he admitted.

" 'I have come to wonder and to marvel at the
workings of Almighty God, that He might have
granted me this joy. Too many years separated us,
but they were years of preparation, each for the
other. I would have loved him regardless of his
secret and blessed the fact of it.' "

"Do you think Sebastian loved her as much as
she loved him?" she asked softly.

"I'm certain he did," Stephen said. He glanced
over at her. "You've never seen it, have you?"

"Seen what?"

"Come, and I'll show you how much Sebastian
loved her."

He stood and held out his hand for her.

A few minutes later they were at Langlinais. He
led her through a doorway and to a place she'd
never before seen, not even in her visions.

The timbers that had once supported the roof of
this chamber had long since crumbled to dust. The
back wall had caved in upon the hall, and bricks
lay in an orderly pile, a monument to destruction.
There was rubble in the middle of the chamber, bits
of stone and wood that looked to have fallen from
the second floor.

But there were clues as to what purpose this
chamber had once served. A few shards of ruby-
colored glass hinted at a once magnificent stained
glass window. The placement of an altar rail was
still marked in the stone floor.

Anne followed Stephen through the chapel to where a large statue dominated one corner. A woman and a man stood together, their figures life-sized and carved in white stone. She was lovely, the first blush of youth having left her face, but the hint of it was there still. Her smile appeared to hide a secret, the twinkle in her eyes hinted at mischief or a deeper humor. The man who stood beside her was dressed as a knight. His face reminded her of Stephen's, his smile gentle and restrained, but the expression in his eyes matched that of his companion. His fingers held the woman's in greatest gentleness, the gesture, even carved in stone, one of deep reverence.

"This is Juliana," Stephen softly said. "Their graves were moved, but this effigy must have been too heavy to transport. It's remained here ever since their deaths."

"She was very beautiful," Anne said, awed.

"I wonder if she was truly so or if Sebastian only saw her that way. He had the effigy carved after her death. It is said that he described each feature in such loving detail that the sculptor fashioned her likeness exactly. Then, when it was done, Sebastian went to their chamber and lay down to die."

Anne touched the statue's arm, almost surprised to feel the cold stone beneath her fingers. Juliana's smile was so real, the look in her eyes one of such transcendent joy that she looked almost alive.

"Sebastian showed his love by this statue, while Juliana did so with her chronicle. Deeds versus words," she said softly.

"Perhaps it is the way of men and women," he said, turning to her.

"Except for poets," she said, "who would give the lie to that theory."

"Who is Alexander Scott?"

She glanced at him, surprised.

"You mentioned him that day and said it was not appropriate poetry for the moment."

She could feel her face warm.

"It was something I heard," she said.

"When you were silent and listening?" he teased.

She nodded.

"Tell me." His smile dared her, and she was not above a challenge.

> " 'The thing that may her please
> My body sal fulfil,
> Whatever her disease,
> It does my body ill.
> My bird, my bonny ane
> My tender babe venust
> My love, my life alane,
> My liking and my lust.' "

His smile had slipped a bit or simply changed character. "Another man ardent in his thoughts of a woman."

"Did you hear no poetry in London?"

"Scores of it. Reams of it," he said. "Too much to wish to quote. Most of it was written for only one purpose. When that was accomplished, I doubted the words survived."

She smiled, well aware for what purpose the poetry had been written.

"Did you like London?"

Stephen touched Juliana's hand. A curious benediction. Anne placed hers beside his.

"There are parts to London that are surprisingly beautiful. But then you turn the corner, and there is squalor. One moment you're in a building crafted with the skill of Inigo Jones and the next in a street with buildings built up so much the sky is hardly visible." He smiled, obviously reminiscing. "I can speak, read, and write five languages, but there are places in London where I cannot understand my fellow Englishman. It took days for me to decipher that 'stren' meant the Strand, and 'wostrett' Wood Street. Sometimes I felt as if I were woefully out of place there, that it was a grand jest that everyone but I understood."

"I've felt that way sometimes," she said.

"Have you?" He glanced over at her.

"Don't you think everyone does?"

"Even at Dunniwerth?"

"Haven't you noticed," she said, only half teasing, "that it's possible to be the most alone when there are other people about?"

"When I've been in a crowd lately, it's been a battle. I've less time to worry about whether I'm lonely than whether I stay alive or not."

"Do you ever talk about it, Stephen?"

He smiled down at her. "You will find that soldiers rarely discuss war. What time not spent in battle or endlessly traveling to or from one is spent in celebrating life."

She could not hold back her smile.

"What are you thinking, with such a look on your face?"

"It's an immodest thought, one a sheltered girl would not think," she said sweetly.

"I've a feeling Dunniwerth did not shelter you as much as support you, Anne Sinclair."

She laughed. "My mother would agree with you, Stephen. And so would Hannah."

"You have still not answered my question."

"My thought was that there had been quite a bit of celebrating life at Dunniwerth," she said, glancing away. "Especially after the men returned from war." In fact, there had been a decided increase in the number of babies born almost exactly nine months from the day the men had returned. But no amount of coaxing would induce her to say that.

"Is there a suitor in your life, Anne? A young Scot waiting until you finally ease his suffering and say yes to his proposal?"

"No." *They could not compete with you.* A thought that she did not voice.

"Just no? No list of men you've spurned?" There was a tight smile on his face.

The miniature of Sarah floated into her mind at that moment. She smiled, absurdly pleased that the irritation appeared equally shared.

"What about Ian? He watches you closely. I would not be surprised if he had been seated in a tree observing our meal."

Such a comment surprised her. "Ian?" She shook her head. "No," she said emphatically, "never Ian."

She walked away from him then, stood and faced what must have been the ruin of a magnificent window. She'd never seen the chapel before, yet it seemed rife with echoes of ceremonies of long ago, of witnessing marriage and knightings and baptisms and burials. She was certain that if she tried, she could hear those sounds, entreaties to heaven itself. Immortal whispers of mortals. As if to prove it, a gust of wind swirled around her skirts, cast leaves and small pieces of plaster into the air.

It began as whispers.

Forgive me, for all my sins, my God. Thank you for bringing her here to me, that forever long as I might live, all my days and nights will be made bearable by the memory of her face, the sound of her voice.

Then the echoes became words spoken aloud, proud declarations that rang in the corners and seemed to sing on their own.

Will you swear to be my vassal, Jered, for all the days of your life? To grant me loyalty and honor, and protect mine as you would me?

I swear, my lord, on my honor.

Affirmations shouted through the room, echoed by an angry infant's cry, a tyranny of the feted and loved.

This child, and how shall he be named?

Harold of Langlinais, brother. Known as his father's heir and pride.

The imagined words lingered in the air, a benediction of sound, a hint of the life lived here. Not only in joy, but in sorrow, too, and all the emotions in between.

They could have been spoken. Once. Now the chapel was a sanctuary for only the wind.

Stephen came and stood beside her, placed his finger on her cheek, exactly as gently as he had on Juliana's. "Why do you look so sad?" he asked softly.

"It seems a place for sadness," she said, granting him the truth.

She remained still and quiet, trapped by fascination. There was a look in his eyes, one she'd never seen before. As if he felt the same enchantment as she did now.

His finger poised upon the lobe of her ear, held there by the stillness of his body, a habit he had of seeming to become stone. His eyes were as motionless, but in their depths she saw them widen, their black centers expanding.

A cloud passed over, blown by a playful gust of wind. It seemed to trap the sun behind it until it was colored luminous, tinted rose and peach and yellow. The statue of Juliana was touched by an errant sunbeam emerging from that cloud. It dusted the smile on her face with radiance until it appeared as if she smiled tenderly.

Her hands brushed against his chest, not to forestall, but rather to entice. Her fingers opened wide, felt the warmth of his skin beneath his shirt. She lifted her head, watched as his lips neared hers. Then let her lids flutter shut as he kissed her.

It was like being welcomed. His lips were soft and warm, the touch of his tongue both shocking and evocative. Her mouth fell open beneath his, her hands clenched his shoulders.

Was life given in the power of a kiss? She felt her body change, her breath grow tight. A sensation like fire raced through her, as if a cord tied all the various parts of it to this kiss.

One hand wound around his neck, the other strayed to his cheek, thumb pressed against his jaw as if to hold him closer. His skin was almost hot beneath her palm. He pulled her to him, the tightness of their embrace accentuating all their differences. Curves against solid muscle. Hollows pressed into hard flesh. His height and strength. Her softness.

It was almost as if a chasm divided them, one that could only be conquered by the flesh. Their joining was necessary and almost painfully needed. Something within her whimpered, craved it. Demanded it. Something wild and yearning and ancient.

She pressed up against him, felt his hand upon her back. An urging she did not need.

An odd time to fall in love. Or perhaps it had happened fifteen years ago when she was a child cowering in her bed and he was a boy suffused with grief. Perhaps her soul had reached out to him then with love and understanding. But it didn't matter when it had happened. Only that it had.

The love she felt for him was not that of a child. It was not a soft and comforting thing. It was strong, a beast of intent. One that had been dormant for so long and now demanded attention and sustenance. Completion. Acknowledgment. Fulfillment.

He stepped away, the kiss ended as quickly as it was begun. On his face was a look of surprise. Or regret. *Do not let him speak of apologies.* A plea she voiced in silence.

Twice he'd kissed her. Twice they'd been lost to passion, the two of them. Would they to pretend now that it hadn't happened? As if each of them were turtles that retreated into their shells? How could something this powerful be ignored? Or perhaps she was wrong and he did not feel the same.

Were there words to measure this longing? If so, she did not know them. Or they had never been crafted. Not in English, nor in Gaelic. Perhaps in his Latin there were such sentiments. Something to express the pain of this moment and the near beauty of it.

When she'd first seen him, he had startled her. Then she'd felt only a strange sort of sadness because he had not recognized her and she had found it difficult to reconcile the man of her visions with the silent man whose eyes were blank and flat.

But she'd grown to know him, and they'd each imparted part of themselves to the other.

She knew, finally, that she loved him. Not the vision but the man.

He raised his head. If there was regret in his eyes, she didn't see it. Or did not wish to. But even that thought was stripped from her as she turned and saw them. Her hand brushed his arm.

"Stephen."

He followed her gaze.

Ned was approaching them. Behind him was a man dressed in livery. He looked oddly out of place, a peacock among pigeons. His trousers and jacket were a jonquil yellow; his cape a sky blue. There was a bouncing yellow feather on his hat. His boots of pale brown leather were over-sized, lace hanging from their thigh-high cuffs.

In contrast, Stephen's garments looked almost Puritan. His white shirt was loose at the neck and flowing at the sleeves; his black breeches and boots were coated with a fine dust.

Yet there was no doubt between the two of them who was the Earl of Langlinais.

Stephen nodded to the messenger, then turned back to her.

He did not have to tell her; she knew it without a word being said. This idyll, these moments of peace, this time of sweetness was at an end.

Chapter 15

The view of rolling hills and green-bearded land was serene and without a flaw. The flowers were beginning to bloom in the gardens and the trees bud in the forests. A bucolic scene.

If she'd had to be injured, Hannah decided, at least it was a pleasant place to recuperate.

She had been led to her chair by Richard, who'd walked up and down the hallway with her. She allowed him to accompany her, feeling an amused tolerance for this man that surprised her.

He was now, he said, attempting to find something that would give her a better disposition. Something to make her sweet. She hadn't told him that with other people she was considered quite charming. It was just with him that all of her comments seemed acerbic. She wondered why that was and why both of them enjoyed it so.

She turned and folded her hands in her lap, wishing that she had something to occupy herself.

The faster she healed, the quicker they could return to Dunniwerth.

But one blessing had been accomplished by her

injury. Not once had Anne mentioned her visions, nor had she attempted to cajole her in allowing her to continue on her quest.

She turned, sighed with acute boredom, and stared out the window.

There were some moments in her life that had seemed to occur in slow motion. As if her mind decreed that the reality of it be given to her a droplet at a time, the better for her heart to bear either the pain or the wonder of it. As she sat staring out at the scene before her, Hannah realized that this was just one of those moments.

Anne walked beside a man. They were followed by two other men. Once they stopped and conversed, then continued to walk toward the house. The breath grew tight in Hannah's chest. There was a look of such longing upon Anne's face that she marveled the rest of the world could not see it.

Hannah directed her attention to the man who stood beside Anne. He was tall, possessed of broad shoulders and a way of walking that declared ownership of the very land beneath his feet. There was a bandage on his arm. A mystery solved, then. She'd heard that the earl had been treated for a putrid wound.

"I've had cook prepare you a heartier broth," Richard said, entering the room.

"Is that the earl?" she asked, pointing at the man who walked toward the house with Anne.

Richard glanced in that direction and then back at her. "That's Stephen Harrington," he said, "the Earl of Langlinais and your host. I want you in your bed, Hannah. You've had enough excitement for today."

Stephen.

She did not argue with him, a fact that caused him to frown. She nodded and allowed him to help her back to bed.

"Here, I have something for you. A remedy known far and wide for its medicinal properties. You cannot fault it."

There on his palm were three tiny tablets. "Anderson's Pills," he said. "It will ease that headache of yours."

"How did you know?" she said, reaching out for the tablets. "Do you bill yourself as a mystic, too?"

"Like Culpepper? I do wish you knew something about him. It would be great fun to debate his methods. Do not chew them," he warned, handing her a cup. "They are to be swallowed."

"Why is the earl up and about and I am barely able to escape from this room?"

"Because your injury was slower to heal," he said. "Now let me examine your side, and tighten your bandage and be of great charm in order to make your life miserable."

"Are all your patients treated with such assiduous good cheer?" He helped her lean forward, and the motion was unexpectedly painful. She closed her eyes again.

"I wouldn't cause you pain, Hannah. Truly." It wasn't fair that his voice was so gentle. "And I've rarely had a patient who's amused me so much."

"Do you make a practice of visiting all your patients so often?"

"It is a pleasure to come to Harrington Court."

He moved to stand in front of her. Hannah stared

at the ceiling as he thumped on her chest, made her cough again.

"What sort of man is Stephen Harrington?"

"I could have answered that question a few years ago. But I am not so certain now." He laid his cheek against her chest, and the sight of him lying there against her so intimately discomposed her. "War has a way of changing a man. I know it's changed Stephen. A year ago he would not have thought to take leave without permission from the king. But he did so without thinking to bring his men home. Every day that passes means he is in that much more disfavor."

"He will return, then?"

Richard removed the sheet slowly, placed both hands on her waist. Once again she looked away. His fingers were warm and gentle even as he secured her bandage.

"He can do nothing else. The king is determined to win the war and needs men like Stephen behind him."

"You are not, I take it, a Royalist," she said dryly.

"I do not believe in the divine right of kings. And I think our sovereign has forgotten that he rules by the consent of the governed, not by some dictate from heaven itself."

"Yet you are here, in the stronghold of a Royalist."

"I have much to be grateful to Stephen for, Hannah. He made me a wealthy man." He said nothing further, a tactic that he must have known would only incite her curiosity.

"How?" she said, finally surrendering.

He smiled at her, looking absurdly pleased. "For years I'd heard tales of the *Santa Helena*, a galleon that sank in a hurricane in the Caribbean over a hundred years ago. She was rumored to have been carrying more than two tons of silver destined for Spain in her hold. I'd not the money to finance such a venture, but Stephen had."

"A sunken ship?"

"That was the beauty of it. She was supposed to have been caught on a shelf of coral not twenty feet from the surface. I knew I could chart her voyage and Spanish divers would help me find the coral right enough."

"I take it you did?"

He nodded, smiling. "It took three years, but I did. I can still remember it, Hannah. She was barely below the water. Just sitting there all those years waiting to be plucked of her treasure like a virgin with an itch."

She looked away, focused on the ornate ceiling above her.

"Forgive me, Hannah."

She nodded, knowing that if she spoke, her amusement might be revealed. He was the most contrary man.

He straightened, opened his chest, withdrew a squat jar. He handed it to her. "I want you to rub a little of this camphor on your chest at night. It's to prevent a watery cough. And no, before you ask, it contains no hair of dog or blind man's spit."

She wondered if he knew how much he amused her. "You take all the joy from my day, Richard. But you didn't answer me. Do you find it difficult to be here when you and the earl have such divergent political views?"

He closed his chest, snapped the lock into place.

When he finally spoke, his words were thoughtful. "I know that there are places in England where the country is divided. That brother fights against brother and father against son. But not here. Here a man is not despised because of his views."

"And a woman? Is she safe here?"

His skin turned bronze. "You are indeed safe here, mistress," he said. "I would never touch you without your leave, Hannah." He picked up his chest, bowed slightly to her, and left the room before she could recover from her surprise.

She had been speaking of Anne. But he, silly man, had thought something else entirely. Her cheeks warmed as she stared open-mouthed at the closed door.

She closed her eyes but was revisited by the image of Anne's face as she'd stood talking to Stephen. It made her feel as if time was standing still. In Anne's face was all that she might have felt once, the muted joy, the fervent hope.

Hannah leaned back against the pillow and closed her eyes. How long had it been since she'd left her island? Being away had given her a sense of freedom, like a child's escape from lessons. And once tasted, she wondered if she could ever return again. Strange, fey thoughts from a woman who was not given to them. She had lived in a pragmatic world since the day she'd agreed to the bargain that still linked her to Robert Sinclair.

Pain filtered up through her thoughts. There was no sense in attempting to push the memories back.

They existed with a life of their own, strong and vibrant, filled with regret. An aching bittersweet longing. Not for the first time, but the hundredth or more, she wished she'd never met the laird of Dunniwerth. She'd been captivated by his charm, the sweet resonance of his voice. His smile.

They'd met at a fair, this man of Scotland and she of England. They'd looked at each other once, the moment so tender that it seemed as if they'd known each other forever. Another fey thought, perhaps, but it had felt as if they'd loved before. Sweetly and passionately for years and eons.

Bid me farewell, then, Hannah, if you must. But say it to my face. Do not give me your back. Words he'd said when she tried to leave him the first time.

She had stared straight ahead, managing not to flinch when his hands gripped her shoulders. His touch was gentle, but it made her tremble. They had come so close to coupling but had not indulged in that final sin. Yet she wanted him to touch her as no other had. To feel him once, that was all she asked. To lie beneath him and hold him, then to let him go. It did not seem to be too horrible a thing to want. One touch of love, and then she would send him back to Scotland. Back to his heritage. Back to his wife.

She turned and raised her head, lifted herself to meet his kiss. After that, there was no talking. She'd gotten her wish, and it was worse than wondering. She'd lain with him in a field, their bed the sweet grass, their ceiling a blue and sunlit sky. So many years ago, and she could remember every moment of it. Their farewell had been a torture. It had been, after all, too great a price to pay, that knowledge she'd sought. She'd known what she would forever miss.

She'd paid a price for her yearning. She'd lived her life on an island, one of land and one of mind.

She was a long way from her childhood prayers, but she remembered them now and said another one, that she might heal quickly so that she and Anne might be gone from this place. Before history repeated itself.

Chapter 16

~~~✦~~~

Stephen didn't bother greeting the royal messenger, simply walked back to Harrington Court as if the man were not following him. A momentary delay of the inevitable. The man didn't look cowed by Stephen's irritation. No doubt he was used to Prince Rupert's infamous rages.

Once inside, he slipped his finger beneath the seal of the letter, read the contents with little surprise. It was as he had expected. Charles was furious. He was being summoned to the king.

He had no love for Oxford, and it had nothing to do with the town. It was the king's base of operations, the place most occupied by sycophants and courtiers.

He glanced over at Anne. A laird's daughter, a Scottish lass with a luring smile and something hidden in her eyes. It was there as her attention turned to him. He felt himself smile. Not only outwardly but inside, where the warmth spread throughout his entire body.

He was not a man given to lying to himself. Therefore, he faced the truth without flinching. He could have, perhaps, avoided the summons and the royal disfavor by leaving a few days earlier. According to Richard, his arm was healing faster than expected.

Was there a look on his face, then, that warned her? There must have been, because her face changed as he watched. There was a look in her eyes that told him she knew what he was about to say.

"I've been summoned to Oxford."

She said nothing, merely stood and waited for him to continue. He could imagine her then as the child she'd been, watching the world around her in silence.

He almost smiled at the picture his mind furnished of her. Her hair would have curled the same and been restrained by the same shade of ribbon. Her cheeks would have been round, her lips a bow shape. Her eyes, those warm, brown eyes that looked at him levelly now, would have been large in her face. And utterly charming. Had she wheedled herself out of her chores and punishments? Or been the darling of Dunniwerth's inhabitants?

She finally spoke. "When?"

"Tomorrow morning," he said.

She seemed too pale, but he could not be certain. The foyer was draped in shadow.

"You must stay until your friend can travel," he said. "I will leave instructions for Ned to provide enough men for an escort for you when you're ready to leave."

She nodded.

There were people around them. The messenger, Betty, the men of his regiment, who stood silent, waiting for their orders. It was not the time to bid her a more proper farewell or even to offer her an apology again if she wished one. For the second kiss. For his thoughts. For this moment when he had to leave.

She had, in such a short time, become his friend. A companion of his mind. A partner to his thoughts. She would haunt him, he suspected, like the other ghosts of his regrets, with thoughts of what might have been.

Knowing her had broken open something within him and exposed him to himself. As if he were a nutmeat and the shell he'd thought to be himself only needed easing aside to understand the true man beneath. She'd brought to him questions he could not answer and wishes that could not be fulfilled.

Someone called to him, and he was trapped there, poised on the sword edge of time. He could not say a proper farewell to her, so he said nothing at all. They exchanged a look, but it was too short for all that he'd wished to convey.

In the end, however, it would have to be enough.

His farewell was so easily done that she could only stare after him.

His boots echoed loudly beneath the dome of Harrington Court. She looked up. A frieze was carved below the frosted glass. Women in diaphanous garments stood next to cherubs, extended arms and hands for the ribbons borne to them in the beaks of birds. A scene of heaven? Were angels so scantily garbed? They wore no wings.

The sound of voices traveled through the corridors and hallways. Shouts turned to whispers and whispers became audible.

"Send word to the rest of the regiment in Lange on Terne, James," Stephen said. He gave orders easily, this commander of men. The leader of a regiment.

"We need enough provisions to see us to Oxford."

"Ned, give Faeren an extra measure tonight. He'll earn it tomorrow."

The day had turned gloomy, the sky dark. The first rain came in heavy drops that struck the windows and could be heard tapping on the domed roof. A giant wept. If so, he stole her tears.

She turned her head, and Betty stood there. Her smile was tentative, as if she bore bad news but was ever conscious of her comportment.

"Hannah is asking for you," she said. The smile flickered on Betty's face, solidified and fixed there. "She seems a bit upset," she said. "Rang her bell something fierce."

Anne sighed. A summons, then. One that she did not relish. But she straightened her shoulders and climbed the stairs.

She hesitated on the threshold a moment before entering the room.

Hannah was sitting up in bed, her gaze on her hands. It was a pose of reflection, of inward thought. Silence could be a weapon, one that Hannah used effectively. It would not be the first time she'd done so.

Anne entered the room, sat on the end of Hannah's bed, waiting patiently. She'd learned that the loser in this battle of wills between them was the one who spoke first.

Hannah had not hesitated to chastise her as a child. The first occasion had been when she was nine years old. She couldn't recall the exact circumstances. Either she hadn't wanted to leave when Hannah suggested it, or had wished another treat when Hannah had declined. Some childish wish not fulfilled to her specifications.

"My father is laird, and I don't have to do anything I truly don't wish to do."

"Do you really believe that?" Hannah had looked surprised.

She'd nodded her head exuberantly, certain that the older woman would be cowed by her consequence. Instead, Hannah had only laughed and held open the door of her cottage so that Anne might leave it.

"There are those who would spoil you, young Anne of the mighty Sinclairs. I would make you wise. But you, of course, have already achieved wisdom and are far beyond what I might teach you."

She'd stopped half in and half out of the doorway, looked up at Hannah's face.

"You won't let me come back if I leave now, will you?"

Hannah smiled. "There are signs of your wisdom even now."

"I don't want to go."

"Then you must apologize for your words, Anne. And you must learn from those who would teach you. The first lesson is to never make another person feel diminished by what you have or who you are."

A lesson she'd learned, like all of them. But she was no longer a child. Perhaps Hannah recognized that fact, and it was the source of her sharp look now.

"Were you going to tell me?"

"About Stephen?"

"Would there be another secret that you have kept from me?"

"Perhaps."

It evidently wasn't the answer Hannah was expecting. Her look of surprise quickly vanished, however, beneath her look of irritation.

"I did not tell you because I wished to postpone this moment, Hannah. When you would ask me what I planned to do. When I would have to tell you I don't know."

"Have you told him about your visions?"

"No."

"Why not?"

A thousand answers. In the end, they all coalesced into one.

"Ever since I came to you, you were determined to protect me, Hannah. Sometimes I wondered if you did so in order to spare me the truth. I'd long since believed I was not evil. You taught me that. But what if my visions were worse? What if all this time it was only my mind playing tricks on me?"

"You didn't believe he was real?"

"I believed it," Anne said. "But . . . what if I were mad?"

At the look on her face, Hannah smiled softly.

"I often wondered if I had wished for him to be real so much that I'd invented him for my playmate. I was lonely enough to do so. I love to draw and do so well, I think. But what if the same talent that lets me see a flower and place its image upon a page also allows me to dream and flesh it out until it becomes something that seems real?"

"Why did you never tell me of your fears before, Anne?"

"There are some things not easily said, Hannah."

"Do you think he will believe you mad?"

Anne smiled. "He might well think so." She sighed. "My visions have always ruled my life, Hannah. For a while I didn't want them to rule his as well."

"Do you think he will fall in love with you, Anne?" Hannah's tone had a bite to it. A bit of anger, perhaps even a touch of fear.

"It no longer matters what I wish," she said. A truth issued in a voice that almost trembled at it.

"Because you are already in love with him." An announcement, not a question.

"Am I?" Her words hung in the air between them.

"Are you not?" Hannah's voice softened. "I would not have you hurt, Anne."

"You would have me live on an island, Hannah." She turned and smiled at her friend. "And I will not do that, not even for you. But as I said before, it no longer matters what I feel or do not feel for him." She stood and walked to the door. "He is leaving in the morning."

She closed the door softly behind her.

* * *

Thomas Penroth looked down at the vista below him. The information his lieutenant had provided him had led them here. Harrington Court shimmered beneath the glittering rain. The great house would indeed be a prize to hand to Parliament. But even more so the man inside it. The Earl of Langlinais. The thorn in his side. The irritant worth marching his men and cannon in pouring rain.

He turned and surveyed his companions. The bulk of his troops made camp some two miles behind, just west of Lange on Terne.

"We will be in place by mid-morning? Even in this downpour?"

One of his aides nodded. "Yes, General." The assent meant his men would be marched all night. Sometimes a necessity in battle.

He turned and raised his spyglass to the sight of the house again. He wished he knew if his earlier thoughts were true, that the earl was involved in a plot to seek help from the Scots. Regardless, Stephen Harrington would be cut off from any assistance, English or Scot.

The earl had evidently expected difficulty. He had dispatched one of his scouts just an hour ago. The earl should have taken the precaution of sending them out in tandem, Penroth thought. There was less danger of them being removed one by one. But the earl's mistake would be to the Parliamentarians' advantage.

General Penroth smiled in anticipation.

Chapter 17

Stephen placed the codex back into its coffer, locked it away where it would be safe. One last survey of his desk assured him that he had left nothing behind.

A branch of candles lit the way to his suite of rooms. The sound of muted laughter echoed through the corridor. A last tankard of ale, one final night of camaraderie before returning to war. The remainder of his regiment had arrived at Harrington Court that afternoon in preparation for a dawn departure. Wives had been kissed good-bye, sweethearts promised a safe return. He wondered how many pretty maids employed here would weep into the corner of their apron come morning.

He entered his suite, closed the door softly behind him. He'd not had a manservant since leaving London and had not felt the lack. In war there was so little privacy that he relished the moments when they came. A valet or personal aide would have been an intrusion. But tonight he felt too solitary. As if he, among all of the inhabitants of Harrington

Court, was the only one to be alone and without companionship.

Sleep was not, surprisingly, difficult before a battle. Perhaps it was because his mind decreed that his body needed rest in order to fight for its survival the next day. Against a tree, on a sagging cot, huddled beneath a blanket, he'd managed to sleep. But tonight, he suspected, rest would not come as easily.

Until he'd received the summons from the king, he'd not realized how much anger had been a part of his decision to return home. Charles listened to men who flattered and fawned, not to men who'd fought the battles and faced death every day. Or he paid heed to his nephew, Prince Rupert, a man who did not mind using the men of the Langlinais Regiment of Horse as chess pieces or cannon fodder.

His respite from the war had not changed the nature of it.

He didn't anticipate returning to it. Yet he would. Another inconsistency in a life filled with them. He was no Roundhead, yet he was considered as stern as a Puritan. He secretly questioned the Royalist cause; at the same time he was sought out and lauded by those who had the king's ear. He hated war, yet his regiment was the most victorious of all the Royalist cavalry.

But the incongruities of his life stretched beyond the battlefield. His life in London had not been a celibate one, yet the last two years had been temperate. In a house filled with people he was lonely. He was a commander who counseled respect for women, yet his waking thoughts and nightly dreams were filled with images of a woman he was honor-bound to protect.

He should have said good-bye to her. Anne. What would he have said? What could there be said? *Wait for me.* The timing was uncertain. His survival was uncertain. *Stay.* A statement he could not have made. The message would have been clear, honorable intent. But he could not make promises to anyone other than the king.

Duty. Honor. Loyalty. They had never been such strict taskmasters as they were now.

Anne turned the door handle to his chamber, pushed it open silently.

He stood at the window, staring off into the distance. He might have been anyone in the shadows of night. A Roman soldier, or a Greek masquerading as a god. He might have been a pagan, his face bearing the lines of strong forebears. Men who'd lived in forests and worshipped deities, and who called upon the heavens to deliver them from the rumble of thunder and the fear of lightning.

She entered the room, closed the door behind her, each motion cloaked in silence. But her footfalls must have whispered against the wooden floor or her breath been too loud, because he turned.

He studied her in the faint light.

"You should not be here, Anne." It was the voice of the commander.

She nodded, walked slowly toward him.

"No," she said, agreeing. "I shouldn't be. But you will be gone tomorrow, and that should not occur either."

Her fingers reached out and brushed against the fabric of his shirt.

"Go away, Anne." His voice was a ribbon of whisper.

She dropped her hand, but she didn't turn and leave the room. Instead, she tilted her head back and looked at him. His eyes were dark with shadows. No twinkling stars, no hint of humor. Perhaps there was anger there. Certainly wariness. Prudence. Circumspection. All those various emotions that indicated that he was more adept at restraint than she.

She should have felt shamed. A woman of Dunniwerth was not to offer herself without benefit of marriage. Or if she did, it was to a man who was bound to her by oaths and promises. What of visions? And a sense of wonder? Were they not bonds as strong? What of the feeling that he and she had been destined to stand this way, in silence and in surrender, each battling their separate wills and their worlds?

The silence seemed white and fragile, a hush of snowflakes. Or the hours before dawn when even the birds still and bury their heads beneath their wings. Even the candles did not sputter but glowed quietly.

He said nothing else, spoke no further words of banishment. But neither did he welcome her. He might have been a statue. An effigy of stone that nonetheless breathed.

She closed her eyes. Let her heart speak. Or her mind. A hundred different times she'd seen him cascaded into her thoughts.

Stephen.

A boy, a youth, this man. Smiling, frowning, laughing, experiencing life in all its fullness. This moment was only another piece of a greater picture. A vision that she created with longing. A scene that she could replay a thousand times in her mind.

Stephen.

A cry from the soul. A fervent and nearly insane wish.

She felt, rather than saw, his movement. His hands reached up and gripped her arms. Not tightly, but not gently, either.

Her lashes fluttered open, her head tipped back.

His face was fierce, his eyes narrowed. His lips were compressed tightly.

"There are men coupling with women tonight. But they will not remember their names in the morning. Is that what you want, Anne?"

"Yes," she said. "The coupling, Stephen, not the forgetting."

He removed his hands from her as if her sleeves had grown fiery.

"I am neither a Puritan nor a despoiler of innocents, Anne. But a man somewhere in between. Go back to your chamber."

His face eased into an expression she more readily associated with him. A carefully controlled watchfulness. As if he guarded even the look in his eyes.

She reached up and placed her hands on either side of his face. "It is my life and my future, Stephen. It is not yours to guide or to protect."

"Someone must, Anne," he said gently.

"Do you think I have not thought about this?

That it is something I do lightly?" Her thumbs brushed the corners of his lips. "Tomorrow you will leave, Stephen, and I will never see you again."

Her words dared him to refute it, to say something calming, speech that hinted at a future between them. But he remained mute.

"If you send me from here, Stephen, let it be because you do not want me," she said, the words pushed past the constraints of her pride. "Not because your honor bids you to."

"You're either too innocent or too brave, Anne, I don't know which."

"Courage is easy when you have nothing to lose," she said. "And if my innocence is such a burden, then recommend one of your regiment to rid me of it. Give me an hour, Stephen. I will return more experienced, if that is what you wish."

His fingers pressed against her lips.

She clasped his wrist, pulled his hand free.

The candlelight was reflected in his eyes. Where they had been watchful before, they seemed to glow like fire now.

"I can offer you nothing, Anne."

There, the truth of it. The sheer barrier that stood between them. She did not rip it aside by asking him for more revelations of intent or emotion.

She had come to him in love. And carried her heart within her cupped hands. There had been bridges built between them, those of laughter and learning and Latin. She wished one more. A joining at its most elementary.

She wanted to have the image of him naked in her mind. A vision to carry for the rest of her life.

A recollection that she might retrieve when she dreamed of him. She wanted to feel his skin against hers, to be indoctrinated into the sisterhood of women with lambent eyes and soft, curving lips. She wanted to bid farewell to him with the taste of his kisses still on her mouth.

She did not require his vow of love for that. Or his pretense. Tomorrow he would leave, and all the wishing and wondering and hoping wouldn't keep him safe. She'd learned that. A silly girl had left Scotland, certain that circumstance would keep her from being harmed. Instead, Hannah had been injured and Douglas was missing. She accepted the responsibility, the knowledge that it had been her actions that had caused those things to happen. Just as she shouldered the guilt for them.

This moment was no different.

She accepted all that might come to her from this act.

"Give me what you can, Stephen. This night."

She thought she might be able to hear his thoughts at this moment. He was perplexed by her, she knew that. And yet, as much confusion as she engendered in him, there was another emotion, too. One that thrummed between them as strong as life itself.

She held both his hands, cupped them together, and placed a soft kiss on the two joined palms. She laid her cheek against the bowl of them. "I don't want to wonder," she confessed. "For all the years left to me, I don't want to wish I had come to you tonight and feel regret that I did not."

His fingers curled against her skin. The rasp of his indrawn breath told her that he was not unaffected. Not the statue he would have her believe him.

Her arms moved toward him. So slowly that they gave him ample warning. But he stood immobile and mute before her as she wrapped them around his neck. One more small step, and she was so close that a breath could not separate them. Her bare toes touched his boots.

For a moment he did not move, then his hand fisted in her hair, pulled her head back. This man was not severe, nor stern. Certainly not controlled. His breathing was as rapid as hers.

"Give me tonight, Stephen."

His mouth descended on hers, his lips hot and hard and insistent. This was not gentle exploration but demand. There was darkness behind her lids, a heaviness in her limbs. She strained upward to meet the insistent kiss, to part her lips and inhale his breath and feel the touch of his tongue. Not seduction but welcomed passion. She was no innocent at the moment of her deflowering as much as a woman craving the same delight as this man. The fact that she had never experienced it meant little to her.

"I want to remember this," she said, countering the ticking moments. "Make me remember."

With each breath her awareness of him expanded, as did a sense of life itself. His finger beneath her chin tilted her head up at a better angle. The heat of his breath warmed hers. His heart mimicked the beat of her own. His hand upon her back felt heated, fingers and thumbs pressing against her clothed skin.

The fabric of the dress felt too coarse, too confining, as if her body swelled and readied itself in anticipation for this act of mystery.

His palm curved around her breast. His mouth inhaled her gasp. Not one of protest, but rather awareness. Delight in a touch. His thumb brushed against her nipple, encouraging it to peak beneath the fabric. Her fingers spread wide then gripped his shoulders.

He pulled back from their kiss. She stood before him, eyes wide, staring up into his face. His hand still cupped her breast. There was a look in his eyes she'd never seen before. It was not gentle nor was it tender. A warrior's gaze.

His thumb reached out and brushed across her bottom lip, as if measuring the distance from corner to corner. He was master in this, effortless at seduction. She closed her eyes at the feelings his touch evoked, then just as quickly opened them again. There was a look on his face, an inquiry in his eyes, a slight smile on his lips as if he contemplated her capacity for surrender. She answered not with a word but with a gesture.

When he would have moved his hand, she held her own over it. She pressed his hand upon her breast and held it there.

He smiled and slowly reached out and pulled her laces open. He undid the knot with practiced ease. Delicately. Slowly.

Her own breaths measured the movements of his hands. And silently implored him to hurry. With each ticking moment, he spun out the act, treating the baring of this inch of skin as an almost sacred ritual.

Finally, her bodice gaped open, the shift bared.

He bent and kissed her between her breasts, a soft kiss on the thin linen that covered her body. A brand of heat and lips and intent.

She trembled. Slowly, so exquisitely slow that she could count the heartbeats until he did so, he pulled down the shift and touched her bared skin with his fingers. Just that. A touch of one fingertip against her skin.

A slight smile was his reaction to her gasp.

Her head fell back, her hands clutched at him. But he gently brushed her hands aside, reached down and pulled her dress over her head. Just as quickly the remainder of her garments followed. In seconds, a fraction of the time it took her to get dressed in the morning, she was naked.

Her hands reached to cover herself, then fell to her sides.

It was not fear she felt at this moment but a melting warmth. As if Stephen had kissed her for hours and her heart still raced with the feeling of it.

"I've dreamed of you this way," he said, a confession that stoked a fire deep within her. "I wondered if your breasts were full, the tips brown or pink." A stroke of fingertip upon a nipple accompanied his words. "They are neither," he said, "but a soft shade of coral." His fingers measured the curve of her breasts, his thumbs brushed against the nipples slowly.

Her eyes closed, her fingers fluttered against his shirt like tiny butterflies adrift in the wind.

Remember this. A command that pierced the languorous haze that enveloped her. Remember how his voice sounded. Low and almost rasping. Breathless. The stroke of his finger upon her skin, the callused palm brushing against her breast, the fingertip so gentle upon her nipple.

And this. He kissed her between her breasts, his breath hot, his lips tender. And then upon her breast. Not shocking as much as delicious. He traced a path too slowly to her nipple. Her fingers pressed upon his cheek as if to hurry him. She felt his smile against her skin. Then only the touch of lips and tongue.

Both hands cupped her breast, framed it for his kiss. He glanced up, saw her watching him. The tip of her tongue brushed against her bottom lip. His mimicked the gesture upon the tip of her breast.

Her eyes fluttered shut when his lips encompassed her nipple, sucked gently. A ribbon of dark feeling ran through her.

"Sweet," he said, and another sensation drifted over her, a heat unlike anything she'd ever known. It was as if she had been opened up inside and had been left vacant and black and receptive. Into this void he came and filled all the various parts of it with himself.

He straightened, kissed her closed lids one by one. Gentle insistence. She blinked open her eyes. Innocent or wanton, it no longer mattered. He held out his hand, and she put hers atop it. He led her through the doorway to his bedchamber. Then to his bed. Naked, she accompanied him, the journey one of blurred desire.

It was a word she'd heard. One to measure emotion. Fear and hate and anger and joy. They were all emotions, too. But she'd never known the meaning of this word. Desire. Or that it was this powerful. She would have defied any custom or any country for him. For the touch of his hands and the seduction of his kisses she would have done nearly anything.

How could she bear more?

She put her knee atop the mattress, turned and watched him. He returned to the other room, retrieved the branch of candles. Placing them on the candlestand, he undressed quickly. Each garment being removed revealed more of him to her greedy eyes.

There were men of all sizes and shapes at Dunniwerth, and she had seen her share of bared legs and chests. They were burly men, her Scots clansmen. Tall and strong with arms like tree trunks.

Stephen's muscles were finely honed, not from tossing cabers but from wielding a sword, riding a stallion. She studied him with none of the maidenly reserve he might well have expected from her, but with an utter and frank delight.

The candlelight cast shadows over him, illuminated him as he turned and tossed his shirt to a chair. His buttocks were round, with flat planes over his hips. A place for her palms. A thought she ached to test.

When he turned, her scrutiny revealed an even more amazing sight. He was aroused, full and heavy and thickly. A man in his prime. When he walked closer to the bed, she raised herself up on her knees and reached out her hand.

Did she startle him with her action? She didn't know. Fascinated, she touched him. He was so hard he felt like iron and so heated he felt like fire. The tip of him was flanged. She traced her finger around the head delicately and watched him jerk beneath her hand.

He pushed her gently to her back, joined her on the bed, and raised himself up over her on one elbow. "Are you sure you're not a sorceress?" he asked, his smile lending wickedness to the words.

I am a witch, aren't I? Words she'd uttered as a child. A great fear then. She smiled at him. "No," she said. "I am not sure."

He bent and kissed her, an enchanted enough journey through the spiral of desire. The night was cool, but she did not feel it. His fingers acted as fire, his palms braziers.

Her breasts were measured with fingers and hands and lips. "*Mamillae,*" he said softly, as he trailed his fingers over the curve of them. "*Papilla*" was mouthed against a nipple.

"Latin?" she asked, the passion she felt augmented by a fierce tenderness.

He nodded, smiling. "*Bracchium,*" he said, trailing a line from elbow to wrist.

Her fingers traced the edge of his smile. He reached up and removed her hand. "*Digitus,*" he said, kissing the tips of her fingers. "*Digitus pollex,*" he murmured against her thumb.

She began to smile, charmed by his seduction. Latin and lust, it was a powerful combination.

Remember this. An admonition to herself to keep this moment in her mind. How could she not?

"*Armus.*" An annointing kiss to her shoulder. "*Umerus.*" A word spoken against her upper arm. A tingle followed his kisses, a shiver of awareness as he trailed his fingers over her body.

He bestowed a necklace of kisses around her

neck. "*Collum*," he murmured as he did so.

"*Basiatio*," he said against her lips. "A kiss."

Her foot, ankle, calf, knee were all named in order. *Pes, talus, sura, genu.*

He made her repeat them softly, and she did so, the Latin words taking on a carnal lure when spoken in candlelight and whispers.

His fingers brushed over the apex of her thighs. "*Cirrus*," he murmured against her lips. "Softly curling hair." Her legs widened, an effortless invitation. Or plea.

"*Osculum*. A little mouth," he said, his fingers softly discovering her. He stroked languidly, seeming not to notice that her breath had stilled or her fingers clutched his shoulders. It was an intimacy of touch that startled her.

Desire. The hunger of it surprised her.

"*Flosculus*. A little flower." His fingers opened her, stroked softly, tenderly. "*Delicatus*," he said, his lips at her temple, his breath on her closed lids. "Delicate. Sweet."

His finger slid inside her with infinite tenderness. Her fingers clutched his shoulder, her breath halting and then starting again.

"*Caelum*," he whispered. "The vault of heaven." He withdrew his finger slowly, inserted it again. The slick friction of it made her tremble.

She turned her head, burrowed against him. An instinctive wish for protection in the most vulnerable of poses.

He kissed her, his tongue as gentle as his fingers, exploring her mouth with intent and languid strokes even as his fingers urged her to a place she'd never been before. Thoughts of him had made her feel achy, and dreams had sometimes awakened her with her breasts sensitive and her body restless. Now she knew why. Her mind had proposed their joining, and her body now urged completion. It was no longer something to be desired. It was an act of necessity. If that was passion, then she was adrift in it.

The sound she made was almost a moan, but it had a note of demand in it. The kiss she returned was no longer passive or exploratory. It nipped at his lips and dueled with intrusive tongue.

Her hand reached down and touched him. Her eyes opened as she fisted him gently.

"What do you call this?"

There was a soft smile on his face as he reached down and moved her hand. Not away but over the length of him. She followed his lead, fascinated by the half-lidded expression in his eyes. As if the rapture she felt was mirrored in him.

"*Penis.*"

"And here?" She stroked the curve of his buttocks, flattened her hand over his hip, trailing her nails over his skin.

"*Clunis, nates, puga.*"

He bent and sucked a nipple, then used the barest edge of his teeth to scrape against it.

Her eyes closed as she fisted him. His finger slid inside her and her hips rose. They played at this and tormented each other. It was an exquisite, trembling delight.

Desire was no longer a black ribbon. It was a fiery red string that tensed her muscles and spread along her skin. Her teeth bit at his lip and he laughed into their kiss.

She wanted to be taken. To be finished with this. And never to have it end. She was wild with it. She pulled at him, slapped at his chest. Heard him speak but was done with Latin.

He entered her slowly, an ancient act of possession. She widened for him, welcomed him in silence and eagerness. In his eyes was passion, not calm, not restrained.

She closed her eyes, suddenly wanted to change her mind. Her hands clutched at his back even as her hips jerked upward.

Her mind centered on the sensation of being stretched and invaded inch by inch. She wanted to cry out for help. To be severed from this terrible bond. It was too much. Not pain but almost so. He was so large within her that her body gripped him tightly. An act of possession at least as demanding as his.

He stilled, his weight balanced on his right forearm. His left hand brushed the tendrils of hair back from her face. He placed a tender kiss upon her lips, breathed against her cheek. A fine tremor marked his breath and the touch of his fingers upon her ear.

She opened her eyes, placed her palm upon his cheek. He turned his head, kissed the center of her palm. Silence, stillness, restraint while he waited for her to welcome him.

Remember this. How could she ever forget?

It was at that moment she felt her most defenseless. She had wanted this and in doing so had counted the cost of it. But she had not known how completely she would be required to surrender herself. Not simply body but will. And dominion, per-

haps, over what she'd always known as hers. The
pounding of her heart, the measure of her breaths.
Even the emotions her body might own and know.
At this moment, she understood what he had
warned her against with his cautions.

Sharing this would change her forever. She
would no longer be only herself, but a part of a
greater whole. Her memories of herself would be
entwined with those of him. She would never be
as naive in body and never as innocent in mind.

He rolled over, slowly, carrying her with him.
She understood when he winced at the movement.
His arm.

He reached up and gripped her hands, pulled her
down to him. She sank like a stone onto his chest,
a tiny cry her only protest. His hands plotted her
skin from the curve of her hips to her shoulder,
encouraging strokes of soft fingers, even as his
breath rasped in her ear.

She inhaled the scent of him, her lips pressed
against the skin of his shoulder, tasted him. He
turned her face up to meet his kiss, and she welcomed it. A mindless darkness. A swift return to
desire.

His hands gripped her upper arms, pushed her
up so that he could kiss her breasts, tease her nipples. His hips thrust up again, a final, insistent act
of dominion. Her head arched back, her lips
pressed tight to hold the cry within.

His fingers brushed her lips as if in praise, then
traced a line from chin to throat to breasts. Learning her with his fingers. Starting little fires where
he stroked.

She closed her eyes, adrift in the feelings he

evoked. Between her thighs not simple pain but an ache. A feeling of being conquered, invaded. Possessed.

He placed his palms gently against her stomach, his thumbs pressing into her softly, intrusively, until they met where they joined. A surge upward sent him deeper. One of her hands covered her mouth, the other splayed on her stomach, the tips of her fingers brushing his. A provocative touch, one that hinted at delicacy and restraint even as he surged within her.

His thumbs slid over her flesh into heated parts that were swollen and tender. Sensitive to the circling touch.

She was enveloped in the feeling that so separated them and joined them at the same time. His thumbs rotated against her, in her, pressed against where he entered her. The ache became greater, changed in nature. Slowly subsided and faded beneath the hunger.

She blinked her eyes open, stared down at him. His hair was strewn against the mattress, his face flushed with passion. His eyes blazed at her even as his fingers stroked her flesh. He smiled then, such a soft and tender smile.

She was startled to feel so many emotions in that moment. Not regret. Wonder and tenderness, delight and desire. But the most powerful of all the emotions she felt was joy.

At Dunniwerth, she'd been protected, carefully cordoned off from single men. She'd been an object of affection and respect. The laird's daughter who walked among them in safety as if she had been somehow elevated not only by her rank but by her maidenhood. Yet on this night she was a woman who was capable of passion. Not daughter, not visionary, not friend or survivor. Only a woman. His.

It seemed to be a memory recalled, a feeling that they'd come together before in laughter and ecstasy. A dream of those moments surged into this one. A recollection of what had been a thousand years ago. A promise of what could be, if circumstance were different and fate did not have greedy claws.

She raised herself, pressing up on her knees so that the ache of his possession was eased. His hands gripped her hips, restrained her. But she was in throes of something more powerful than his wishes or her desires. She closed her eyes to savor the sensation of him sliding out of her slowly. It maddened her. She sank down again as deliberately.

He made a sound something like a startled laugh as she did it again. Her head fell back as she concentrated on the feeling, the exquisite torture of it, the slow, languorous delight of feeling him deep within her.

It speared her heart.

Her fingers trailed along his stomach, her nails scraped against his skin gently. She felt his muscles contract. His hips rose even as he pulled her to him.

She shook her head, the sensations unbearable. Her hands tingled, her tongue felt cold, her breasts heated and flushed. She was sensuous and womanly and feral.

He surged within her; at the same time he pressed his hand on her hips and forced her down.

A look of intense pleasure crossed his face. Again he raised his hips, demand inherent in the gesture.

She'd thought the act one of physical joining, never realizing that it could involve her soul. That she might splinter into a thousand pieces and all of them chained each to the other. A bit of moonlight attached to a string of stars. But more than that. A breath of joy, so pure and sweet that it chilled her with its perfection.

Her breath caught and then expanded. A gasp turned into an inarticulate plea. A moan, a sigh. A prayer.

"Remember me," he whispered even as she soared.

He was chided by the sound of God. The mutterings of the Almighty, who was not pleased with his actions. He frowned at the voice, then retreated willfully into recollections of Anne. The curve of her waist and the line of her hip. The soft, surprised moan when he'd loved her the second time. She'd beaten her fists against him in time to her release. He smiled in his sleep.

God, however, was continuing to complain. He uttered a stern warning in a voice that growled with the sound of poetry. Stephen turned in his bed, the ropes creaking beneath him as God spoke. Was he doomed to some celestial punishment, then, for the joy he'd felt last night?

He reached out for Anne, then remembered she had left him a few hours ago. Draped in candlelight and kisses, she had slipped through the hallway to her chamber.

The rumble of angel voices chastised him. God

was not content to deliver him a silent rebuke, evidently. He had summoned the seraphim to quote poetry to him. Male angels?

Sleep vanished in an instant. He blinked open his eyes, listening to the drone of voices. Thousands of voices. He'd faced that sound too many times. Parliamentary soldiers had a penchant for marching into battle chanting psalms. A ploy, he'd long suspected, not only to demonstrate that God was on the side of the Parliamentarians but to give the poor foot soldiers something to think about other than the cannon bearing down on them.

He rolled from his bed and rushed to the window. This side of the house faced Langlinais. It was not until he reached the other side of his suite that he saw what he'd feared. There before him were thousands of soldiers marching on Harrington Court. He recognized the banner immediately. General Thomas Penroth.

He had not been fast enough in returning to battle, it seemed. The war had come to him.

Chapter 18

Stephen turned as William entered the room. "Have you assembled the men?"

"Yes, my lord," William said.

"Then let's begin," he said. William followed him down the hallway to the ballroom.

He'd never played host in this room, but his youthful memories supplied him with details of stuffy air and the overpowering fragrance of thousands of beeswax candles, the pungent aroma of ladies' perfume, and the odor from velvet, lace, and silk needing a good airing. He'd been six the last time he'd been required to attend one of his father's parties. On that occasion he'd been paraded about with much fanfare, his attire a duplication of his father's favorite suit of clothes, his hair styled in the same fashion. The night had not ended well, he remembered. He'd been feted as only an heir might be in a sea of indolent and hedonistic nobles. He'd been fed so many sweetmeats and wine that he'd been sick over a dowager duchess's new yellow kid shoes.

At least his father had never summoned him here again.

He looked at the sixty men who comprised the Langlinais regiment. He knew these men well, had grown up with most of them, had come to depend on all of them.

The plan to ride for Oxford could not have been worse timed. The Parliamentarians had trapped them here as ably as the other inhabitants of Harrington Court.

"I need a volunteer," he said without preamble. "Someone to ride for Colonel Blagge."

"I will go, my lord." James stood. He'd originally come from Kent and was one of the best cavalry officers.

"I've a brother with Penroth, my lord," Samuel said, standing and joining James. In another war that news might have brought on some reaction. At the very least, angry muttering. But there was only silence at his announcement. Families had been torn apart over this conflict, even as the ideas and causes once deemed worth fighting for became dross as the war lingered on.

"It might be easier if you choose me, my lord. That is, if I'm caught."

"I can only spare one of you," Stephen said. He nodded at Samuel, the decision made. "Let's just hope you don't see your brother any time soon," he said and proceeded to outline the fastest way to reach Blagge's troops.

He left them then, intent on only one thing, to determine for how many days they could withstand Penroth.

Instead, he was lured by the sound of laughter.

He followed the sound to the kitchen, a labyrinthine journey that wound through storage hallways where barrels of their sand were stored. It was used for cleaning, but would be moved to the hallways soon to help put out fires if Penroth began to bombard them.

He pushed the door ajar. Betty, Ned, and what looked to be the majority of the staff stood watching Anne. She sat at the head of the long table, intent upon her drawing. Her fingers flew over the page.

A burst of laughter accompanied each successive viewing of a drawing being passed from one to the other. It was not difficult to deduce that the subject of the amusement was one of young maids, whose cheeks were a lively red. But she looked as if she enjoyed the attention. He stepped forward, held out his hand, and the drawing was placed in it by one of the younger downstairs maids. She giggled without turning, passing on a bit of fun, unknowing that she did so to her employer.

It was only then that he realized the room had grown quiet. The one person who was patently ignoring his presence was Anne, and she was intent upon her drawing. When one of the maids would have slipped away, he shook his head, a gesture to induce her to stay.

Anne finished the drawing with a flourish and held it out to Betty. Betty covered her mouth with her hand as if to stifle her laughter, but it rolled forth anyway. She handed it to Ned, who took one look at it and began to laugh. But what surprised Stephen the most is that his taciturn servant reached over and grabbed Anne's hand and raised it to his mouth for a smacking kiss.

Stephen smiled, which seemed to release them from their silence. He was absurdly grateful to her at that moment for bringing laughter to them at a time that was neither amusing nor lighthearted.

She glanced over at him then, and they shared a look. Too intimate for strangers, too warm for friends. He moved aside, motioned to Betty.

He gave her the instructions he'd meant to impart, left word for Ned, and slipped out of the room.

Stephen called out to her knock, and Anne pushed open the door. He looked up and smiled as she entered. He had not lit a candle, and the soft light from the windows cast the room in a pewter glow. An almost intimate setting.

She did not speak when she entered, merely turned and closed the door behind her. It shut with a small click.

Propriety was shut outside the room with her action. They both knew it. Codes of behavior were passed down equally well to Scottish as well as English women. They were each aware that she should not have closed the door, just as neither remarked that it was too late to worry about proprieties. She had sobbed in his arms, and he had lured her to taste passion.

Of all the numerous rooms at Harrington Court, she thought, this one would always be the most special. She had knelt at his side in this room, marveled at his courage, and whispered her secret to him in Gaelic. Here she'd felt delight, wonder,

envy, and jealousy. They'd begun their discovery
of Juliana's chronicle in this room and begun an
idyll of another sort.

"You didn't stay," she said. Her hand reached
out and cupped his cheek.

"I find it difficult to be in the same room with
you," he said.

She felt a spike of hurt at his words. But then
his hand gripped her wrist, but not to pull her hand
away. If anything, he anchored it there. The bristle
of his cheek abraded her palm, her thumb brushed
against his lip.

"I harden when I look at you, Anne Sinclair."

"Do you?" She felt her cheeks warm even as the
words blazed a trail of fire within her.

His eyes darkened as she watched him. She
pulled away, finally.

She sat at his side, not looking at him. Instead,
she concentrated upon the pattern of the intricate
carving of the desk.

"What can I do to help you?" It was no secret
he had spent the day preparing for the siege.

"Do what you're doing," he said. "Keep people's
spirits up."

"It does not seem such a valuable task," she said.
"Not like firing a musket or cleaning a gun."

He smiled. "Can you do either?"

"I can fire a musket, but I cannot hit anything,"
she confessed. "And I know enough to tell a barrel
from a priming pan. But that's about all."

"Then you should occupy yourself with tasks
that suit you."

"What about you? Is your task only that of commander?"

"There is little enough I can do until I receive word back from the king." There was a look on his face as if he wished to add something, but he remained silent.

Was the situation as bleak as she suspected? Every member of the household was subdued as if bent beneath the weight of fear. Their voices were reduced to whispers, their smiles coming less often.

And in the midst of it, this perfect island. This man.

She should not have been so content.

"Even the commander must separate from the man occasionally," he said, smiling. "A moment for himself from time to time." It seemed to her to be a wicked smile, one deliciously so.

He pulled the codex to him. "Shall we read?" he said, and raised one eyebrow. If he knew that she had been entertaining thoughts of a more carnal nature, he didn't show it.

He opened the book and began to read.

" 'Sebastian agreed to give the Templars what they wanted, but to do so he had to travel to the fortress of the Cathars. He was determined to leave me behind, just as I was determined to travel with him. I was his, in heart and soul, even if I could never touch him.' "

Words that rang with a curious similarity to her own thoughts.

I have seen you all my life, Stephen. I have slept on a pillow and breathed your name as I fell asleep. I have drawn your picture over and over and over again until I had your face just so. That one crease of dimple on the left side of your face, the small lines at the corners of your eyes. If she were truly filled with Sinclair courage, she would turn to him, press her fingers against his lips. She would tell him what she was. A visionary, a seeker, and perhaps a witch, after all. Because what she felt for him was some type of sorcery.

" 'I had never seen him attired in anything but his monk's robe. But the man who stood before me in the sunlit bailey was the warrior I'd heard so much about, Sebastian of Langlinais. His armor gleamed in the sun, his tunic matched the shade of the ruby mounted in the hilt of his sword. The journey to Montvichet was one of sadness. Every step I felt as if Sebastian was growing further and further from me. I felt as if time was my enemy.' "

Another point of kinship. Too close to be comfortable.

" 'The fortress of Montvichet was a sad place, one of whispering shadows and haunting voices. The women of the fortress had been besieged, and although their suffering had been terrible, they had withstood the privations for six months. Their fate was one of great sorrow. Once at Montvichet, Sebastian showed me what he would surrender to the Templars. It was a chalice he'd been given in the Holy Land, one of gold and crimson glass. He would lead the Templars to believe that it was the Holy Grail and thereby save Langlinais.' "

Anne glanced up. There was an expression of disbelief on Stephen's face that must mirror hers.

The cup Christ used at the Last Supper, the Holy Grail, was an object of veneration and unbelievable reverence. The Earl of Langlinais perpetrated a hoax. Not on just any group, but on the powerful Knights Templar.

Anne felt as if the breath had been stolen from her.

"Could that be true?"

"If it is, I can understand her reason for burying the codex," Stephen said.

"But why write it at all? To put it down on paper seems a dangerous thing to do."

He turned to the front of the codex and reread Juliana's words. " 'My task is to impart the truth of these matters to all who come after us who would know of the true story of Langlinais Castle and the threat that stands between us and lasting peace. Would it be that such words were never read, then all that is Langlinais will remain fast and without peril.' She and Sebastian must have known that the Templars would try to use the legend of the Grail to enforce their power."

"Did they?"

"There have been rumors for centuries that the Templars had the Grail in their possession. But they were disbanded in 1312. Most of them put to the sword or tortured. They never posed a threat to Langlinais."

"But they might have."

He nodded. "Perhaps the codex was protection, in a way."

"But it cannot be the miracle she spoke of," she said.

"I find myself as mystified by Juliana as you."

Anne propped her chin on her hand and leaned toward him as he continued to read.

" 'The Templars accepted the Grail as real, but they trapped Sebastian and me at the fortress of Montvichet. The ruse had succeeded in satisfying their greed but nearly cost us our lives . . .' "

Stephen's voice faded, and he turned to her. "I would have sent you to safety if I'd known Penroth was so close, Anne."

Her hand reached out of its own volition, guided not by thought but by an instinct as old as time. When her fingers rested upon his hand, he smiled. Did he realize that his smiles came more often in the last few days? As if some little-known door had been opened inside him, and they'd all begun to spill out.

Each member of the Sinclair clan had contributed to rearing her, just as they had to educating her. Each bit of life wisdom had been instilled with an accompanying bit of physical emphasis. She'd been given a tap on the head or had her ears pulled when she was not paying attention. Her hand had been squeezed and she'd been pulled into a boisterous hug for doing right or for no reason other than for being Anne. She'd been patted and kissed so many times that as a child she'd wondered if she would have the imprint of a mouth or a pair of lips permanently embedded on her cheek.

It was obvious that Stephen was not used to such gestures. When she saw him as a child, hurting, swept away by grief, she'd wanted to comfort him. Even as a girl of eight she'd wanted to hold his hand or sit beside his bed and speak to him of silly things that might make him smile.

A feeling that had only grown through the years.

He had been so much a part of her life for so long that the shadow of him lingered, even as the reality of his presence took hold. Yet that image was less formidable than this man.

He ran his fingers over the top of her hand, tracing the undulations of her knuckles. It was as if he touched her intimately. Memories of other touches intruded. A stroke upon her naked stomach with his palm. A kiss to her nipple, a press of lips against her throat. Her eyelids fluttered shut as she was caught in a web of her own making. One crafted of memory and wishes.

"Anne." A word of warning. A soft and low sound. How beautiful her name sounded when he said it.

She blinked open her eyes and smiled at him.

His eyes were dark. What was he thinking? Recalling memories as easily as she did? Of the moment she'd gasped into his mouth or clenched his shoulders so tightly that her nails had left her mark on him? She would go to sleep tonight with the thought of him and wake to the touch of his hands on her. But it would only be the sheet on her bare leg or the corner of the pillow brushing against her lips.

Wanton acts and even more wicked thoughts. No wonder the kirk preached against them. Even now the wish to be loved by him made her limbs feel heavy and the air so thick it was as if she bathed in it instead of breathed it.

With each stroke of his thumb across her flesh he divested her of a little more will. It was as if she'd discarded each restraining thought as she sat there, letting them trail down to the floor like a wafting kerchief.

Love me. The words trembled in the air between them. Held silent by the knowledge that it was not the time or the place. *Do not leave me.* Selfish thoughts. His world was in jeopardy. A thousand swords glinted in the distance as soldiers arranged themselves for the sole purpose of harming this man.

She admired him, even as he sat beside her, a small smile playing on his lips. All the qualities that made him so perfect in her eyes were balanced by his failings. She'd heard him shout at William for something nonsensical and not deserving of the rebuke. And growl at Betty when she would have chastised him about eating more of cook's soup. He was occasionally impatient, a perfectionist when it came to his orders being followed. He didn't speak easily of those things that mattered to him, but she'd come to believe that she belonged on that list.

He had a streak of fierceness that accompanied war well and a layer of compassion that did not.

But enumerating his attributes and his faults did not explain why she loved him. For that she was left to the mercy of her mind and heart. It was simply so, and she accepted it as easily as this moment.

"Is all well with you, Anne?" he asked gently.

"No," she said. She stood and he did, also. Then she extended her arms around him, laid her cheek against his chest. "Now all is well," she said, with a small smile.

His hands came up slowly, reached her arms, and gripped them. It was a tender touch, one that swept from wrist to elbow.

He bent his head and whispered against her cheek, the words traveling in a slow, delicious trail to her ear.

"What troubles you?"

The future.

But that, too, did not matter. Not as much as the touch of his arms around her and the solid thump of his heart.

She pulled herself back and looked into his face. There was an implacable resolve that told her he wanted an answer.

There had been too many times when she could have told him about her visions not to recognize that this was not one of them. Still, she laid the bricks in place for the wall that would be erected between them by his disbelief.

"Have you ever had something happen," she asked him, "that changed your life?"

"Unfortunately, yes," he said, a half smile on his lips. "War has that effect."

"Have you never had something occur that confused you? That you could barely believe at the same time you welcomed it?"

"I met a woman once, who knew of my childhood hiding place although no one had shown her. She spoke my name before we had met."

He had never before mentioned these things, leading her to believe that he had forgotten. Or had not noticed.

She stepped back. Her hands fell to her sides. Her heart pounded so hard that she could barely breathe. Had the moment been forced upon her, then? The truth, spoken when it was not convenient, but when he demanded it?

A knock spared her.

"My lord?" they heard William call from the other side of the door. "Penroth's camp is signaling. Shall we let the messenger through?"

Stephen called out for him to enter. When he did, he answered the question, his gaze still not leaving her face. "Yes," he said. "Give him safe passage."

They stood for just a few moments looking at each other, a silent island in the presence of William and behind him other members of the regiment.

Then someone asked a question, and the bond was broken.

Chapter 19

"**I**t's all your fault, you know, that you're trapped here," Hannah said.

"I'm not trapped," Richard said with some equanimity. He moved his chess piece and sat back. "I simply took advantage of Stephen's offer and settled into a room here. After all, I had two patients to treat."

"You might be back at your own house."

"True enough, but how would I live without your biting wit? Your dulcet tones?"

She smiled at him. It appeared to discompose him more than her frown.

"I want to be gone from here," she said, moving her pawn. She had no hope of winning this silly game, but it appeared to give him pleasure if she at least made the pretense of wanting to.

"Why? Have you some pressing need?"

She looked at him in amazement. "Other than ten thousand bloodthirsty troops ready to slaughter me in my bed?"

"Six thousand," he corrected. "Can't be more than that. Maybe a few hundred less."

She narrowed her eyes. "You seem too calm, Richard."

"I am quaking in my boots. However, I'd rather put on a show of courage for your sake, Hannah."

"For my sake?"

"Indeed," he said, smiling. "It seems to irritate you. Besides, if the truth be known, they are Parliamentarians. Surely I am safe enough."

"I do hope they take that into account when starving us out."

He lifted one eyebrow.

"Is that your only reason for wishing to be gone from here?"

"Cannot I simply want to be safe?"

He shook his head. "You are much too devious for that. You have a streak of cunning about you, my dear, that's not altogether wholesome. However, I confess to wanting to be a pirate at one time, so it strikes me as altogether fascinating. Would it have something to do with Anne?"

"I am not cunning."

"Have you never called her daughter?"

A chess piece rolled to the edge of the table, hung in the air for a long moment before clattering to the floor. She stared at him open-mouthed.

"Has no one ever commented on the resemblance?"

Numbly she shook her head.

"I am not merely speaking of appearance, my dear, but of temperament. She appears to have a stubborn bent, just as you do."

"I am not stubborn."

"Next you'll tell me that you're a fragile flower of Scotland."

"I'm English."

"That explains the acerbic wit. I understood the Scots to be more dour of nature."

"How did you know, Richard?"

He did not, thankfully, pretend to misunderstand her. "When she turns her head, she looks like you. And when she smiles in a certain way. I see also, Hannah, although I hesitate to offend you by saying so, a youthful Anne in your flashes of humor."

"No one has ever known."

"I doubt that. Perhaps they never commented upon it."

"There was never occasion to see us together," she said, looking down at the table.

He sat back, all pretense of being absorbed in the game gone. "There is no reason to look so stricken, Hannah. There are too many young girls who've found themselves in your plight. I've delivered my share of babies born on the wrong side of the blanket."

"I didn't want that for her. To be thought of that way." She lifted her eyes. He was looking at her, a warm expression on his face. Not the revulsion she'd expected to find should anyone ever discover that she'd been both wanton and unwise.

"What happened, Hannah?"

She said nothing for a moment. She had never told the story. How odd that it should feel right to do so now. "I fell in love with a man I could not have. A common enough tale."

"But you are not a common woman. There must be more to it."

She smiled, thinking that he really was possessed of a deadly charm.

"Robbie was married. A fact I did not discover until it was too late. He returned to Scotland, and I remained in England. My parents banished me when they discovered I was with child. There was no one to turn to who would welcome a woman in my condition."

"So you traveled to Scotland."

She glanced up, surprised. She nodded. "The journey took longer than I'd expected. I had little money and walked a good deal of the way. Every once in a while a farmer would let me ride in his wagon. But eventually, I reached Dunniwerth."

"I imagine you were a great shock to your Robbie."

She gave a small smile. The years had taken the sting of pain from that time.

"He was stunned to see me. So was his wife. But something good always comes from something bad. At least that's what my grandmother always used to tell me. They had been married seven years, and Maggie had never been able to have a child."

"So the story was put about that Anne was Maggie's child. What was to happen to you?"

"If I wanted to stay, I was to remain on the island at Dunniwerth and become the wise woman."

"A harsh payment."

She shook her head. "No, not really. I had no place else to go, and this way, I could at least be near Anne. For a time after she was born, Maggie came to stay with me. It was given out that she was recovering from the birth. I nursed Anne until they found a wetnurse for her."

She stood, folded her arms around her waist. Those days had been among the most painful of her life. She'd watched that small face and known a love like she'd never believed possible. When she'd handed Anne over to Maggie on that last day and watched her walk away from the cottage, she'd wanted to die. She'd prayed for it, in fact. But death did not come that easily. Gradually she had begun to live again. To take an interest in the world around her. It was a pleasant life, one without highs or lows. Still, there were moments that sufficed for pleasure and contentment.

"I didn't see her again for eight years," she said, recalling the day Anne had come to her doorway. Her heart had nearly stopped with the joy of it. The first thought she'd had was that Robbie had taken pity on her loneliness and longing and had sent her daughter to her.

"What did you do all those years, Hannah? How did you bear it?"

"I went to fairs in the autumn. Tilled my garden." She looked up at the ceiling. "Grew herbs and learned how to heal broken wings and ease the suffering of an animal that escaped from a trap." She smiled. "And became a friend to the daughter I loved so well. Those moments were among the most precious of my life."

"It is no wonder you've a wagging tongue," he said with a gentle smile. "You've no one to talk to all this time."

She began to smile, then to laugh, understanding that he used insults the way other men used flattery, to coax and cajole. She didn't bother to tell him that it worked. Her mood was lighter than it had been a moment ago. By his smug smile he told her he knew only too well.

He studied her. "You're afraid it will happen again."

She turned and stared at him. "You have an uncomfortable knack of doing that, Richard."

"Of doing what? Keeping you off balance? It is my ambition, my dear, since your bandages were removed."

"Don't call me my dear."

"I've been doing so all along. Have you just now noticed?"

She frowned at him.

"Do you think Anne is in danger of doing what you did?" he asked, returning to subject at hand. "Of falling in love with the wrong man? Or of doing something that will lock her up on an island forever?"

"I wouldn't have that happen to her, Richard. Sometimes love isn't enough."

"Do you still love him, Hannah?" he asked. His question was addressed to the chessboard. "After all these years?"

She had wanted, just once, to see Robbie again. To thank him for those years. For allowing her to be part of Anne's life. If it was true that he'd ruined her, it was equally so that she'd participated in her own shame, had enjoyed the act with him enough so that memories of it had given her hot and feverish dreams for years. Yet he'd rescued her when a lesser man would have turned his back. And had not forbidden his daughter to come to her.

"I will always love him, Richard. He is Anne's father. But love is like a flower. Without sun and water it will not grow. And whatever doesn't grow must eventually die."

He smiled at her. "Hannah, that was almost poetic."

She could feel her face warm. "You are a silly man, Richard."

"No one has ever called me that before," he said, his smile growing in scope. "My daughter will be pleased. She has been fussing at me to be more daring in my dress and my demeanor."

She stared at him, absolutely flummoxed. With only a few words he'd dismissed the tragedy of her life. Not only had he made light of the story, but he'd stripped any shame from it.

"You warned me once that those who listen at doors never hear any good about themselves. Now I know why," Anne said, stepping into the room. "I might have learned I was a bastard."

Hannah's blood turned to ice.

"I came to ask if you would like to come to the garden with me. It is safe enough there. A few moments out of doors seemed like a nice diversion."

"Instead, you've found another," Richard said, standing. He looked from one woman to the other. He said something, made his excuses, left the room. Or at least Hannah thought he did.

She stood slowly, faced the woman she'd known as friend but had never acknowledged as her daughter.

"Why did you never tell me?" Anne asked, her eyes flashing with anger. "There were numerous times when you might have said something."

"What could I have said?"

"The truth? Ian certainly made it a point to let me know what the gossip was."

"What would it have served? The truth was that

you were the laird's daughter. What did it matter who your mother was?"

Anne looked away, focused on the window and the view beyond. She took a deep breath. "I could not go to my father with those tales, and my mother would have been too hurt by such words."

She turned, faced Hannah. It occurred to Hannah that she had rarely seen Anne angry. The emotion seemed to snap in the air between them.

"But you knew. I came to you with all my secrets. All my fears. You could have eased them with a few words."

"And stripped you of a mother's love." Her own anger began to build. "What would you have me say to a child? That your mother isn't your mother? That the woman you knew as friend was your mother? What good would it have done, Anne?"

"We'll never know, will we? You never spoke of it. I think, Hannah, it was less to protect me than it was to shield you. I have been grown for years. Does the same excuse suffice?"

"Why do I think your anger is not solely at me, Anne?" She studied the younger woman.

"I do not need to be sheltered; I am neither a child, nor am I a fool." Anne moved away, toward the door, then turned and glanced back at Hannah. "It all makes sense," she said. "Why you rarely spoke about my parents; why they never asked about you. Why you hardly left the island."

"The ruse was done with you in mind," Hannah said.

Anne smiled thinly. "I cannot believe that your sole reason was my happiness. My father wanted an heir. My mother wanted a child. You wished security."

"You see things in absolutes, Anne."

"Do I? Or only as they are?" she asked softly.

She left the room without a backward glance.

Chapter 20

Anne looked up as the door to Stephen's study opened.

"I knew you would be here," Ian said, frowning at her. "You always seek him out. Everyone else is gathered in the kitchen and here you are, pining for him."

Her entire life had been turned upside down, her knowledge of herself split in two and joined again in a misshapen ball. But in this matter, at least, things had not changed. Ian still played the bully.

"Stephen is not here," she said softly.

"But you still remain. Why?"

"Does it matter?"

"He does not want you. You may have succeeded in becoming a diversion for him. But there is nothing else for you."

There was such anger on Ian's face that it startled her. Was he enraged at her or at Stephen?

That question was answered in the next moment.

"We should have left here before we were trapped," he said.

Anne was bewildered. "And you blame me for that?"

"Who else? It was you who wanted to come here. Why, Anne?"

What would he say if she told him that she and the English general Penroth had the same motive? Both of them had the same purpose—they wanted Stephen.

Anne suspected, however, that she would lose, either to Penroth or to Stephen's honor.

If she had not left home, would her life be in such shambles? Or would she simply have wondered, for the rest of her days, about the visions that had enchanted her from childhood? Which was better? Full knowledge or blessed ignorance?

Another question whose answer she knew. She would gladly pay any price for these days.

"Why did you never return to Dunniwerth in all these weeks, Ian?"

His gaze never left her face. "I have been charged with your well-being, Anne. I could not leave you here."

However respectful he might be of her father, and however seriously he took being entrusted with her safety, there was a part of her that would never trust him. They had never been friends, only adversaries. The lonely child and the bully who'd tried to wound her with words.

"Come with me, Anne," Ian said, his voice now kinder. As if he'd heard her thoughts or intuited her misery. "You can sketch those sitting in the kitchen."

"So that we can all pretend to be amused?" She

shook her head. She had been unable to draw caricatures these last few days.

He frowned at her, then left the room.

She found, oddly enough, that she could not draw Stephen. To place the image of his face on paper was more difficult than it had ever been before, as if her heart was filled to the brim and the act of sketching him would tip out the tears carefully guarded there.

She often found refuge in his study when he was with his men in the ballroom. That large chamber served as both a training ground and practice yard.

The room where she sat echoed with his presence even when empty. Many times she went to Juliana's desk, and simply stood there with her hands resting on the sloping surface and finding a strange comfort in doing so. A connection to this woman who had lived so long ago.

This morning she went to sit at Stephen's desk, leaning back in the ugly lion chair that had been the source of his disdain. She suspected that he did not rid himself of the ugly animal chairs because they were part of his history. He was a man who prided himself on his heritage. As her clan did. The behavior of each Sinclair was held in check by rules handed down for generations. A code of honor as strict and inviolate as that Stephen of Langlinais followed.

Did men live only to fight? She'd witnessed such exuberance on the faces of the men of Dunniwerth when they'd marched off to war. There had been two occasions in the last ten years when they'd left Sinclair lands in order to fight the English. The words they spoke were those of reluctance, but the sparkle in their eyes belied it. They hid their enthusiasm behind such exalted concepts as honor and pride and country.

It sounded grand. But in the end what did it mean? That they loved the idea of fighting more than they did staying with their wives and children? That it was easier to lift a claymore than it was a hammer?

Perhaps there was something she didn't understand. But when it was over, when the siege of Harrington Court was through, when Stephen Harrington, Earl of Langlinais was captured and taken to London, what would be the final result? Would the world have been made a safer place? Would the crops grow better, children live past their infancy? Would men become more wise? Would the world be enriched somehow and made more beautiful? Or would it change anything? Other than his life and hers?

It would not alter the outcome of the war or make the world a better or a worse place.

She sat where he had so many times, looked out the window to the right of his desk. Here she could see the vista to the east. If she ignored the signs of encampment, the landscape appeared peaceful. A mist settled over the meadow. A variety of shades of green colored the trees and bushes and grass, from almost blue to emerald. A lovely sight, this land. Not, however, worth the cost of his life.

The codex was before her, bound tight again within its wooden cover. She placed her hand gently on it, feeling a sense of awe that there had been only three people to touch it.

Her thoughts were so filled with Stephen that it was with little surprise that the door opened and he walked in. He was intent upon his thoughts, his gaze on the floor. He looked up, blinked at her, and then smiled. A slow, dawning smile that warmed her from her toes.

She stood up. "I've been at your desk," she said.

He did not seem irritated or even startled by her admission. Only waved her back in the chair.

"Perhaps I can tempt you into the role of steward," he said. "Although I will admit, it's an easy enough job under a siege."

"No survey of the crops to do," she said, smiling.

"None," he agreed, his own smile in place.

"No sheep to shear."

"Or lambs to count."

It was silliness they engaged in, the banter of two adults who ridicule a topic the better to tolerate one that is not mentioned.

"There is little enough to tally," he said, the words shattering the illusion that it was only play.

She didn't pretend to misunderstand him. Nor did she dismiss his words with a smile. "How many more days until we're out of food?"

He seemed to study her, as if gauging her stamina for the truth. She wanted to tell him that her quota for bad news was absurdly low at the moment. But she didn't, sensing in him a need to tell someone else his inner thoughts. So she smiled and returned his look with a steady regard of her own.

"Less than two," he said. "It was the devil's own luck that we were preparing to leave the morning Penroth arrived. Otherwise, he wouldn't have trapped the entire regiment here."

"What are you going to do?"

He closed the door behind him, walked to the window, and stood there looking out at the mist-enshrouded landscape. He stood silent and still, so resolute in that moment that she could have guessed his words. Something daring or profane in its sacrifice.

But he surprised her.

He turned and smiled at her. "Do you know, I've pictured you as a woman of the court. With your hair in curls and a beauty patch on your cheek."

"Have you?" His intent look made her smile.

He nodded. "But I've decided that I like you better as you are with just your hair tied back with that ribbon."

"You do?" She should not be so absurdly pleased.

"And your green dress with its frayed laces."

She felt a flush of embarrassment tempered with laughter. "I have hardly the wardrobe of a lady of court."

"You don't need one, Anne. You outshine them."

How easily he charmed her.

He came around the side of the desk, looked down at her drawing board. "What are you working on?"

"The knight of Juliana's. Something about him disturbs me, but I cannot place it."

His fingers hovered in the air above her drawing. "Have you never worked with paints?"

She shook her head. "No, although I've longed to. Perhaps one day."

"I hope you do," he said. His tone was bemused, his attention seemingly caught by the drawing of the knight. She'd drawn him with the shield across his body in much the same stance as Juliana had portrayed.

"There is a great similarity between you and Juliana," he said. "Both of you talented in things that do not interest most women."

"Or perhaps it is only that we are privileged to be given the chance to engage in them."

He glanced over at her.

"Circumstance favored our interests. Juliana's convent fostered both her and her talent. My father would have indulged me in whatever I pursued. I doubt there are that many women who have such good fortune."

"An interesting thought."

"People are interesting," she said.

"Life at Dunniwerth certainly sounds so."

She smiled at him. "No less so than at Langlinais. Do you not think of what the castle might have been like in Juliana's time?"

"Knights and damsels and codes of honor?" He turned and looked at her. "Our family motto dates back that far. Duty, honor, loyalty."

"As onerous as mine," she said, confessing more than he knew. "A Sinclair is always brave."

"Difficult doctrines to accept."

"Or live up to," she said.

"Must you?"

"Being a woman, you mean?" She wasn't even irritated by the question. She doubted, however, that her equanimity might have been the same had another man asked that question of her. "I am the laird's daughter. An example to follow. Even if you could discount that, the fact is I'm a Sinclair, and Sinclair women and men are supposed to be equally brave."

"Don't Sinclair men protect their women?"

"Yes, but the women sometimes guard the men. In their hearts if not with their claymores."

"What will you do with the rest of your life, Anne?"

The question was as sharp as she'd known it would be, just as she'd known that he would ask it eventually. He was a man who felt responsible for those in his care. She'd given her innocence to him, albeit willingly, and therefore he had incurred a debt. One that he felt, even if she did not.

She was not, however, a parcel to be carefully tied and wrapped and bundled together in order to send it off to its destination.

She sat back in the chair, faced ahead, her hands curved over the absurd lions' heads.

"I will marry," she said calmly. "Someone who adores me. I will have children and grow old and wise." The words came sweetly, with no touch of the hurt she felt.

He said nothing, simply moved away.

She felt a twinge of shame. Not enough to recant her words. In the next moment she was glad she had not.

"Select your husband well," he said, his voice soft. "Make sure he's of genial temperament."

"Like you, you mean?"

He turned and glanced at her. His smile had an

edge to it. "I find I am not excessively genial when it comes to you, Anne Sinclair."

She leaned back in the chair and watched him. "You do not show it. I must commend you on your manners."

"I have been reared to be polite."

"It is a good thing I have not been," she said. "One of us can be honest at least."

"There is a time to be honest and a time to remain silent," he said, his attention focused on the figurine in his hand.

Since she had used the same rationalization for her inability to tell him of her visions, she remained silent.

"Yet I find that I am almost painfully honest with you. I wonder why that is?" He glanced at her.

"Perhaps because I am simply a traveler through your life," she said.

He raised one eyebrow. "Is it the siege that brings out your irritation or my presence?"

"No . . . just your absence," she said, staring straight at him. "Something you've refrained from mentioning for all your claim to honesty." She knew it even as she watched him. An uncanny sense gifted her with the knowledge of what he planned to do. Or perhaps it was only there in his eyes.

He placed the figurine back on the shelf and stood in front of the desk.

"You're going to surrender, aren't you?"

He extended his hand to her. She slapped it away. The gesture seemed to surprise him.

She stood, the desk still between them, her eyes sparking.

"Is it your aim to make me angry so that our parting is easier?" she asked.

"Will it work?"

"No," she said. "I'm already irritated at you; a bit more anger will do nothing but keep the flame bright."

He smiled then, his look genuinely amused. "Then will charm accomplish my aim?"

"There is nothing humorous about this."

"Perhaps not, nor as tragic as you perceive."

"They will kill you, Stephen."

He said nothing.

"Am I to congratulate you on your sacrifice, kiss your cheek, and send you on your way?"

Still there was no response from him.

"When?"

"Soon."

"When?" She wanted the hour, the minute, the second it would happen. But he would not give it to her.

Instead, he suddenly gripped her hand and pulled her around the desk.

She went, resisting, into his arms. She didn't put her arms around him and return the embrace. She was afraid if she did, that she would not be able to let him go.

A Sinclair is always brave. No, not always. She wanted, with a child's desire to beg him to stay. To not do this thing. To not give himself up for her sake—for anyone's sake. There was no one worth the sacrifice. But she said nothing.

"I will be safe," he said. The words were soft, meant to be reassuring, she was certain. They failed in their mission. "They will not harm me. I'm worth too much to them as a figurehead. An object lesson, if you will."

"Other men have thought the same," she said. "But they have been hanged."

He pulled back and smiled at her. "You must have faith in me, Anne. I would not willingly walk into danger with my eyes wide open."

Yes, you would. In order to save someone else. You have a surfeit of honor, Stephen.

If she had no courage, at least she had pride. But even that she would have given up at this moment if it would have convinced him. She knew, with a sense of honesty at least as great as his, that he would still leave her.

Chapter 21

Stephen stood at one of the dormer windows on the third floor. From here he could see the array of men. Hundreds if not thousands of tents spread out for as far as he could see.

He had known for days that they weren't going to be rescued. In addition to the message to Blagge, he'd sent the royal messenger back to Oxford with a request for troops. Whether or not he'd gotten to Oxford was unknown. If he had, the king might not have had the troops to send. Or perhaps he would not have sent them as punishment. A lesson for the Earl of Langlinais that it was not wise to disobey a royal command.

Stephen had faced General Penroth on the battlefield numerous times before; each knew the other's strengths and weaknesses.

He glanced down at the letter in his hand. The paper was wrinkled, the penmanship perfect. The wording was a masterpiece of understatement, enumerating the terms under which he was to surrender. Left unsaid was what would happen if he did not. But then, he didn't need Penroth's words. His mind had furnished images only too easily.

You have five days in which to consider these terms of surrender. If I have not heard from you at the end of that time, I will have no choice but to view your silence as hostile.

For those whom you shelter, I offer safe passage to the nearest town.

For those men who have served under your command, pardons as long as they do not take up arms again.

For yourself, imprisonment in London, there to be tried for your crimes against Parliament.

Six thousand men against sixty were hardly favorable odds. All Penroth needed to do was roll up his cannon and bombard Harrington Court until there was nothing left but dust and splinters. Even easier was to simply starve them out. Parliament would thereby acquire a rich estate with little or no effort.

He'd returned to Harrington Court not prepared for a long stay. He'd remained in winter quarters with his regiment. Spring was the time for planting, but war had taken its toll of schedules, even those of the land. What foodstuffs had remained after the long winter were barely enough to feed the thirty-odd servants, let alone the men of his regiment of horse.

He was responsible for the safety of over a hundred people at Harrington Court and even more at Lange on Terne. Women and children and old men with nothing to do but to sit and pontificate on the state of the world and anticipate the next day.

If its inhabitants were guilty of any sin, it was pride of place. If there was something needed, it was to be found at Lange on Terne. No reason to journey all the way to London for it, especially in these troubled times. There were merchants and shops, wares and bakeries. All manner of produce might be found on market day, as well as the plumpest guinea hens and the fattest pigs. And Lange on Terne, the natives said, had naught of the stench of London about it. Here a goodwife could hang out her linens without fear of them turning yellow from the foul air.

He knew most of its inhabitants by name, had played with the children of the village when he was a boy. For hundreds of years Lange on Terne had depended upon the castle of Langlinais for its sustenance and protection. Today the responsibility was the same.

He returned to his suite. There was nothing more to be done. Nothing that could be done.

The words of Juliana's chronicles were too pointed. The siege of Montvichet had ended in tragedy. If he did not do something, the same fate would befall those at Harrington Court.

Two mullioned windows flanked the fireplace at the north end of his suite of rooms. He walked to the left window, stood looking down at the expanse of countryside below him. Harrington Court was built facing away from Langlinais, as if shunning the medieval fortress. Why had he always felt an affinity for it? Because it was his heritage? Because men who lived there had been his ancestors? Perhaps. Or perhaps his imagination had been caught by the idea of codes of knighthood and honor.

The castle seemed to glow in the moonlight like a place alight with ghosts. Perhaps it was haunted by all the men he'd admired, whose shades rose up to chastise and question and condemn.

Even the soil gave witness to their walk upon the world. The path down the hill, across the bridge, and through the baileys had all been worn into the earth over time, hollowed out for him by those who had gone long before. Perhaps his dreams were nothing more than echoes of their lives.

Did spirits stand vigil on him at each tower of Langlinais? In each room of Harrington Court? Did they line the roads and watch in silence as he passed? Were they bitter because he breathed and they did not? Or were they kind in their pity, knowing that the ending that had come to them would come to him soon enough?

He was the seventeenth Earl of Langlinais, and throughout his life the responsibility of being so had always been there. First as a goal. He must measure up to the previous earls, be as wise, as intelligent. He must study as hard, learn as well as all the men who'd come before him. He had been concerned that he might not be able to continue the dynasty that stretched so far behind him. Or that he would be unable to protect the village and the people who'd always depended upon the earls of Langlinais.

He stood at the window and watched the moonlit landscape. From time to time a campfire blazed or was extinguished. Tiny pinpricks of light not unlike stars.

Angels winking at him. A saying he'd been told in childhood. One given to ease his fears. He'd been awed by the majesty of the sky above him, and by the great gulf that existed between the earth upon which he stood and the heavens. He'd felt small and insignificant and terrified.

He was the Earl of Langlinais, he'd been told, and could never be less than that. Until his life and experience had expanded to include more than this place and this heritage, he had believed it. True, he was ennobled by a title, but in the greater scheme of things, it truly didn't matter.

The boy who had been afraid of a night sky made himself known again. That same child had sat and promised God that he would be good if He did not take his mother from him. Loss, then, that was part of what he felt. As a boy, he'd pounded his pillow in the darkness and refused to speak his mother's name for one whole month. He'd even dared God to take him, too. Anger. Grief.

He mourned for what was his and could never be again. Not simply a house or a home. But an era, a time. A legacy that would be no more.

He'd fought with his mind, his heart, and his body to protect what was his. To credit all the men who'd gone before him and would come after. The blood of warriors flowed through his veins in addition to men of words and stately deeds.

He asked forgiveness of the ghosts of his heritage. They seemed to answer him. The earl who'd been rumored to have been in love with the queen, who had been Elizabeth's advisor on affairs with Spain, would have counseled a parlay with Penroth. But then, it had been said of him that he would bargain with the devil. The man who'd started it all, who'd fought at William's side six hundred years ago and been awarded Langlinais as a prize for both his loyalty and his fierceness in battle, might have wished to fight. Never mind the cost for those he held dear. And the earl who had built Harrington Court after that terrible year when the Terne had flooded the old castle so badly it was no longer habitable, what would he have said? He would have been the most practical of the group, advising that Stephen look upon the situation with logic and sense, devoid of emotion.

It was nearly impossible to do so.

Had Penroth waited until now before he'd offered terms? He possessed a devilish instinct for coincidence or perhaps he simply knew the desperation of their circumstances as well as Stephen did.

He stared out at his world. "Surrender." He spoke the word aloud, but it made the decision no easier. It clawed at him.

He was suffused with a curious kind of resignation. As if all that he had done from the beginning of his life until this point in time was for this one deed.

He, like most of his men, had been untrained in war. But he'd learned the brutality of it soon enough. He had not wanted to kill, but neither had he wished to die. He had become a soldier because his country had split apart in thought and ideal and he'd been forced to choose. His courage had been tested as he lived through each day.

Around him slept more than a hundred people. Or remained awake as slumber was chased away by fear. Their fate was his. Their futures placed lovingly and with great faith into his hands. They trusted him to do what was necessary, just as they believed in him to save them.

It was oddly fitting that he should recall one of the Psalms the Parliamentarians were fond of quoting as they marched into battle.

O lord how are my foes increased,
Against me many rise

There was only one thing he could do. He'd known it for days. However much his mind circled around it, it always came back to surrender.

He glanced down at the coffer on the table beside him. Another regret. Perhaps he would give the coffer to Anne, have her take the codex somewhere safe. Protect it, that it might be read a hundred or more years from now.

He wanted to tell her what he'd discovered. Words that had startled him and confused him and then amazed him. He would go to her chamber and tell her. Only that.

His smile was a silent rebuke, an effortless ridicule of his intent. If he went to her chamber, it would not be to tell her of the Langlinais miracle but to leach some comfort in her arms.

Would she know how much he needed her tonight? He would not say the words, but perhaps she would know and extend her arms around him. Lover and friend.

He left the room before he could convince himself that it was not wise. That honor decreed he treat her with discretion, with gentleness. But she answered his soft knock within moments, as if she'd waited for him. One sign, then. A few more, and he would stay.

She'd lit not one candle but a branch of them which stood outlined in the flickering light. Shadows graced her face and accentuated the reddish hue of her hair. Her hand stretched out and greeted him, lured him closer. Just that, an outstretched hand. Nothing else. Not a sign, then. It was a night of farewells and poignant partings, not omens.

Once before they'd stood together like this. A night of loving to last a lifetime. Memories to be pulled from their resting place when the world turned black with powder or death rode too close in battle. But that night would also be recalled in more peaceful times. Perhaps for the rest of his life. A night of passion he'd not dreamed of before, of both conquest and longing. Of desire sated and rewarded.

Tonight he came to her. The moment repeated again. The need for forgetfulness and a wish to add to that store of memories.

Even as he stood in silence, he vowed that he would love her once not in parting but in joy. This he silently promised her, even as he accepted that it might not be possible. He made another promise, one he could ensure was kept. If she allowed him to stay. Tonight would not be swathed in sorrow. Not in the shadows of grief.

He would enchant her, as she had him.

"Forgive me," he said, his voice kept low. Out of respect for her? Or because he did not want to have the world hear him beg?

There were secrets to her mind and person, mysteries in her eyes. In the slight smile she wore when

looking at him sometimes. In the passion she so
artlessly gave and shared. She opened her arms.
Welcome and forgiveness in a gesture.

A sign, then, of how close to madness he must
surely be, that he pressed her face gently to his
chest and sighed into her hair.

"I need you," he heard himself say in horrified
fascination. "I need you." Again, as if the initial
capitulation had not been enough. Again and again
and again, this surrender. Practice, then, for what
he must do in the morning.

Help me. Ease me. Make me forget for a while.

She'd guessed so easily what he'd planned to do
before the thought had become solidified in his
mind. It seemed as if she intuited the exact moment
of his surrender now. Or did she see the knowledge
in his eyes?

She wound her arms around his waist. She held
him tight to her as if the words he did not speak
would sever them otherwise.

He'd held her so when nature itself had split the
air around them. Held her when the thunder roared
and lightning flashed. The passion that sparked between them was as strong. But she'd not been
afraid then. Even in her innocence, she'd matched
his need and gifted him with a wonder he'd never
before felt.

When she pulled away, he was humbled and
awed. On her face were tears. They glazed her
cheeks and reddened her lips. He'd sought a sign,
an omen, a signal. As he stared down into her face,
he found that he didn't need one after all.

She did not cry easily or often. How did he know
such a thing? The same way he knew that her tears

were for him and the morning to come, and a hundred such when time separated them and wars and politics and religious unrest. All stupid reasons. All silly notions measured against this woman.

Anne. How simple her named sounded. How plain for such a glorious creature. Anne. He wanted to call her something different, something unique and rare and unusual, that was never uttered by any other voice. A name that would indicate to her how he felt, how he wanted to thank her and praise her and show her, in some tiny fashion, that he would hold the memory of her smile in that sweet spot in his heart where all such memories rested.

He had thought himself adrift in near madness to think of her so often, to dream of her so deeply. But in her look was the same possession of thought. To be so open in her vulnerability was an act of the greatest courage.

The candlelight was too bright, the moment too ripe with feeling.

Some women were lovely even in their tears. Anne was not, a discovery that sent a surge of tenderness shooting through him. Her nose was pink, the whites of her eyes nearly red.

He'd shared passion with her, and it had been wondrous, something that made tawdry and minor other joinings in his lifetime. But now she offered him something more. Not mere passion, not solely exquisite physical pleasure, but part of herself.

Do not. He wanted to tell her to shield her eyes or cover her heart, but not to show him her soul so easily. He might bruise her accidentally or wound her with his actions. But she stood silent, as she had a habit of doing, and dared him to look inside her. To take or to reject what she so effortlessly offered him. The gift of herself.

She offered and he would take. He knew that even as he reached out and bared her shoulder. Her dressing gown was borrowed or made for her. Cast off from one of the servants or crafted from the bolts of cloth kept in the sewing room. He didn't know, nor did he care. His only interest was in stripping it from her.

He felt hollow. A man without a soul or heart or even thoughts at this moment. They trembled in the air between them, all the separate pieces of himself, to be gathered up by either of them.

My soul. I shall need it if I pass through to heaven. And am challenged at the gate for all my misdeeds. Shall I number you among them, Anne?

It did not surprise him when she answered, her soft voice proof that he was indeed adrift in confusion. Enough to speak the words he had not wished to say aloud.

"No, Stephen, my dearest. Do not regret me."

"A command again. You have a habit of doing so." His smile curved even as he kissed her bare shoulder.

She tilted her neck, an invitation to feast on her throat. He could not deny himself. He kissed her there, where the pulse of her was hot and rapid. Life beneath his lips. A life all the more precious for being hers.

"My thoughts," he said, content to continue this madness with her. "You are in them always, as if you have invaded my mind. You are not content to simply be in my dreams."

"You have been in my sight all my life," she said, the words crumbling beneath her sudden, surprising sobs. She began to cry so hard that he gathered her up into his arms and held her tight.

"All my life," she said, as if it were a confession.

Her tears were those of grief, mourning held too long within. He did not ask for what she cried. Whatever answer, it would too closely parallel his own thoughts.

Instead, he could only hold her while the storm raged within her, survive these minutes with a silent endurance. If he ever thought himself numbed by war or uncaring, that would be when he summoned this memory to mind. Or if his freedom were curtailed and his life forfeit, he would think of this time. Each of Anne's tears seemed tinged with acid, and each of them bored through his chest to find his heart. The recollection of these moments would prove that he was not jaded after all. Rather that he was proficient at feeling too much.

The flickering of his anger was unexpected. But it grew in that moment to be a wall through which he viewed the world and anything that would come between him and her.

The hollowness of him expanded until he felt only a shell. But it curved and wound itself over her. A hermit crab, perhaps, summoning a home.

He had not lost his senses in wine, but his thoughts were no less drunk. Or fevered.

Valere iubere. Beautiful words. Words that fell in a soft, rolling lilt from his tongue. *Valere iubere.* To bid farewell. A strong parting, one of optimism, victory, great health. Not a surrender to circumstance or to men who fought for causes he could not espouse.

He should not be here. Remonstrated with himself even as he bent his head to kiss her. *Make me remember.* She had said that to him once, and he'd not been able to forget. Not one moment of the night they'd shared. They'd laughed and lingered and explored each other. Yet when he touched her naked skin now, it was as if it were the first time. Her fingers tangled with his. Her eyes wide, her lashes spiked with tears, she encouraged him and welcomed him without a word spoken.

Her flesh was warm as he cradled his palms around the curve of her full breasts. Warmed them as she closed her eyes with the feel of his knuckles brushing her skin.

They'd teased each other with words before. Soft words that had draped themselves between desire and propriety. Their speech had tripped along a cliff of need, been tender and evocative.

Not this time. This time he welcomed lust. It would burn away the sorrow they each felt and would not acknowledge. He wanted to bind her to him with passion. To make her weak and wasted from it, from him. To take her tears and taste them and transform them into weeping of another kind.

He needed to spill himself within her. Not honor, then. Not even duty. Only need. Naked and intractable and necessary.

He would make her whimper in the faint light and be as ensorcelled as he felt.

"I want to taste you," he said, not bending to whisper the words in her ear, not lowering his voice. He stared into her eyes and watched her cheeks deepen in color.

He parted the garment slowly an inch at a time. Then bent his head and nuzzled her engorged nipple. Sucked it into the heat of his mouth. He heard her gasp, felt her hands flutter on his shoulders.

He sucked harder, a gentle insistence, passion's game. Then used the edge of his teeth to scrape the length of the nipple.

Her breathing grew louder or his hearing more acute. He wanted her to scream in his arms, to grow wet with his play. To beg him to enter her, to sob his name.

The other breast was teased with his lips while he fondled the one he'd deserted with tender fingers. Her nipples were sensitive, easily aroused. He'd learned that during the one night they'd shared.

She closed her eyes. He touched her closed lids with one gentle finger, remonstrance in a touch.

"No," he said, gently. "I want to see your eyes, Anne."

She had a habit of blinking slowly when she was moved. A curiously evocative gesture. One that hardened him still further.

In the candlelight her eyes appeared almost black. The centers had expanded, the look in them was beyond passion. Something more dangerous, perhaps, as if a part of her recognized his game for the tenuous control it represented and goaded him to continue.

For a second, a moment, his hand hovered at the apex of her thighs. Then he gently touched her.

She blinked again, that slow, arousing blink even

as she tugged at her bottom lip with her teeth. He wanted to tell her that it was his game of seduction, that she could not sway him from this goal, but words were too difficult at the moment.

His fingers found her wet and hot. Nature prepared her for him even as he ached to be inside of her. His thumb brushed over gently swelling flesh. When she gasped, he repeated the gesture.

"Is it nice, Anne?"

She looked shocked at the question. He repeated it, accompanied it with a tender smile and a soft, teasing touch.

She nodded.

"Is it nice?"

She understood finally. "Yes," she breathed, the sound no more than a sigh.

"Do you want more?"

He inserted his longest finger gently, sweetly, slowly inside her. Her plump breasts had been sucked into arousal, their nipples deeply red and gleaming with his kisses. Her dressing gown hung from her shoulders, framed them, and made the sight even more arousing.

Anne with her eyes black with passion and her cheeks pink and hot.

He kissed her temple, breathed the words against her ear.

"Is it nice, Anne? You must say if you want more."

He felt her shiver.

"Stephen."

She should not have said his name. Not in that husky voice. It made him want to thrust against her, spill inside her now instead of teasing her to fulfillment.

Who was being bound in lust?

She was hot and wet and slick and so tight that she gripped his finger as he entered. His thumb stroked her flesh where it swelled.

"Say it," he demanded.

"Nice," she said, her head falling back, her eyes closing. An artless siren. A sound escaped her. A moan of delight or need? Either heated his blood.

"Do you want me inside you, Anne?"

He'd shocked her again. Her eyes flew open, met his. But instead of looking away or lowering her eyes, she smiled. A long, slow smile that fanned the flame inside him.

"With all my heart," she murmured.

"Then you must do as I say," he said. His look was heated, her smile one of complicity.

"Ride you, Stephen?" she asked softly.

She learned quickly. But then, she was a woman of candor and daring.

He took her hand and led her to her bed. She lay on it before him, acquiescent, but not sweetly so. There was a look in her eyes that made him wonder if she would match his audacity.

"Will you do anything I ask?"

"Anything." It was a murmur, sweetly fashioned by curving lips.

"You must ready me for you."

She smiled, as if she knew what a fallacy that remark was. He'd been hard since he'd begun to think of her.

But she raised up on her knees and unlaced his shirt, aided him in removing it.

Her tongue reached out and touched his nipple. "*Papilla*," she said softly.

She unlaced his breeches, thrust both hands within, and widened them until he heard the stitches pop.

Both her hands gripped him. One slid to the base, held him there, as the other gripped him as if he were a stalk of wheat and slowly slid to the head.

"*Penis*," she whispered.

She bent down and placed a kiss on the head. Anointed him with the daring touch of her tongue. "*Basiatio*," she murmured against his flesh.

He was on fire.

"I was wrong to teach you Latin," he said, as she pulled him to her.

He half tumbled onto the bed beside her. Their mutual smiles made their kiss one of delight, the sheer exuberance of their lust for each other changed their laughter and transformed it into whispering words and smiles dusted against skin.

"Spread your legs for me," he said, and she did. Without hesitation or question.

Slowly he inserted a finger within her. She was wet and hot. Her fingers splayed across his chest, combed through the hair there. He chose that moment to withdraw his finger. She closed her eyes, breathed one long gust of a sigh when he began to stroke her softly.

The sight of his tanned hand buried between her white thighs was impossibly sensual. So much so that he didn't chastise her when she closed her eyes again.

He bent forward, sucked at her nipple. Gently,

slowly, elongating it as he drew back then let it escape from his mouth. His mouth was so hot that it felt he might burn her. He repeated the gesture over and over, all the while slowly slipping his finger inside her, teasing her with his fingers.

She began to tremble. A shimmering tension that radiated from the core of her, one that he felt and recognized. He slowed his movements, not willing to end it yet. He wanted to keep her on a precipice of arousal. So that she would sob for it, cry for it. Scream for him.

"Is it nice, Anne?"

The sound she made was neither assent nor denial, but almost a moan.

His smile had long since disappeared. He was concentrating on her, the flush of her breasts, the gasping breaths she made. It helped to keep his mind from the almost pain he felt at the moment.

"Do you want me in here?" He accompanied the question with a long slow slide of his finger inside her. Her thighs clamped against his hand, trapping it.

"You must say, Anne."

"Yes," she said, opening her eyes. Her fingers trailed up the length of him and down again. In the soft, lambent glow of her eyes he saw a challenge and a surrender. Both equally wished for and as earnestly felt by him.

"I want to be right there," he said, demonstrating exactly where in one protracted stroke of finger. She trembled even as her legs widened.

The expression on her face was the same as that night they'd loved. Interest, curiosity, and something learning to be lust. In the faint light it was more than that. It was a woman's look. A fascination with the beast that showed itself so eagerly, bobbing in the air for a chance to bury itself in the soft heat of her.

He reached down and stroked himself. His finger was wet with her, and he anointed the head with it. Once more he inserted his finger. Once more pulled it out and bathed himself with her wetness.

"I want to be in you," he said, his own voice a rasp of sound. "But not yet. This will have to do."

He pulled himself back and squeezed himself with both hands. It was exquisite torture. "You are this tight," he said, closing his eyes as he spoke. He rocked his hips forward in an instinctive thrust. His body wanted release even as his mind declared he wait.

He opened his eyes.

"Do you want to touch me?" he asked, a smile curving his lips.

"Yes." A soft and breathy response. Something like greed in her eyes.

"Not now," he said softly.

"Please."

"If you are good," he promised.

"Come inside me," she whispered. "Now."

How quickly she'd learned the power of words. Of looking at him with hunger in her gaze. He wanted her to touch him, wanted to be inside her.

Instead he smiled.

"Do you want my finger in you again?"

"No. I want *you*."

He leaned over her, braced on his right arm. His fingers speared into her hair, kept her anchored there. He leaned down and kissed her. Soft, darting kisses that left both of them hungering for more.

"You'll have me, then," he said, the pain of needing to be inside her almost too much.

He arranged her at the end of the bed, stood between her thighs.

She lay before him like a pagan offering. A woman glowing in the light of the candles. She was, simply, perfect. A surge of possessiveness nearly knocked him to his knees. His. She was his. Only and always.

He watched her as he entered her slowly. So slowly that his mind screamed at him to hurry, that his blood pooled in his loins and the world stilled and nothing mattered but the feel of her around him.

He inserted himself an inch inside her. "Are you sure this is what you want?"

Her arms lay outstretched, her hands clasped the sheet between fists. Her eyes opened, her gaze met his.

"Yes," she whispered. A sound as loud as a shout.

He moved an inch. His palms stroked her thighs. She lifted her hips in an effort to get him to move, closed her eyes.

Another inch.

"Don't be greedy, Anne."

She bit her bottom lip. He wanted to lick it.

His hand pressed against her abdomen, his thumb pressed into the furrow protected by the delta of hair. She turned her head, her eyes clenched shut. But the hands that gripped the sheet did so with increased ferocity.

Another inch.

"Am I hurting you?" A tender question. One that belied his sudden wish to impale her on himself.

She tossed her head from side to side.

His thumb circled and rotated along the swollen folds. She drew up her feet, anchored them behind his thighs. Pulled him to her. Tenacious in lust.

"Is it nice, Anne?"

The only sound she made was a soft hum.

He moved slowly, his hips thrusting an inch at a time until they were pressed together, groin to groin. One more thrust buried him.

"Do you like that?"

She opened her eyes. She looked dazed. Passion could do that. So could longing. It grew until it was almost pain. Until nothing else was as important.

He bent and bit one nipple gently. Her hands fisted on his shoulders, beat at his back.

"Do you want more, Anne?"

Her answer was not a sob. Not even a cry. She reached up and dragged his head down for a kiss. She seduced him with lips and tongue. Her hips arched up and thrust against his. The effort not to spill his seed had him drawing back.

"Please, Stephen." An aching plea. "Beloved." A whisper that struck his heart.

He thrust once and felt the earth shatter.

Only then did he hear her scream.

Chapter 22

◦◦◦◦◦

Hours later she roused. She had not drifted to sleep so much as had been catapulted there. Wakefulness came with the same suddenness.

Stephen was not at her side. Instead, there was only emptiness. A quick survey of the room located him. He stood at the window, looking out at the view.

He stood before her in unselfconscious nakedness, the only covering the bandage that bound his left arm from elbow to wrist. His legs were corded with muscle, his arms roped with it. His chest plated and hard and dusted with hair.

He stood there, his face set into stern and unapproachable lines. Did he know, for all his severity, that he was more than handsome? She had seen him in all manner of poses from boyhood to now, and she'd never ceased to marvel how princely he looked. It was as if nature, knowing his rank among nobles, had endowed him with extra height and breadth. Given his eyes a more intense hue, dusted midnight with a hint of royal blue. His nose was proud, as a Roman's might be. A conqueror's, at the very least. And his lips were full, but not too much so. Perfect, she thought, as she studied him.

"I've never realized how truly handsome you are," she said.

He looked startled. He did not receive enough compliments, she thought, if they made him so uncomfortable. She could think of a hundred things to say. A considerate host. A man of great talent in languages. A magnificent lover. She felt her cheeks warm.

It was his fault. He was not the least disturbed by his nakedness, while it seemed to strip sense from her.

His smile was not untinged by tenderness but blurred by some other emotion. Bemusement, wonder, confusion? She didn't know.

She wondered how he could not see the words in her thoughts. She loved him. Not an eloquent statement. But simple. Complete. She did not want to surrender this man. She wanted to live with him. She didn't want to be a martyr to war, she wanted to learn about love and all its permutations. She wanted to be irritated at him, find reasons to dislike him, argue with him, ache to throw something at him at the same time she wanted to worship his body and admire his mind. Salute his spirit and feel awe for his courage. She wanted life with Stephen.

But those thoughts, as many others, went unvoiced.

The candles were still lit. He'd not slept as she had, then. He turned back to the window. She had evidently startled him with her compliment. He, in turn, shocked her with his next words.

"Sebastian was a leper," he said, his words addressed not to her but to the night-darkened window.

She raised up on one elbow, draped the sheet around her.

"You've finished the codex."

He nodded.

"Can you read it straight through again? From the beginning?"

"Now?"

"We have no more time, Stephen." It was a gentle reminder that even the seconds were precious.

He pulled on his breeches. In moments he was gone from the room, leaving Anne to stare up at the ceiling.

He was a complex man, one she'd come to understand. Not the whole of him, but glimmers of who he was. Even if he loved her, he would never ask her to stay. Not as long as he was going to war. A man of noble purpose.

In that, he had greater resolve than she. She wanted to beg in an un-Sinclair way. She wanted to extol her own virtues and plead with him to offer her a glimpse of a possible future. As leman or friend, lover or wife.

She'd received her wish and learned of the parts of his life she'd not known and heard him tell her what he felt. It would have to be enough, perhaps, to last the rest of her life.

He returned, closed the door behind him.

She raised herself on her elbows and surveyed him. She could almost see him adorned in armor, his hand outstretched, the sword he carried gleaming new in the morning sun. A man not unlike Sebastian. A man of honor and valor, just as this man was. Gentle, for all that he had killed.

"I'll read what you don't know first," he said, moving to sit next to her on the bed. He opened the brittle parchment pages and began to translate.

" 'An accident divulged my lord's personal secret. He rescued me, and in doing so, I touched him. It had been strictly forbidden between us. I had been a biddable girl, having been raised all these years at the convent. It was not a decree I understood, but I abided by it nonetheless. Sebastian led me to the smith's hut on that horrible day. I thought that he would thrust my hands into the flames. Instead, he confessed his great secret.

" 'I had come to love him even more than I feared him. But even so, on that occasion, I trembled. I knew that the moment would bring a revelation, and I did not know if I was brave enough to hear it. Sebastian had chided me often for my timidity, stating that it was a habit I had chosen rather than a matter of my character. But on that day, I wanted to claim cowardice rather than to hear his words. I had been right, after all.

" 'Sebastian had been confined to prison after being captured by the Saracens. It was there that he was kept in a dark and dank cell, the only hope for the future his ultimate ransom. But during that long year, my beloved was stricken with disease, the most horrible and hideous fate for a man as strong and vital as Sebastian. He had become a leper.

" 'My lord had feared to summon me to his side because of his disease. But he was pressed to because of the Church. If he had not sent for me, a cleric would have come to Langlinais. The church would have discovered that he was a leper and cast him out, away from home and kin. As it was, he'd hoped to find some solace at Langlinais, to remain secluded from the world and from me.

" 'The Church calls such as Sebastian the undead and speaks the Mass of Separation over them. But he was too alive for such punishment. I was certain he planned to leave me, to go into hiding as a leper, to live out the rest of his life in silence and loneliness.

" 'That morning at Montvichet I viewed the most horrible sight of my life, Sebastian attired in a leper's robe. They would have taken me away from him, and this I could not allow them to do. I declared myself a leper in order to be with him. It was a decision that angered my lord but gave me peace. Life without him would have been intolerable.

" 'The Templars took our men, even as my lord gave them the Grail. It was evident that they believed it was a relic of great importance. But it was not the treasure of the Cathars.' "

"Sebastian's leprosy was one secret. The Grail wasn't the other?"

"No," he said. "Nor was the Grail the miracle Juliana spoke of."

She frowned at him.

"Remember the statue, Anne."

She sat up, draping the sheet around her. "A statue of Sebastian and Juliana," she said, reasoning aloud.

"One that was carved toward the end of his life."

She looked at him, eyes wide. "But there was no sign of leprosy."

He nodded at her. The beginning of a smile appeared on his face.

"There is no cure for it."

"Exactly."

"The miracle of Langlinais," she said, smiling. "But what is the treasure?"

At her look, he bent his head and continued to read.

" 'It is a sorrow that no one will know of the miracle of Langlinais. That my lord was cured of his disease. The danger is too great for Sebastian. But I will know, and these words will speak of it. Of the bright white sun of Montvichet and the moment that Sebastian was no longer afflicted. The leper became a man again and my beloved. The joy of this great miracle will be with us for the rest of our lives. So, too, the gratitude that we each felt.

" 'We went home to Langlinais, Sebastian, his loyal squire now made knight, and I. It was a journey I'd not thought would take place. There was laughter and love to mark our passage home. But there was one more secret. The true reason Sebastian had been summoned to the Cathar fortress. The treasure that Magdalene had left for Sebastian.

" 'I discovered the secret of the Cathars as I read a codex hidden at the bottom of the basket of scrolls. I read it disbelieving and afraid. Not only of its contents, but of its potential danger. It could alter the world as we knew it. It was for our protection that Sebastian brought the codex back to Langlinais. In case the Templars threatened us. But its presence was a danger, and Sebastian and I de-

cided to send it far from here, with our newest
knight.

" 'The codex was written by the Cathars for their
protection. I have copied the codex as completely
as I can and hidden it here as protection if it is ever
needed. If the Templars or the Church come to
Langlinais, this copy will protect us. The original
scrolls will remain safe, guarded as the treasure
they are.' "

" 'I came to love Sebastian not because of his
appearance or even because he was kind to me. But
because I sensed in him the same loneliness I felt.
My heart reached out to heal him and in the doing
found itself touched and warmed.

" 'Others may not see Sebastian the way that I
do, but he speaks to my heart with his voice and
his gaze. I thank God that he was brought home.
No longer a warrior, but the Lord of Langlinais.' "

When Stephen finished, he closed the codex.

"What do you think the rest of the codex contained?"

"I don't know," he said, touching the edge of the
parchment. "The pages were too badly damaged
some time in the past. Probably water seeped into
the tower from the flood. The pages cannot be separated."

He looked over at her and smiled. "Perhaps there
are some things we are destined never to know."

"I hate the thought of her words being destroyed
that way."

"Regret has no purpose, Anne," he said gently.
"It makes you sad, but rarely aids a cause."

Juliana's words came back to her. She had received her miracle. Was it too much to wish that Langlinais might see another?

"We can reread the codex from the beginning," he softly said. "Or engage in other discoveries."

He placed the codex on the table behind him, stood, and waited for her answer.

The emotion running through her heated her breath, tingled the tips of her fingers, and pooled between her thighs. It was more elemental than need, and although fueled by love, it was neither delicate nor refined. It was not even affection. It was a craving for this man lit by candlelight, touched with a golden glow. A greed and a hunger she'd never expected to feel.

She opened her arms for him.

Chapter 23

❦

"**H**e has agreed?" General Penroth stared at the messenger who stood before him. The man's horse was lathered; he was breathing hard.

"He says he is willing to surrender only under his conditions, sir." The words were exhaled in tiny gusts. Penroth considered the idea of advising his lieutenant that such speeches were better spoken with breath. But he said nothing. The news was too good to be irritated by its method of delivery.

"Are you certain? The Earl of Langlinais offers terms?"

"I've the document here, sir. It's addressed to you."

Penroth opened it, grinned as he read the words that would give him a prestigious Parliamentary victory with little further effort. The inhabitants of Harrington Court were to be given safe passage. The town of Lange on Terne must remain intact and not be occupied. Stephen Harrington also demanded unconditional pardons for his regiment. As for himself, the Earl of Langlinais was prepared to

270

surrender to General Penroth as soon as terms were agreed to and he made his farewells.

"Shall I send word back to him, sir?"

"Very definitely, my boy. Very definitely. You may tell the Earl of Langlinais that his terms are accepted."

The faces of his aide and officers reflected Penroth's glee.

"Are you sure this is what you want to do, Stephen?" Richard asked.

"It's what must be done," Stephen said calmly. He studied the map in front of him with some intensity. His study had served as headquarters for the past day. He'd given each man in his command a directive, a role to perform in order to ensure that the departure from Harrington Court would be orderly. But he wondered if he could enlist Richard's aid in the most delicate of missions.

"I wish circumstances were otherwise," Richard said.

" 'A thousand wishes form a life; a hundred breaths a gale'," Stephen murmured, then wondered from what source the adage had come. He rolled up the map and placed it in his dispatch case then turned and smiled at his friend. Richard looked entirely too worried.

"I need some organization in the departure of the servants, Richard. Will you assist me with it?" There were thirty servants employed at Harrington Court. They could call the huge house their ancestral home with as much truth as he himself. Their grandfathers, their fathers, perhaps even their great-grandfathers had served the Earls of Langlinais.

"You know I will. What will happen to them?"

"They are to be escorted to Lange on Terne. It's the safest place to be. They need to leave the house in small groups. They've lived here all their lives, they know the route to the town well enough."

"I'll meet with them now."

Stephen rolled up the map, stuck it in his pack.

"Tell them that it's better to stay there." War was bad enough without being homeless and hungry.

"Are you really going to surrender, my lord?" William's face was a study in contrasts. Hope balanced against sick horror.

"I already have, William," he said. "I want you to take advantage of the pardon offered. You've family in Lange on Terne. Somewhere to go."

"I am your aide, sir."

Stephen didn't smile although he wanted to. Or thank William for his loyalty.

"You would be serving me better by staying in the town."

William frowned, stepped away, and left the room. Gestures done with stilted steps and precision that came from restraint, not military drill.

"Is there nothing you can do, Stephen? Other than offer yourself up as sacrifice?"

Stephen raised an eyebrow. "What, an earnest Parliamentarian counseling me not to surrender?"

"If you don't get your neck chopped off as an object lesson, you'll swing at the end of a rope."

"Not a palatable end."

His desk was clean but for one sheet of paper. He handed it to Richard. It was a list of each of the inhabitants of Harrington Court, their closest relatives, and their choice of destination. He would

ensure that they would be cared for and safe before
he left them.

"And your guests? Have you made provisions
for them?"

"Yes," he said, shortly.

"She is an interesting woman," Richard said
thoughtfully. "One with her heart in her eyes."

"You noticed that, did you?"

"How could I not? She is normally so argumen-
tative that it is a shock when she's silent."

Stephen leveled his gaze on Richard. "You are
not speaking of Anne, are you?"

Richard looked startled, then embarrassed if his
flushed face was any indication. It was a unique
situation, Stephen thought, to see the man who'd
upbraided him often enough relegated to stammers.

"Women are a great source of fear, Stephen. You
live without them and you're afraid you'll never
find one to love you again. You live with them and
are afraid that you'll never be able to make them
happy. A conundrum."

"Not a logical frame of mind, Richard."

"What ever made you think life was logical?"

Stephen glanced at him, noted the smile.

"Take your own life, for example. You added to
the family fortune on a whim. Even now you ag-
onize with yourself because you know the king is
wrong. But that is based less on logic than on your
heart."

He stood, inspected Stephen's bandage one last
time. "You're a man of emotion, however much
you'd rather emulate your father."

"Would I?"

"I suspect it would be easier for you. Less troubling."

"Is that what you've learned being a ship doctor? How to see inside a mind?"

"I myself am not exempt from such difficulties, Stephen. I find myself heartily attracted to a woman who insults me at every turn. She has no respect for my profession, is not at all concerned as to my financial status, and seems to think that I dig in graveyards for ingredients to put in my medicines."

There was such a look of disgust on Richard's face that Stephen almost smiled. On a different day, he would have. At another time, perhaps, when his mind was not so fixed on his duties. And his farewells.

Anne. That was destined to be a difficult meeting. One that he's postponed until the very last moment. Would she understand what he had to do?

Would Richard? He glanced at his friend. Richard was intent upon the list, his frown making him appear more fierce than he was. He was a kind man, a friend despite their political differences.

He turned and clasped his hand on Richard's shoulder. The closest he would come to a farewell. The most overt gesture he could manage right now. All his emotions were being held in check for another moment to come. One only hours away.

Richard was not so reticent. He clasped his arms around Stephen's shoulders. A quick parting, one without words.

Dunniwerth, Scotland

Robert Sinclair entered the room, watched his wife. She was seated in her favorite chair. On her

lap were a few of the drawings that Anne had done
as a child. Pictures of him and Maggie and other
occupants of Dunniwerth. When he'd first seen
these drawings, he'd suspected that his daughter
possessed a wicked sense of humor. A line here, a
curve there, and a grin could easily become a leer
or a slight paunch the rounded barrel of a stomach.

He had grown adept at gauging her moods by
what she drew. When she was annoyed by someone, the sketch of that person was exaggerated.
Such as the times when she was angry with him.
She would draw him with his beard trailing to the
floor and his eyes shooting fire.

"She was so much better at this," Maggie said,
glancing up at him, "than she ever was at embroidery." Her smile was reminiscent as she studied the
drawings. "Do you remember how she tried to convince me that the spots of blood on her work were
actually tiny rosebuds she'd fashioned?"

He nodded, his heart heavy.

He walked to the window. Little more than an
arrow slit, it made for a chilly room in the winter.
But then, they rarely used this room in winter, preferring the sunnier chamber to the west. But it was
near summer now, and there were breezes that
smelled of sturdy barley and flowering things. Sunlight filtered into the room and danced on the car-
pets Maggie had caused to be placed on the floor.

"I'm going to find her, Maggie," he said. "The
scouts I've sent out say that there are reports of a
group traveling south. I've plans to follow that
route."

"I'm surprised you have not left before now,"
she said, placing the drawings on the ground and

standing. "Weeks have passed, Robert."

"I had to know in which direction to travel. Or did you want me to chase around like a dog in a feud with his tail?"

She smiled and shook her head at him.

"You'll take care of yourself, Maggie?" he said, walking toward her. "You'll not go to your bed and cry for two days?"

She reached up and flicked at the leather jerkin he wore. A dismissive gesture, just like the smile on her face. But he was not fooled.

"And you, you'll not be thinking you're a younger man? Doing something foolish?" She patted him with both hands. She had a habit of doing that when she said good-bye to him. Placing her hands on him all over, as if to reassure herself that he was hale and hearty. She did the same when she welcomed him.

"You'll send word to me if you hear anything?"

She nodded, her worry apparent.

She leaned close, laid her head against his arm. "Please be careful, my dearest."

"I am a Sinclair, Maggie. We are not simply careful, we are victorious."

Her smile, for all its charm, held a trace of sadness and was gone too quickly.

Her palm rested against his face. He placed his own atop it. A look too deep for words passed between them.

"I'll miss you with my whole heart," she whispered.

The tenderness in her eyes was almost his undoing. He did not deserve her love and affection.

Nor her loyalty. But he'd been blessed with it all these years.

He reached out and with two fingers gripped her chin. He turned it gently, his eyes narrowing as he saw her tears. Her eyes glinted with them. She never cried. But maybe she was worn down with worry over Anne.

He kissed her hard, then made himself walk away.

Richard came for Anne at dusk, his face somber. He, too, was dressed for travel, but his journey would be only the few miles to his home.

The inhabitants of Harrington Court were to meet with men of the regiment just this side of the river from Langlinais. They would then be escorted to Lange on Terne. Anne's journey home would be more dangerous. She was not certain Hannah, Ian, and she could even cut through the Parliamentarian army, let alone head north to Scotland. The only other alternative was to remain in the town. It was a decision that would have to be made by all three of them. Something she'd learned from this journey. That her wishes could sometimes endanger others.

How many people had Stephen saved with his sacrifice? How many would realize what he had done?

"What is to happen to him?" she asked.

"I promise that you will see him before you leave." It was not the answer she wished. She wanted to know if he would die because of this. Or if they would simply release him, exchange him for other prisoners. Would they take him to London to parade him about as a prize? What was his fate? But Richard had walked away, as if proximity to her was a dangerous thing.

Stephen would see her long enough to say good-bye. From that meeting she was to take all that she was to have for the rest of her life. Every breath, every word, every glance would be compressed and stored lovingly away. To be unearthed when she could bear the loneliness no more.

She had been prepared to do that once. Then twice. How odd that the idea of it made her angry now.

She left Harrington Court by the kitchen entrance. There were tears and hugs and soft words exchanged by those who lingered there. She slipped away from them, her composure fragile.

Hannah and Richard stood at the garden entrance, no more than shadows. They did not speak as they walked slowly down the hill, the speed of their departure dictated by Hannah. Halfway down the hill, her hand reached out and gripped Anne's, and for a moment Anne thought it was because she needed support in the long walk. Then she understood that the gesture was more in the nature of giving comfort than needing it.

Ian spoke from behind her. "Why do we have to skulk about like ghosts?"

It was Hannah who silenced him before Anne had a chance to say a word. "Because we do."

Langlinais appeared like a specter in the moonlight. So, too, the shadows of people who walked slowly down the bank of the river on this side of the castle. They were escorted by members of the regiment, their murmurs barely audible in the night

air. Harrington Court would be empty soon and
Stephen made a prisoner.

Richard stopped and turned, gathering Hannah
close to him. Together they were a small, huddled
group. He bent his head to Anne's.

"You are to wait for Stephen at the tower," he
whispered. "He's asked that you show no light. Can
you find your way?"

She nodded. The steps to the east tower were as
familiar to her as Dunniwerth's many paths.

"I'll go with her," Ian said. She stayed him with
her hand on his chest.

"No."

"It will not be safe," he insisted.

"No," she said again. She didn't want him at the
castle. She wanted to say good-bye in her own way.
Her tears would be her own, not witnessed by Ian.
The boy he had been was too strong a memory to
feel friendship for him now.

It was Richard who stepped between them, then
turned to Anne.

"We will see you in time. Godspeed, Anne."

One by one, the inhabitants of Harrington Court
faded away until she stood alone.

She stood there watching darkness fall over Langlinais, feeling a curious emptiness. As if the very
spirit of the place were seeping away. Saying farewell in the most tender and bittersweet of voices.

She walked slowly to the tower entrance. A glow
infused the castle, made it appear as something out
of a dream. But it was only the moonlight, full and
rich and white.

No wooden door stood there, guardian against

invader. Only a rectangular space that opened up to a cavernous darkness.

She was not frightened of the dark, and it seemed a good thing as she took one step after another up the spiral stairs. The night sky beckoned her, sending a shaft of blue-hued moonlight through the opening at the top.

How many people had taken those steps and stood upon this timbered floor? How many faced a vista of spangled darkness and a moon shining bright in an early sky? Had they each felt as she did now, with her heart beating loudly in her chest, and her breath caught by such beauty?

The trees along the Terne were black tinged with emerald. Shadows clung to the ground, hugged the river and hills, casting them in relief, rendering them larger than before. Even a bird, soaring toward the moon on wings dusted by night, appeared grand and awe-inspiring against the full disk of moon. A sparrow turned eagle.

She had never before felt such enchanted beauty. It was a moment of poignant serenity like the instant before a song, a hesitation just a second before a dirge began on the pipes, or a solemn breath before a flute's perfect note. It was a promise in the air, as if it trembled with anticipation. A spellbound tower in an enchanted castle.

It was somehow oddly fitting that she sat there in the silence and waited for Stephen of Langlinais.

Chapter 24

❧

Stephen walked into the kitchen, intent upon one of his final tasks. A farewell.

It was a room that mirrored the spirit of the house. It boasted four large windows now darkened with the encroaching night. On each sill there were two bright red flowerpots filled with trailing ivy. Dishes and silverware were arranged on blue shelves mounted against crisp white walls. The copper was brightly polished, and the watery gleam of pewter reflected the glow of the fire.

"I've no wish to leave you, my lord," Betty said, drying her eyes with the corner of her apron. Stephen had arranged with Richard for her and Ned to live in his household for a few months while they made plans of their own. There they would be safe. Even Penroth would not bother a Parliamentarian as prominent as Richard.

Betty had been his second mother. And Ned? A store of valuable knowledge had come from Ned, who'd spoken to him as he'd curried the horses, the words almost unintelligible formed around the stem of his pipe.

"You'll not want for anything for the rest of your lives," he said now, giving Ned the name of his banker and a letter that bore Stephen's crest. The document would serve as both an introduction and written verification of Stephen's wishes. Even in time of war, the monetary system flourished. Fortunes were made or lost regardless of year or political climate.

"We could not, my lord," Betty said, ignoring the elbow jab from her husband.

"You must," Stephen said. He smiled at her and she sighed. A gesture of capitulation and one he'd rarely seen from Betty.

"It's time to go," he said gently.

She squinted her eyes at him. When he'd been a boy, that look had preceded a scolding. Even the fourteen-year-old earl had not been exempt from her occasional disapproval. But now all she did was grab him and hug him fiercely. He held on for just a moment before she released him. Ned only pumped his hand up and down and smiled. An expression that looked as forced as his own.

"Be careful," Stephen said, and they only nodded.

He watched them for a moment as they walked down the hill. They were the last. The house was settling in around him, soft murmurs of sounds almost like that of a sleeping cat. As if Harrington Court slept. Or dreamed.

The act of surrender had been as carefully choreographed for him as if it were a pageant. There was a curious spectacle to it. He was to walk out of the front door of Harrington Court and meet with a representative of General Penroth. From there he was to be taken to the general's tent, where he would formally surrender not only his home but his person to the Parliamentarians. He would be sent to London, there to stand trial. For all his words to Anne, he doubted the possibility of clemency. He would, no doubt, be sentenced to die.

He had no intention of going to his execution without at least trying to escape. There was more warrior in him than statesman.

One of his ancestors had devised the holder in his hand. A candle fitted upon a spike and a parchment shade, oiled and cut into a curve, surrounded it on three sides. He lit the candle now. The effect was a diffuse glow.

He turned and walked through the entrance to the public rooms and from there into the green room, so called because of the emerald silk adorning the walls.

This chamber was out of a nightmare, an excess of ornamentation with curlicues painted on the green silk fabric. Gold tassels hung from the seams. Even the plastered ceiling had not been spared and was painted in varying shades of ochre and umber.

He stood in front of the black granite fireplace. Above it, hung against the emerald brocade, was a massive sword. Sebastian's sword.

As a boy he'd been barely able to lift it. Now he did so easily. Still, he felt admiration for the man who'd carried it into battle. It was always kept polished. Even now it gleamed in the light of the candle. He had begged the maids to let him do the chore as a boy, and they had willingly relinquished their duty. He smiled now at the dupe he had been.

But he could still remember the joy he'd felt as

he'd rubbed the steel until it gleamed. Now he traced the line of the pigeon-egg-sized ruby in the center of the hilt.

He left the room carrying the broadsword, placed it on the table in the kitchen. He began to tour Harrington Court. His mind furnished memory as he went. A boisterous boyish voice. His own. His mother's soft tones, Betty's remonstrances. The echoing boom of his father's shout, the sound of Anne's soft laughter.

He entered his study, placed the candle on his desk. He placed the coffer with the codex in his pack along with a few other items. The most valuable treasure, the scriptorium desk, could not be taken with him.

His fingers rubbed the blackened wood. Age had imparted a sheen to it, a patina that no carpenter could duplicate. He walked behind it, placed his hands on the sloping desk. Juliana might have written her Chronicles here.

He left the room finally, completed his tour of the second floor, then the third.

An echoing emptiness suffused the house, and as if it knew its fate, it seemed to sigh.

On the third floor, he began to touch the draperies with the candle. Tongues of flame followed his descent to the second floor. Then to the first.

His prayer was elemental. *Give me the strength to finish this.* And then, an imploration to all those unseen ancestors who appeared to watch, horror-struck from the shadows. *Forgive me.*

Anne stood, her fists braced on the edge of the merlon, staring at Harrington Court. Lights flickered in the upper stories as if a party were being held and a thousand candles had been lit.

A shadow ran down the hill, its back hunched. A wolf, not man. Or a monster, perhaps.

He ran across the bridge, then halted in the lower bailey, looking up at the tower. She separated the shadow from the man as Stephen placed his pack on the ground.

She heard his footsteps on the steps, stood beside the opening, her attention directed not upon his arrival, but on the conflagration.

The glow from Harrington Court lit the night sky, set into relief the ruins of Langlinais.

"Have they fired it?" she asked when he arrived at the top of the tower.

"No," he said, "I have."

She looked at him. "Why?"

"Losing is not in my nature, Anne. If they want Harrington Court, they'll take it on my terms."

"And you, Stephen?"

He glanced at her. He was moon-draped shadow. "The idea of surrendering myself has even less appeal."

"Why did you not tell me?" It would have saved her hours of worry, not to mention grief.

"There was no time." He stepped closer, reached down, and extended his arm around her. "Did you think I would abandon you, Anne?"

"No," she said, allowing herself to be mollified by the gentle kiss he placed on her temple. "Only do something idiotic and courageous."

She could feel him smile against her skin.

She turned in his arms, her attention drawn back to the sight of the fire. The great house was an inferno now, the flames leaping from the ground floor to the roof. Only the stone lions guarding the kitchen gate appeared exempt, their aloof majesty lit by the glow behind them.

She knew why he had done it. So that a stranger would not sit at his table or marvel at the fireplaces carved at the behest of an Elizabethan earl. They would not stride through hallways adorned with frescoes and boast of the capture of this house. Not one man whose name was not Harrington would ever marvel at the thirteenth-century woman who'd been a scribe.

But he had been so much a part of that place. And this one where they stood.

One by one the windows began to shatter. The house groaned as if all the voices from the past rose up in muffled consternation. One last protest before they were forever silenced.

"It sounds as if it is alive," she said.

"It is a place of stone and brick," he softly said. "Nothing more."

It was more, and he knew it well. Did buildings hold memories? Did they hide within their shells the recollections of joy or sorrow?

She turned to him. His gaze was not on Harrington Court, but on the moonlit castle around them. From here the open chambers of the great hall and chapel could be seen. Then beyond, to all three baileys glowing in the light of a full moon.

Memories were here for him. Here was his childhood refuge, the place he went to feel alone, at peace, or free. It was his sanctuary.

Stephen.

He glanced her way as if he'd heard her.

"It is only a building," he said again, and his voice was strong and resolute. Too much so.

"I prayed for a miracle," she confessed. "I was somewhat happy when General Penroth first appeared. I thought it would keep you from going to war."

"An odd miracle."

"I think it is a lesson from God," she said, smiling. "Do not question His miracles."

"God does not like to be tested," he said. Juliana's words.

He held out his hand and she clasped it.

Billowing black smoke created a nimbus around the grand house, seemed to stretch to the moon. An eerie sight, this moonlit night. As if nature had lit a candle to better illuminate the destruction of Harrington Court. The Parliamentarian soldiers milled around the structure, witnesses to the conflagration, as she and Stephen were from the safety of the tower at Langlinais.

It was a time of farewell to all that the Earls of Langlinais had been and would never be again.

She felt awed by him. The earl, the commander, the man.

It had been obvious he could not defeat Penroth's forces, and to protect those within his domain he had not tried. But he had not given up, either. Even now, as he stood watching his heritage burn to the ground, he did so with resolve.

She reached up to him, framed his face with her hands. The tears she'd tried not to shed bathed her face. Her mouth trembled with the effort to hold silent her sobs.

He leaned against her. Sighed. Only that.

She held him then. Simply held him. Words were too much.

They descended the steps slowly, but instead of following the path of ascent, Stephen veered to the left. A few steps more, and they were in the chapel.

The statue of Juliana and Sebastian gleamed in the moonlight. They approached it silently. Stephen placed his hand on Juliana.

"I used to think that she looked like my mother."

"Did she?"

"No," he said. "But I do not think them dissimilar. My mother had blond hair and eyes that changed, either blue or green, depending upon what she wore. I remember being fascinated by them when I was a child. She had a way of walking that seemed as if her feet never touched the ground. At least it looked that way to a small boy. She was gentle, with a kind word for everyone. But it was her laughter I remember most. She always found something to feel joyous about, be it a newly opened flower or a rock that I brought her shaped like a frog. If she cried, I never saw it."

Anne's gaze was intent on Juliana's face. Stephen saw a curious resemblance in the moonlight. Both women of strength. Perhaps Anne was less biddable and certainly more fierce, but there was a connection between them. Or perhaps he wished only to see it.

They left the chapel finally. In the moonlit bailey, Anne let loose his hand, staring as she twirled in a slow circle as if she wished to imprint everything about the castle in her mind.

He had never told her how much Langlinais

meant to him. She'd somehow known. What he felt for the ancient fortress was in his blood, was in his very breath. He was the direct descendant of men who had died to protect it.

It did not take much imagination to envision a day in the past, a moment of its glorious heritage. The bailey was awash in sunlight. A horse, as black as the crows that perched in the nearby trees, pranced in anticipation. His bridle and harness were adorned with shining silver, his saddle dotted with the same metal insets. His rider effortlessly controlled the large horse, even as he smiled with the same exuberance. His grin flashed as bright as the armor he wore, silvered chain mail that stretched from neck to wrist and ankle, topped with a sleeveless crimson tunic. His sword belt was heavily embroidered in red and silver, and the weapon it held bore a ruby embedded in the center of its hilt.

A knight as great as any of Stephen's childish wishes.

He turned and stared at the fire that consumed his home. They had expected of him a perverse elegance in his surrender. Instead, he had delivered to them his birthright in the only way he could.

He wondered what Sebastian of Langlinais would have said to his idea of surrender. He could not help but think he would have approved. Templar or Parliamentarian, four hundred years ago or today, mailed armor or Puritan garb, they were still invaders.

Anne walked toward the bridge as he turned and glanced up at the east tower. Perhaps it would last another four hundred years. But he would not be here to steward it.

One day, perhaps, a child might well stand here and look about him at a weed-choked ruin. He might wonder at the people who'd lived here before, the men and women who'd inhabited this place. He would never know of Sebastian and Juliana and a host of men and women culminating in him.

He was the last of his line, the last Langlinais man, and he stood and paid homage to not only the past, but the future that must surely come.

The dawn sky promised it.

They followed the bend of the river for about a quarter mile to where it was shallow enough to cross on foot. There Richard and the others waited for them.

There were thirty of his regiment who had chosen to come with him.

"What happens now?" Anne asked.

"Now we take you home to Scotland," he said.

At her look of surprise, he only smiled.

"I'll go with you, then," Richard said.

"Wouldn't your abilities be better used here?" Stephen asked, frowning. "The army would be grateful for your healing talents."

"I am serving the army quite well, my boy, if I but shield Penroth's troops from Hannah. I should garner a pension for my efforts," he said. "Besides, I've grown fond of the woman. I'll let her whittle her teeth on me instead of your young bones."

"Someone should have clubbed you over the head long ago." The voice that threatened such bodily harm belonged to a tall woman who stepped out of the shadows. Her blond hair shimmered in

the moonlight, her face was attractive. But it was
her frown that captured his attention. It was equally
bestowed on Richard and him.

Hannah. Strange that he'd never met her in all
this time.

The older woman continued to study him. Almost as if to reassure herself he was real.

"I would not choose to be clubbed by any one
but you, dearest Hannah," Richard said, bowing
over her hand. Stephen raised an eyebrow at the
courtliness of his friend's gesture. An intriguing
woman, he thought, as they exchanged looks. But
her enmity to him was difficult to understand.

She did, however, allow Richard to assist her in
mounting her horse. As she did so, he looked over
at Anne.

"I think your friend dislikes me."

"She doesn't dislike you, Stephen," she said
calmly. "She simply does not trust you."

"Why?"

"First because you're male," she said with a
smile. "Secondly, because your name is Stephen."

"Would I be more favorably received if I were
named Harold, then?"

"Yes," she said surprisingly, and laughed.

It was all the answer he was going to get from
her. He knew that. Even if it made no sense.

His hand reached out and cupped her chin, feeling the sharp line of jaw, the softness of her skin.
His fingers spread out and touched her throat. Her
hands gripped his wrist.

Then she startled him again by reaching out and
kissing the back of his hand, bringing it to her lips
in a gesture of supplicant or worshiper. His knuck-

les were warmed by tender lips. The shadow of her lashes on her cheeks completed the picture and stole his breath from him.

"Anne."

"I despise being afraid," she said. "A Sinclair is not supposed to be a coward."

"I've soldiers who are not as intrepid as you." His smile was sudden, amused, and real. "How are you a coward?"

Her look was direct, allowing for no guile or restraint. "I thought you were going to do something stupid and noble."

"You are not the type to weep into your handkerchief are you, Anne?"

"Because you let the Parliamentarians have you? No," she said, as if she considered the answer. "I'm afraid I would be more like Hannah and wish to club you."

It was not the time for laughter, he thought, but he was grateful to her for it.

Chapter 25

"**I**f you will just roll with the gait of the horse, Hannah," Richard said, "it would be much easier for you. Just roll with it." He made an exaggerated movement of hunching his shoulders, bringing them forward, then arching back. A demonstration of what he wished her to do.

"I do not roll, Richard," she said, her tone one of ice.

She would have liked to think that the journey back to Dunniwerth was being made slower these past days because of the number of cavalry that accompanied them. But in truth she was not up to a canter. She had been quite brave in even mounting one of the beasts again. Even so, a slow walk made her ribs ache, a fact that she'd managed to hide from the others. Richard, however, had an uncanny ability to see through her determined cheer. Even now he was looking at her as if judging the extent of her discomfort. Silly man.

"Truly, Hannah, your look would singe my eyebrows off. Expend the same amount of ire on your horse, and you'd have him tamed in no time. As it is, you will probably bounce all the way to Scotland like that. You look like a mushroom bobbing up and down."

"Dare I ask what part of the mushroom I resemble?"

"Why, the entirety of it, of course," he said. "The way your hair shoots straight up in the sky and back again is the top, and your skinny legs are the stem."

If she'd had a musket, she would have shot him.

"My legs are not skinny. Besides, you are not to look. My skirts are perfectly proper."

"It is true your legs are not skinny, Hannah. But your gait is better. You've settled in quite nicely." With that, he tipped his hat and made his way to the head of the troop.

"I hate that man. May God forgive me, I hate that man."

"He, on the other hand, mistress, is exceptionally complimentary of you."

She glanced out of the corner of her eye. The earl rode close to her. He was dressed as soberly as any Puritan. The twinkle in his eye, however, did not belong with the plain clothing.

She had spoken few words to him over the last three days, but she had watched him carefully. His men appeared to hold him in great respect. He commanded with ease and with fairness. Added to that the fact that Betty had a great fondness for him, Muriel an adoration, and even Richard praised him. A man of great charm.

To be fair, he had, for the last few days, been unfailingly polite to her. Before he had ever met her, he'd provided for her comfort, her care, opened up his home for strangers. A man of great nobility.

A man without a home, who no doubt had a price on his head at this moment. A man who, from the talk she'd overheard, had angered a king.

A dangerous man.

It was all too obvious that Anne adored him. They thought they had been so circumspect. A fool could have intercepted the looks between them. The problem, as she saw it, was that there was no clear resolution. He had never talked of the future. Nor had Anne.

Why had she herself fallen in love with a man she should not have? Why did she look now at a man with red cheeks and bright white hair and feel a warmth around her heart? Perhaps because it was meant to be.

"What does he say about me?" she asked. Her words were a capitulation, even if the man at her side was unaware of it. Her gaze was on Richard, who was riding far ahead of them. He was chatting quite amiably with one of the soldiers. That was the problem with Richard, however. He appeared quite friendly just before he let loose a verbal dart.

"He says you have lovely skin and the most delightful shade of hair. He put me in mind of a Cavalier poet, mistress. Despite his protestations to the contrary, Richard has a great deal of the courtier about him."

"Have you known him long?" A part of her, a more fair and equitable part, chided her for asking Richard about Stephen and Stephen about Richard. However, the first inquiry had been for Anne. These questions were strictly of a personal nature.

For her benefit alone. It would aid her to know the character of the man who so bedeviled her day after day. And made her smile so often.

"Most of my life," he said. "My mother named him my godfather, a role for which he was unprepared. Not because of his aptitude for it," he said, smiling, "but my father's antipathy to him. He thought that physicians and earls had nothing in common, let alone the rearing of his son."

"Do you?" He glanced at her. "Think that physicians and earls have anything in common?" she explained.

He grinned at her. "More than my father would have imagined." His gaze rested on Richard, and his grin faded to a fond smile. "He is a fine man," he said.

"He says the same of you," she said.

"Perhaps we should gather in a group and exchange such pleasantries," Stephen said, smiling. "It might save a good deal of time."

"I confess to not being the type for idle chatter," she said.

His sidelong glance was filled with amusement.

"You sound like Richard when you say that," he said. "I have noted that your temperament seems similar."

She frowned at him. "He says I remind him of a she-goat."

His laughter surprised her and made Richard turn from the head of the troop where he rode and send an inquiring smile in her direction. She simply turned her head and looked away. Silly man.

When they rested for the evening, Richard came to her.

"Will you walk with me, Hannah?"

She was weary enough not to grumble at him. She walked beside him in the faint light. The Scots called it the gloaming. A sweet word for a lonely time of day. They sat beside a stream. The air was warm with a hint of summer. New leaves were uncurling on the tips of branches. From somewhere came the cry of a bird, a melody joined in and repeated loudly. In front of them was the beginning of hills, but even those were touched with a mantle of green.

"My home is a comfortable place," Richard said. He frowned down at the stream before him. "Even though there has not been a mistress present in seven years, it has had the touch of a housekeeper. I've found that women know better about the arrangement of furniture and things."

She slanted a look up at Richard, who stood beside her, his hands clasped together behind his back. He had a habit, she'd noticed, of rocking on his heels. She wondered if it was because he'd been aboard ship all those years.

"Do you miss it?" she asked suddenly, interrupting his speech.

He blinked at her.

"Miss the sea," she explained.

"I was sick for a good two weeks at the start of every voyage. Why would I miss it?" He tone was irritated, his look decidedly so. She shrugged and went back to her survey of the countryside.

"I've a good profession," he continued, "even though I practice it less and less these days. I'm a wealthy man. Did I tell you that story?"

"Many times," she said dryly. "I've no wish to

hear it again. You are to be congratulated for your tenacity and the earl for indulging you in your dreams."

"It was hardly that," he said. "The silver added to his wealth, also."

"What do you think he feels for her?"

"For who?" Once more, she had the decided feeling that she was goading his temper. Since Richard had done the same to her on more than one occasion, she didn't feel dismayed by it in the least. "Sometimes he looks at her in a certain way," she said, "and I wonder if he feels something for her. Then his face becomes blank, and he looks away."

"He's a very private man," Richard said. "One can surmise all sorts of things from his silence. Pride," he continued, with a sharp look at her, "is a very delicate thing in a man."

"Too delicate," she said. "More damage has been done to the world because of men's pride than any single reason."

"And women are not to blame?"

"We mop up the mess, Richard, and tend to the wounds and care for the sick and bear the children. We do not cause the problems."

He raised his eyebrow at her. "Then we should not call you women," he said, "but rather angels. And count ourselves lucky that you consort with us mortal men at all."

"It *is* a sacrifice," she said with a smile.

He frowned at her. "My needs are modest, but my income is more than enough to provide for extravagant tastes. I have invested some of the money from the ship and set aside some for my children in the event of my death. But there remains a goodly amount to fritter away if I've a mind to do such a thing. I've thought of adding on a room for flowers and plants to my house." He looked over at her. "Women like such things, don't they?"

She only raised one eyebrow.

"I could do with some expansion, perhaps. Build another wing. Or a better dining room, so that guests might be more comfortable. More gardens, too. I know nothing about gardens."

"Is there a reason for this determined litany, Richard?"

He didn't answer her, simply continued to talk. "My daughter is a lovely girl," he said. "I expect to be made a grandfather shortly. But they live some distance from my house. I do not see them often. Her husband is a prosperous man. A Parliamentarian, like myself." He looked over at her, as if his political leanings had anything to do with her.

"I believe that I will be safe enough in the coming years. My belief is that the king will lose this war. Do you have some softening in your heart for the Royalists?"

She huffed out a breath. "Richard, I have spent the greater part of my life on an island. I do not care what either side does or does not do. I tend to my animals and my herb garden, and attempt to bring health to those who come to me for aid."

"And have odd ideas about some perfectly acceptable practices," he said.

She was formulating her arguments when she glanced up and noted his smile. It silenced her.

"My son is, I am sorry to say, one of the great disappointments of my life. He has taken himself off to France, and the only missives I ever receive from him are requests for money." He frowned at the stream in front of them as if it were an affront. She suspected, however, that it was his son Richard saw and not the sparkling water.

"The problem with Harold is that he whines," Richard said. "It's an affectation. It's a grating, nasally thing. I find myself disliking the boy almost constantly, even to the extent that I bless providence that he's chosen to live in another country. He is rarely underfoot, but when he is, he's as welcome as a blister on my . . ." He looked over at her, then away again. "I am sorry, Hannah. I have a deplorable habit of returning to the conversations of my youth. Aboard ship there is apt to be little gentility."

"On an island," she said wryly, "there is none. I can say whatever I wish, with only the squirrels and the birds to hear me."

"You are a truly unique woman, Hannah."

She felt her cheeks warm.

He smiled at her, a toothy grin. He was a rather formidable-looking man, what with his shock of white hair and his bushy eyebrows of the same color. His teeth were good. A comment he made next, as if he divined her very thoughts.

"I'm in good health, my teeth are sound, my habits not unduly rude. I've a staff of ten to keep me pressed and combed." He looked over at her again. "Not that I need all of them to do so," he explained. "They mostly clean. And cook," he said. "I do have a cook. She sometimes makes too rich a sauce, but that is not often. Only when boredom sets in. Not that life at my home is excessively boring. It is of a calm and placid nature."

She knew better than to try to interrupt this charming bit of boasting.

"I've a sister. She is a sweet woman, but she lives by herself. A cousin resides with her, and they are no burden. They come and stay with me at Christmas time, however. I think it's important to share the holidays with family, don't you?"

She didn't get a chance to answer.

"I will confess to having few friends. My profession took me away from my home for years. When I returned, it was to find my children near grown. But these past years have been turbulent ones. Stephen is a friend, although I doubt I'll see much of him in the future. I've one or two others, but not of his rank."

He braced his shoulders. "I am told I snore, and I've a lamentable habit of swearing, but only occasionally."

"Is there a point to all of this, Richard?"

He turned and blinked at her. He looked, she thought, rather like an endearing hedgehog at the precise second before it rolls into a protective ball. Eyes wide in terror, blinking at the world, and twitching its nose in alarm.

She stood, walked to him, and laid her hand on his arm.

"I forgive you all your faults, all dutifully enumerated. Whatever you feel you've done or said to me to induce such a lengthy confession, I hereby forgive you. I am tired now and would like to seek my bed, even if it is only a mattress of moss."

"Do you want to return to your island, Hannah?"

Richard asked suddenly. "Is there anything there for you?" His hand gripped hers, turned her so that she faced him fully. "Do you want to live the rest of your life in isolation? You could, instead, spend it with me."

"Is that what this has been? A proposal?"

She narrowed her eyes at him. "Or do you wish another arrangement simply because of what I've told you about Anne?"

He stepped away from her, offended. "Good grief, woman. I confess to having some interest in you in that way, but only after exchanging vows."

It was her turn to blink at him.

"You might have said something," she murmured. "Instead of insulting me all this time." The idea of Richard lusting after her was a fascinating one to consider. She tilted her head and considered him. He met her stare.

"I knew you were worried about Anne. Wished to see her safely home. Tomorrow we'll make the border, and Stephen is releasing those men with families to return to England."

"You wish me to go with you?"

He leaned close, so close that he was a blur. "What in hell do you think I've been doing for the past thirty minutes?" The words were enunciated clearly, each one of them having a bite.

"I didn't need to hear a list of your assets, you silly man," she said, reaching up and grabbing his ears. They were quite large, a point she should insist that he enumerate in his list of flaws. "All you needed to do was kiss me," she said, and proceeded to do just that.

Chapter 26

They rested at noon the next day, the site a curve of meadow beside a stream. Stephen dismounted, held out his arms for Anne. She braced her hands on his shoulders as he spanned her waist and set her down on the dirt road. Next to them, Richard was doing the same for Hannah, the constant bickering between them a source of welcome amusement.

It was obvious that they both enjoyed the sparring.

Stephen extended his arm, and Anne placed her hand on it, not unlike any man and woman out for a leisurely country stroll. Except that the air was thick with dust kicked up by the horses, and the noise created by thirty men dispelled the sense of peace.

Here the earth was fertile, the growth green and lush. Red sandstone peeked from gashes in the land. Rounded hills, shrouded in a pale gray-green mist, were mirrored in small silver lakes. In the distance there was the hint of mountains and gray skies covering snow-capped peaks, as if the earth was shedding itself of its polite drapery and becoming sullen and stark and wild.

It was neither Stephen's map nor the terrain that declared them in Scotland, but rather the gap-toothed smile of a man who spoke in Gaelic. Anne conversed with him for a while, wished him a good day, and turned and walked back to where the others were waiting.

"We've less than two days," she said, "before we come to Dunniwerth land."

They followed the road for a while, stretching their legs. To an onlooker it might appear that they were simply content in each other's company. In truth, silence was easier. Words might have led to the spilling of emotions, and it was simpler to just exist in a dull state, neither enlivened by joy nor tossed into despair.

It did not mean, however, that thoughts were as easily numbed. Two days until he left her. Two days. She did not count the hours. She would bear it because she must. What were the choices? To sink into despair, or to hold herself tight in order not to shatter into a thousand pieces. To keep her silence and endure.

For nearly ten minutes they continued their walk, and in unison turned and were starting back. She wondered if she would recall these silent moments for the rest of her life. Would she regret that she had not spoken? No, because the words trembled on her lips and craved release. Not those that would explain, but instead, beseech.

"Will they lose their pardons by being with you?" she asked finally, looking ahead to the assembled men. Even at ease they congregated in a group, sent men ahead and behind them. She had heard her father say that the measure of a commander was the behavior of his troops. How would he judge Stephen? They obeyed him without question, held him in high esteem, witness the devotion they showed. But there was fondness, too. He was occasionally the subject of a joke, a remark that caused him to raise his eyebrow and stare. He was their commander and occasionally acted as their father. Some of them were so young that they looked barely beyond their first growth of beard.

She'd heard that he assessed fines for drunkenness and disobedience. He did not, she'd been told by James, hesitate to order a man flogged if he raped, or looted, or burned a field. Yet his men had showed no hesitation in following him to Scotland when they might have surrendered their arms and returned to their lives as farmers or tradesmen.

"I doubt the Parliamentarians will fault them for a journey to Scotland. Most of them will return home today."

She turned and looked at him, surprised. "And you?"

"I must be exceptionally careful not to be caught," he said, the edge of a smile curving his lips.

"Won't the Parliamentarians punish Lange on Terne?"

"Because I escaped?"

She nodded.

"They have more to lose by alienating the citizenry than by showing them favor. Lange on Terne is now a Parliamentarian town, whether it wishes to be or not. They will not suffer. Besides, as much as I dislike Penroth for his military tenacity, I've always known him to be fair. Such acts would be beyond him."

"You have evidently given this much thought," she said softly.

"I had to weigh my life, Anne. Whether it mattered enough if I lived or died. In the end, I found that no one would be penalized by my survival."

"Is that the only reason you did not surrender?" She felt the sting of anger. An emotion to be desired as much as humor. "Because you decided no one would suffer for it?"

His laughter rang through the air. "No, my fierce Anne, it's not."

He looked beyond the road to where the mist still clung to the rolling hills. It was noon, but the sun was still a watery globe in the sky, the air damp, although it had not rained. Nature had sensed her mood, Anne thought with a wry smile, and duplicated it.

Because she did not want to look back on these times and regret that she had not told him things in her heart, she spoke now, divulging at least one of her secrets.

"She's my mother," she said, looking at Hannah. A half smile was on her lips, even as she batted Richard's hand away. They were too far away to hear their conversation.

"I know," he said surprisingly, moving to cover her hand with his. "Richard told me."

One of her secrets exposed already, then.

"How do you feel about it?"

She moved away from him, stood at the side of the road looking over the valley before them.

"I might have done the same," she said, obviously surprising him.

He came and stood beside her. An onlooker might think them each engrossed in the view. Instead, she was painfully conscious of how close he was.

"Do you carry my child?" he asked suddenly.

She had not expected that question. She placed her hands over her stomach. A protective gesture. She did not know. How could she? It was too soon.

"No," she said, to reassure him or to absolve him, she didn't know which. Perhaps to release him.

He stood with his back to his men.

"Would you tell me if you did?"

"I don't know," she said, giving him the truth. It was evidently something he did not like by the expression on his face.

She reached up to frame his face with her hands. He didn't pull away, but neither did he move forward. Here was the man who'd led troops across England, who'd fired his home. There was a studied stillness to him, as if he held himself tightly so as not to expose any of himself.

Her thumbs reached to the corners of his lips, and she brushed them softly as if to encourage them to curve upward.

She would never forget him. Not the dawning smile that lit his eyes and seemed to color even the air. Not the sound of his voice reading Latin and translating it for her. Not the look in his eyes when he'd watched his home burn. Her fingers stroked through the hair at his temples. She marked the line of the scar there and held her breath as she traced its path with trembling fingers.

"How did this happen?" A tremulous breath of question that he answered just as softly.

"A stone fell at Langlinais."

"Did it hurt?"

He smiled then, a soft, prompting smile that seemed to be tied to her breath, so tight did it feel in that moment. "I was a boy determined to prove my courage. It no doubt hurt abominably, but I pretended it did not."

"So brave," she whispered.

From the corner of her eye she saw Hannah approach. She quickly stepped back, absurdly grateful for the interruption. She was too close to confession, and it would do no good to speak those words that trembled on her lips. *I love you.*

"I would speak with you, Anne."

She nodded and followed Hannah.

They sat on the trunk of a felled tree, the next seconds spent in gathering their skirts around their ankles, brushing cloth over their knees. Identical gestures Anne might never have noticed a month ago.

All those times when she'd burst into Hannah's cottage came back to her. The instant joy on the older woman's face. The tenderness of her expression, the times in which she'd kissed Anne's face or held her tight in an embrace. A thousand times, a hundred moments. All strung out like glistening drops on a spider's web.

She sat silent, waiting for Hannah to speak.

"Do you hate me, Anne?"

A simple question. "No," Anne said honestly. But it would take longer for the feeling of betrayal to subside.

"I am glad," Hannah said. She pinched the material of her skirt between her fingers. "I would have done the same thing again," she said, glancing over at Anne, "if it meant protecting you. Fault me for that, if you will."

"I do not fault you at all," Anne said. This conversation was difficult, the moment too strained. "Only that you never spoke of it." Hannah had confided in a stranger, but she'd not told her own daughter.

Reason enough for anger.

She'd grown up with one identity and learned to live with who she thought she was. Now, all of her life was suspect. The knowing looks, the whispers that had followed her as a child, they now took on a different meaning.

For the first time, she truly understood what her father had been trying to teach her, about circles, and perspective. Only this time, the circle was her life, and she was standing outside looking in.

The only thing constant, the one thing that had not changed, was Stephen. The visions she'd had as a child, the longing she'd had as a woman, none of that had altered. Yet, in only days he would leave her. Was she supposed to meekly acquiesce to that fate? Accept it with good grace?

"I am not going back to Dunniwerth, Anne," Hannah softly said.

She glanced over at Hannah. Her face seemed younger somehow, less lined.

"I find I cannot go back to the island," Hannah said, folding her hands on her lap. "It will be easier for you if I do not return."

Anne rubbed her palms over her face, pressed her fingers against her eyelids. The back of her neck ached, her shoulders felt stiff. Her breath was tight, and a headache had lodged in her temples and would not be eased.

"It is not because of me," Anne said, her lips thinned with the effort to contain her anger. It bubbled free, despite her will. "It is because of your own choice. It's what you wish to do. Do not hide behind good intentions."

Anne stood and looked to where Stephen was talking to his men. He turned as if he had felt her rage, stared at her. They were too far apart for him to hear her words, but Anne did not doubt he could ascertain her expression well enough.

"It sounds so honorable to think of the betterment of others. So noble." She glanced down at Hannah. "But it's only a cloak, Hannah. What is wrong with wanting something simply for yourself? I would welcome pure selfishness at this moment. It seems more honest."

"There is nothing wrong with wanting something for yourself," Hannah slowly said. "If you are willing to pay the price for it."

"Are you?"

"I always have been," Hannah said surprisingly. "I gave up my life to love your father, and to give you a future." Hannah looked to where Richard stood. "And now I'm going to do what I truly wish. I am going to marry that silly man. He wants me to debate medicinal practices with him, and brew teas and discuss the works of some idiot by the name of Culpepper."

She glanced up at Anne. "But you are right, Anne. It's not for you. It's for me. And perhaps

you are right about the other, too. I was frightened
to be on my own with a child. I wanted the best
for you, but I also wanted to be near your father.

"I've never regretted a moment," Hannah said.
"Or my decision." She appeared to study Anne.
"You are a daughter to be proud of, however it
came about. I have watched you grow into a
woman any mother would cherish." She stood,
joined Anne. "But I do regret any pain I may have
caused you."

She touched Anne's arm gently with just the tips
of her fingers. As if she feared she would be repudiated. "Forgive me," Hannah said.

"It will not be the same without you," Anne said,
forcing the words from her lips. The anger was still
there, but added to it was a sorrow too deep to
measure.

"Life never stays the same," Hannah said. "A
lesson you're learning even now." She looked beyond to where Stephen stood. Anne thought she
might speak again, but she said nothing more.

Hannah turned and walked away. Richard waited
for her, smiled in greeting. Behind him were eighteen men of the regiment. They had families at
Lange on Terne to protect and would be returning
to the town now that they were sure their lord was
at a safe distance.

Anne had the curious thought that the moments
of her life were slipping from her grasp like sand
through her fingers. In only minutes, Hannah would
leave and with her, the opportunity to repair their
rift.

She could not allow that to happen.

Hannah had chastised the child and counseled
the woman. She'd been her friend and held her se-

cret, reassured her. Through it all, she'd given her affection and love. Without explanation or even hope of it being returned.

There was one last thing she needed to do. "Hannah," she called out. The older woman turned. Anne walked to her.

"Will we see each other again?"

Hannah only nodded, her eyes filled with tears. "Yes," Hannah said. "There are not enough wars in the world to prevent that."

"Be happy, Hannah." Anne said, her voice shaking from a surfeit of emotion. The girl would not have said the words, but the woman could not prevent them. "I love you, Mother."

Hannah closed her eyes, then opened them. She took a few steps, then a few more. Her lips were clamped shut, but her arms opened wide. The tears flowed down Anne's cheeks. Long moments later, she pulled away, wiped her face with the backs of both hands.

She stepped back, watched as Hannah mounted her horse. It was difficult to swallow and she could not seem to stop crying. But she offered up a watery smile and a wave, then stood and watched until Hannah and Richard and the rest of the men were no longer visible.

She had the oddest thought that in saying farewell to Hannah, she was also saying goodbye to the person she had once known herself to be. No longer Anne of Dunniwerth. No longer the spoiled child of the laird. Not a woman so certain of her own destiny that she reached out and gripped it with both hands and pulled it to her.

Who was she? Perhaps only time would reveal the answer to that question.

Chapter 27

"You look pleased to be in Scotland again," Stephen said.

"I am," Ian said. "It's a more civilized country than England at present."

Stephen could not argue with that assessment.

Ian rode abreast of him. Stephen had been careful up until now to avoid the man. The brooding look had eased somewhat since they'd entered Scotland, but the dislike was still there in Ian's eyes. So palpable that Stephen could not help but feel it.

He looked ahead to where Anne rode in the center of his men. She turned back at that moment and glanced at him, as if she'd felt his antipathy for the man at his side. He narrowed his eyes as Ian Sinclair smiled at her.

She turned, faced forward again. She sat erect in the saddle, her skirts folded around her. He would have believed her almost oblivious to him if he hadn't noticed her glancing at him from time to time with a look of sadness on her face. As if she were finding a way to say farewell to him.

A bit of appreciation for his seeing her safely home and a kiss on the cheek. A sour thought.

Parting with Hannah had been difficult for her. Yet not once had she spoken of it. He decided that he did not like this habit of hers of holding her thoughts tight to herself. In the short time they had been together, she'd never been cautious before of telling him what she thought. But in the last day, she'd been remarkably silent.

He was struck suddenly by how utterly lovely she was. Not strictly in form, but the essence of her, the wholeness of her. Women of artifice are careful to guard themselves and careful to project only their better qualities. She was not wary of showing him her anger any more than she was her fear of storms. Yet now she sat aloof in the dampness.

"She's been a pest to me ever since she was a child," Ian said, studying Anne. "Always following me around and then telling the girls that she thought my dimple was cute."

"Damning to a man's consequence," Stephen agreed, his tone amicable, but his smile missing. The absence of it didn't seem to affect Ian's sudden, surprising candor.

"I was ten when I first noticed her," Ian said, "and determined to show that I was as manly as my father. She is my laird's daughter, and I will protect her with my life."

"I would expect no less of you."

"Just so we understand each other," Ian said.

The two men shared a long look.

"Does she know you love her?" Stephen asked carefully.

A shake of Ian's head was his answer.

"I doubt I would be as complacent as you, Ian. Or as silent."

"I will always be part of her life. Can you boast the same?"

No, he could not. In fact, he wasn't certain exactly what it was she felt for him. It could range from apathy to antipathy.

Would Ian be the man Anne finally chose? The thought was not one he wanted to entertain.

The future had not been a subject of conversation between them. An oversight, he saw now.

There were times in the last few days when Stephen had known they were cutting through Parliamentarian lines, but they had managed to avoid being detected. Leaving England had made him breathe a little easier. Once in Scotland, though, the danger was less by only a degree.

However, Scotland had something that occurred only occasionally in England. Rain. Incessant rain. This morning was no different. It began to rain again as if nature had known the exact moment he'd condemned the weather. For two hours they continued slogging through it, their eyes downcast, huddling in the misery of being drenched to the skin with no surcease in sight. The air was almost white with rain.

Even the horses plodded along with a dispirited air, their necks bowed, mire up to their hocks. It was a graceless day, and one that nicked at the edge of his temper.

The jingle of harness, an occasional equine snort, a cough, and the patter of the eternal rain all served as a backdrop for his thoughts.

He told himself that she was being wise. Their parting would come in days. It was simpler to pull away now. Not to meet his look, not to speak to him in passing. A kind word might well be misconstrued. A smile might bring forth memories that should not be summoned before their parting.

They seeped into his mind with too much ease.

My home is a huge sprawling place of red brick, aged over the years until it is almost black. Nothing as lovely as this place. Words to describe her Dunniwerth. An apology had prompted a protest. *If I did not feel the same? Would that excuse your honor?* Other words, that spoke of her talent. *My father's map maker taught me.* She spoke of circles and fears and knowing that it was possible to feel the most alone in the midst of a crowd.

The most precious memory of all, a strong woman's vulnerability. A confession spoken in a whisper. *For all the years left to me, I don't want to wish I had come to you tonight and feel regret that I did not.* Yet she did not look at him now, and seemed to barely know his name.

He should congratulate her on her wisdom. Praise her for her foresight. He might, then, be given a small smile, and a whispered farewell. Or did she intend to leave him without a word?

The first sign that there was trouble was a shout from the guard at the rear of the column.

But he'd barely had time to draw his sword before he was surrounded by screaming men.

Stephen berated himself for being so lost in his thoughts that he hadn't noted them, even as he pulled his sword free.

It was Ian who stayed his hand. "It's her father, you fool."

Stephen shouted to his own men to stand down. A command that was met with instant obedience and glances of surprise.

At the center of the shouting Scots sat a mountain of a man. His face was immutable as granite. His beard was white, an odd match for the brown hair on his head.

Nature, that fickle Scottish witch, banished the clouds and dried up the rain. As if she feared the presence of the man who sat staring at him impassively.

It was quite a welcome. Very impressive.

"You'll be English," Robert Sinclair said.

Stephen nodded.

He looked over the twelve men who'd moved into defensive positions. "A fighting force," he said. "But a small one. Do you think yourself such great warriors, then?" He smiled.

"I'm here to escort Anne home, not to fight."

Sinclair nodded, then turned to his daughter.

He neither moved to greet her nor stayed the men who did. She seemed summoned to him by the very nature of his silence. She moved toward him slowly. Their horses were nose to nose before he spoke.

"So, Daughter," he said, his voice deep and booming. "You've finally come home."

Anne nodded. But she didn't look the least cowed. In fact, her chin rose, and she stared at her father.

"With an Englishman who calls you Anne."

She nodded again.

Robert Sinclair turned and glared at him.

Later, Stephen realized he should have listened to his instincts. They told him that Sinclair's antipathy was not based solely on a father's protectiveness. But even if he had known that Robert Sinclair sided with the Parliamentarians, it was too late to do anything about it. He and his men were outnumbered by Scots and in a strange country. Still, he would have chosen a different foe.

It was a pity Sinclair didn't feel the same way about him.

"Is that your Dunniwerth?" Stephen asked late that afternoon.

The huge red-brick castle squatted on the landscape like a giant in a bad temper.

The voice that answered him was laced with humor. "I told you it was ugly."

"It's large," he said, trying to find something of merit to say. "Sturdy."

"It's a fine place," Robert Sinclair said from behind him. Ever since they'd been surrounded by the Scots, Sinclair had been no more than five feet from him. Stephen wondered if he would have mounted Faeren and sat behind him if his stallion had allowed it.

He smiled, a not altogether humorous smile. He would have liked to have seen Sinclair try.

People began to come out of their homes, neat little dwellings not far removed from a small English cottage. Most of the people of Dunniwerth stood open-mouthed as they passed. One woman cried, then shoved the corner of her apron in her mouth.

It was as if they viewed a ghost.

Their horses walked up the road, accompanied by the dawning sound of wails and cries and screams of gladness. There was no gate to Dunni-werth, encircled as it was by a mound of earth. Almost, Stephen thought, like the inverse of a moat. They passed through the earthen wall just as the double iron-studded doors were being drawn open.

A strikingly lovely woman flew down the steps. She stumbled, then righted herself. Anne dismounted, ran to her mother. The two women embraced.

It was a homecoming that called for tears.

He nudged his horse close, faced her father even as his frown turned to a glower.

"She's tired," Stephen said, "and any interrogation can wait."

"It can, can it?"

It was like facing a burly bear, Stephen thought. He nodded.

"And a welcome home?" Sinclair asked. "Will that wait, too?"

The glower changed to a grin as Robert Sinclair dismounted and held open his arms, went and extended them around the two women. As they embraced, it was only then that Stephen saw the tears. Not only on Anne's and her mother's, but on the face of Robert Sinclair as well.

Chapter 28

The dungeons of Dunniwerth were as dim and dreary as the rest of the castle. A lone candle stuck in its own wax was the only illumination. The cell Stephen was in was a small square, not unlike an oubliette. But there was no trapdoor in the ceiling, only a door with a small grate over the window. Altogether, it was sufficient to allow him air but not freedom. He had an odd thought of Sebastian of Langlinais, wondered if his ancestor had been as enraged as he felt at this moment. Sebastian's imprisonment had lasted a year, however. Not the mere hours he'd been chained to a dank cell.

It had occurred to him, in the past hours, that he and Sebastian had a great deal in common. Both of them were men who would much rather learn than fight. Both felt a tie to Langlinais that was greater than most bonds. They had each been prepared to give up their life for a cause they held sacred, only to discover that what had glittered so promisingly was only an illusion.

He had admired Sebastian because he was a warrior, but it was more than his battle prowess he thought of when he recalled his ancestor. It was the statue he left behind, the improvements he'd made to Langlinais.

His courage as he prepared to go into exile, and his sacrifice because of his leprosy. His enduring love for one woman.

The candle sputtered. It was made from drippings, the cheapest method and the most fetid. The faint light revealed cobwebs being spun by industrious and plump spiders. Stephen watched the progress of a pair of flies coming closer and closer to the web.

"Beware, my friend," he said softly. "Trust not in women flies. They'll buzz around you with their diaphanous wings and lure you into danger. Before you know it, you'll find yourself trapped in a shiny web, wondering how you got there."

"I wonder if it's a fate you perceive for yourself?"

An eye peered at him from the grate.

Stephen lay on the stone bench carved from the rock wall, one arm draped over a raised knee. He didn't bother to change his posture when a clang of keys announced that the door was soon to be opened.

"I wonder, too, what my daughter would say to hear herself likened to a fly."

"I doubt it would concern her, sir," he said to Robert Sinclair. "If you have not noticed, your daughter has a temperament suited ideally to herself. She does what she wishes when she wishes, and the devil take the hindmost."

Sinclair's laughter was surprising. So, too, the look of amusement he sent him.

"I see you know her well. Her mother would say that she takes after me."

"Not a charming legacy for a daughter." It was baiting a bear, but he wasn't feeling particularly agreeable at this moment. The irritation he felt after being thrown into the dungeon a few moments after their arrival at Dunniwerth had deepened into rage after a few hours.

Sinclair stood watching him with equanimity. Why shouldn't he? *He* was not imprisoned in a dungeon.

"My daughter says you are an earl and a man of much property."

Stephen smiled. "My house has burned to the ground, and if the king loses this war, my title will no doubt be passed to one of the victors. Or abolished entirely."

"Did she tell you, this daughter of mine, that my title equals yours?"

"No," he said, not unduly surprised.

"But my house is not so fragile that it will burn," Sinclair said.

"I doubt anyone would want to set fire to it," Stephen said. More like tear it down brick by brick and begin again.

He had the distinct impression that Robert Sinclair circled him as a fox might a nest of eggs, interested in devouring him whole.

"Have you any wealth remaining?"

Stephen fingered the ribbon in his pocket. A length of scarlet, to keep her close to him.

"Is there a reason you wish to know?"

"Only to gauge your worth in ransom."

"It does not matter," Robert Sinclair said when he remained silent. "I'm to turn you over to the Covenanters in a day or so."

There was a look in his eyes, one that gave Stephen the feeling that Robert Sinclair was secretly laughing at him.

"My daughter didn't tell you that either, did she?"

"That you sided with the Parliamentarians? No," he said wryly, "she neglected to mention that little detail."

"She's a brave lass, is my Anne," he said. "But too silent at times."

"I can only agree," Stephen said dryly.

Sinclair glanced at the corner where the spider's web sat like a drape of silver. One of the flies had become ensnared in it. The other flew blissfully away.

Sinclair's laughter could be heard for long minutes, then the echo of it vied with the sound of the sputtering candle.

More than a little irony in this moment. He had taken such effort to escape Penroth and the Parliamentarians only to be imprisoned by their allies, Scottish Covenanters. He didn't delude himself that they would be any more sympathetic to his plight than Penroth.

For the whole earth is the sepulcher of famous men, and their story is not graven only on stone over their native earth, but lives on far away without visible symbol. Woven in to the stuff of other men's lives. For you now it remains to rival what they have done, knowing the secret of happiness to

be freedom and the secret of freedom a brave heart.
The words of Thucydides echoed in his mind.
Where had they come from? A boy's mind. A
dreamer's thoughts. A young man in love with
ideals and principles. The greatness of Athens had
fascinated him. The ideals espoused by the histo-
rian had appealed to him. But he'd learned in the
years between youth and age that words such as
freedom and bravery and even happiness were ge-
neric ones. They meant different things to each man.

He wondered if duty, honor, and loyalty might
be as generally interpreted.

Duty. He'd congratulated himself on the fact that
he'd saved the lives of the villagers and the inhabitants of Harrington Court. He should have returned
to Oxford that day, instead of deserting the king
once more. Yet, he'd been curiously unwilling to
pick up his sword and fight again. It had not been
cowardice, but a distaste for the very cause that the
king espoused.

He could not even claim that he had been dutiful
or honorable in the matter of bringing Anne safely
back to Scotland. Another emotion had been at the
core of that impulse, one less open to scrutiny than
most. He wanted her safe and protected. Protected
by him.

But he'd also wanted to spend more time with
her. In his mind, he'd thought they might be enchanted days. But she had not smiled at him with
great charm, nor wished to talk to him of weighty
topics. Nor had she said the one thing he'd wished
to hear. *Stay with me.*

Honor? A nobility of mind? His reputation? How
was honor to be measured? By the manner of his

death? By the grace he accepted it? Not an altogether pleasant thought.

Loyalty. To what?

There was no longer any principle associated with this war. Men might argue that the right of kings took precedence over the common man. Or it might be said that freedom to worship God as a man chose was greater than any loyalty to a monarch. Either way, it no longer mattered. War was, simply put, a test of courage. Humanity versus cruelty. The winner was not always the man in the right. It very often was, he thought, the one who could be more brutal than his foe.

He realized that unlike that boy he'd been, he didn't particularly want to die. He didn't want his bones to inspire the dreams of other young men.

Loyalty? To what? A king who did not tolerate the advice of others? A monarch who wished to govern in absolutes?

Duty, honor, loyalty—a set of principles that had ruled his life.

Sebastian had been dedicated to the knightly virtues. Generosity, compassion, a free and frank spirit, courtliness. Generosity, a lesson Stephen had learned from his father's example. He would continue to aid the inhabitants of Lange on Terne. Compassion. He believed himself capable of it. A free and frank spirit? He had not felt free in years, even though honesty was a trait he prized. Courtliness? Too much experience in it, if the word was taken in its broader meaning. He was tired to the bones of simpering, fawning people who were adept at intrigue and cunning. Even Sinclair was a better opponent. Stephen would always know how he felt.

A knight, however, might think the word to mean the protection of a damsel, a fair lady. Did it matter if the lady fair in question had a will to match his own? Or that there were occasional flashes of anger in her eyes? More a woman of fire than a delicate flower of womanhood.

He really should be angry at her. But that emotion had strangely been stripped from him by another, more powerful realization. One that would change his life and most certainly his future.

Stephen smiled.

Chapter 29

"**Y**ou haven't said why you left Dunni-werth, Anne."

The words were uttered as both a greeting and a warning. She turned and watched as her father closed the door behind him, walked into the room.

There had been numerous times she'd been summoned to this chamber as a child. For minor infractions and other sins less minor. She'd been lectured and chastised and punished here. As a young woman, her father had called her here to speak to her of marriage, of unions and lands and clan loyalties. But through it all, through discipline and discourse, she'd felt loved.

"There was something I had to do," she said.

"You're daft if you think that's all the explanation I'll accept, Daughter."

She smiled. "I'm sorry, Father, but it's the only one I'm going to make." She'd never spoken of her visions to her parents. She did not regret the decision now. It had been a wise choice, even though it had been made instinctively. The child had recognized what the woman had come to know. There were people who could accept what she saw and people who could not. Nor did it seem worthwhile to mention them now that the visions had ceased.

He squinted his eyes at her. "You've changed," he said. "Why?"

She shook her head. The answers were too numerous. The reasons too varied.

"Ian says Hannah returned to England."

There was a look between them. One they'd never shared before. She saw him as he was, neither godlike nor venal, but someone fixed in between. There was greatness to Robert Sinclair, but he had also sinned. And erred in his dealings.

A proud man who'd wished for an heir. Who regretted, perhaps, his indiscretion with Hannah. Had he acted in the best interests of all? Probably not. Who was she to judge him? Her own actions had been foolish and fueled by emotion as strong. Is that the greatest trait they shared? Not their coloring but a fierceness of temperament. She felt a surge of fondness for him. And understanding.

He had protected her and sheltered her and provided a life for her. And during all these years, he'd loved her.

Her voice was kind when she answered him.

"She's going to marry a man she met in England, Father. She deserves a life of her own after all these years."

There was a look in his glance, one that made her wonder if he would speak of it. Finally he nodded, looked away, and then back at her.

"So you know, then?"

"Yes."

"Your mother has been making herself sick with

worry, Anne. I'll have you be kind to her." In his eyes was a look of entreaty.

"Of course I'll be kind to her. She's my mother."

It was the truth. Simply because Maggie Sinclair had not given birth to her did not strip her of the title. Or the love that Anne had always felt for her. She'd been granted the greatest gift of all. The love of two mothers.

"Ian says you have a fondness for this Englishman."

"Ian should not involve himself in things he doesn't understand," she said curtly.

"He thinks he understands you. He would marry you if you gave him any encouragement, Daughter."

"Do you approve of him, then?"

He nodded. "I always have," he said, looking not the least bit ashamed.

"Is that why you left him in charge of my safety when you left Dunniwerth?"

He looked offended by her laughter. "You had ignored him for years."

"He has made my life miserable for years."

"You were a child then."

"With a long memory," she said dryly. "Did you expect me to simply forget how he's tormented me all my life? To awake one day and notice his shapely legs?"

"It's a sight better than noticing an Englishman's."

Her amusement vanished as quickly as it had come. She walked to the window that overlooked the loch. She could see Hannah's island in the distance. Had her father stood here and watched as she did now? Or did he simply bow to fate, and turn away from the woman he'd loved so passionately if for so short a time? An irony of the purest sort, that Stephen would do the same.

"There is something between you and this Englishman, Daughter. I see it myself."

She glanced over at her father. There was a look on his face she'd seen before, but only when she'd done something wrong as a child. It was regret mixed with anger, as if he both disliked the necessity of punishing her and was irritated that she had pushed him to it. The look was effective, even if she was grown and there was no further threat of punishment.

"There is nothing between us," she said softly. The words were a death-knell, uttered in a voice barely more than a whisper. Saying them did not ease the burden in her heart. She might repeat them for a hundred years and at the end of that time it would still be untrue.

Remember me. How could she not help it?

Amor vincit omnia. Love conquers all. But it doesn't, does it? *Audi alteram partem*—there are two sides to every question. The journey had not been a total loss, perhaps. She'd added to her store of knowledge and learned a few words of Latin. Words that had been fed to her on a kiss the night they'd lain together the second time. The conversation of lovers. She closed her eyes.

"If he's what you want, I can persuade him to stay, Daughter. Dunniwerth's dungeon hasn't seen a visitor in a few years." He came to her side, his look intent. "He's there now, awaiting your answer."

She turned to him and placed her hand on his arm. "You cannot procure a husband for me as easily as you would a new wardrobe, Father."

"I'd much rather hear the screams of an Englishman than the twittering of a group of sewing women," he said.

For all his glower, he would do no such thing. Not unless she wished it. Then, Stephen's fate would be dire, indeed. She patted his arm and shook her head. "Let him go, Father."

"Do you want him, Anne?"

Did she want him? Did she want breath?

The days would be bearable because he walked the earth. The nights endurable because he saw the same stars as she did.

Want him? He had always been hers. Since the first vision. A moment when she'd watched him grieve and felt his loss. She told him once, the night before he'd surrendered. *You have been in my sight all my life.* She'd wept as the words were torn from her. But he'd not recognized the truth of them.

He would go to war again, and each night she'd dread sleep because it might bring a vision of him. One in which he suffered. Or died. When that time came, what would she do? Weep into her pillow, or stare, sightless, at the ceiling? Would madness be the gift she was given for loving him and losing him?

Perhaps it was only a matter of time until the children of Dunniwerth would point to her chamber window and speak in hushed tones of scraggly haired Anne, and her invisible lover, of her tears and moans. They would dare each other to call out to her and scream in delicious terror if she looked out the window to see their childish forms fleeing into the courtyard.

Want him? It would be easier not to.

She should wed someone with no ties to these past weeks. Not Ian, because looking at him would forever bring Stephen to mind. Nor a man with blue eyes, because they would be pale mirrors of a midnight shade. Nor a man with black hair with a habit of it falling to his brow.

She would not marry a man with humor or honor or someone who kissed with full lips and whispered forbidden words in her ear. Deaf and dumb and blind, perhaps. A man of cruelty would suffice.

A child or children would follow, and she would pray that they would all be girls with blond hair. Not a boy among them. Else she might whisper to him of a man she'd known once who wore gallantry as easily as a cloak, and garbed himself in honor like a cape. She might wish her child to emulate this man, to be as strong and fierce and brave. But she would coach him to be kinder, and more gentle. To love as easily as he hated. But more than all of that, she would teach him in the matter of constancy. He would pity as well as love, and have compassion for those who loved him in kind.

Want him?

Enough to die for it.

He smiled with such an air of surprise as if he was startled by his own amusement. And he walked with great long strides upon the earth and stood taller than most men. The tailor who sewed his clothes bemoaned the size of his shoulders. Such odd things Anne knew about him.

But she had not known that he commanded with such ease or so impatiently. Or rode with an effortless grace. His hands clenched when he was enraged, his eyes were capable of the iciest look. He could bear the unbearable without a moan. A formidable man. In his arms she'd learned the meaning of words she'd only heard. Felt them in her heart and in her body and in her mind. Perhaps even her soul. Passion. Desire. Longing. Love.

She had seen the boy and had known the man. She had learned what people thought of him, and had become familiar with the person he truly was.

Did she want him? Enough to die for him.

But how easily he was leaving her. Choosing death over life with her, the decision made without regret or compunction or hesitation.

She had become someone else in her quest for him. Yet, he did not even know that. The anger she'd buried these last few days blazed through her. At this moment, it didn't matter if it was directed solely at Stephen or in equal parts to both of them. It warmed her blood, and made her voice steady. Resolute.

"No, Father," she said, her voice filled with quiet fury. "I don't want him."

It was a difficult thing, Robert Sinclair thought, to care for another person. The room in which he stood was his oriel, a strange block of a room added on to Dunniwerth in the last hundred years. It was his eagle's nest, Maggie had said often enough, and was fitted with glass he'd ordered from Edinburgh. It provided him a view of most of his land, including the loch on which Hannah had lived all these years. He was truly pleased at her happiness. It had been a long time coming.

Maggie joined him, leaned her head against his shoulder.

"She knows about Hannah."

"I suspected as much," she said.

He glanced down at her.

"It was the way she looked at me, I think. When she and I hugged. Or perhaps the way she told me that she loved me. She has not often done so."

"Are you sorry she knows?"

"No, she is my daughter. I could not love her more if she had been born to me."

He knew that. Of all the blessings in his life, Maggie's love of his child had been the greatest. It had made the sadness bearable, the agreement they'd crafted among the three of them worthwhile.

"She is so miserable, Robert."

"I suspect the man in the dungeon is the reason why."

"What will you do to him?"

"I would like to turn him over to Argyll's men, but I'm going to let him go, instead."

Her look prompted his smile. "Not my idea, Maggie, but Anne's."

"What will happen to her now, Robert?"

"I don't know," he said, and it was something that angered him. He was a man who liked to be in control of his life. In this case, there was nothing he could do, and it didn't set at all well with him.

Chapter 30

❦

Anne did not want to be at Dunniwerth when Stephen left. She didn't want to bid him farewell with grace and courage and watch as he rode away.

Even now the regiment readied itself for its departure. She had stood at her chamber window and looked down into the courtyard. All the twelve men who'd seen her safely home. She did not trust herself to bid them farewell individually, so she'd contented herself with a wave, a smile.

She was not given to tears, but he'd brought her to them often enough. He would not see them now. If they were to be shed, it would be in the privacy of her bed with the pillow pressed over her face.

There were empty chambers at Dunniwerth. Rooms created for men-at-arms when the barracks overflowed, a few for important guests. She'd ask for one of those in exchange for the room she'd known from the time she was a child.

A change of scene. As if he'd invaded her bed and she wanted no more memories to assail her. In truth that's exactly what it had felt like. He had been her nightly companion long before she'd physically hungered for him.

What would nights be like now?

The thought brought heat to her face and regret to her mind. Not that she had loved him or lain with him. She was not the first woman to have done so outside of marriage. But that her memory was so strong. She might wish to be senile or simple, the better to forget.

She would forget. If she worked hard enough at it, she would.

But now she found herself at the shoreline. There was one boat tied there. The other would be at the island. She got into the boat, touched the rowan wood for luck, and began to row.

Halfway to the island, she had to stop rowing because she was crying too hard. She bowed her head, let the tears come. The only witness to her tears were the fish and the turtles. Long moments later, she swiped the backs of her hands against her cheeks and continued across the loch.

This time Stephen didn't hear the clink of the keys. He was involved in his thoughts. Not those of a spider's web, but introspection of a deeper nature.

When Robert Sinclair entered the cell, he glanced up at him with a great deal of disinterest. Or so he wished it to appear. He had no intention of remaining a prisoner. Not of Sinclair and certainly not of the Covenanters.

The only drawback to this plan was the fact that in order to escape he might have to injure Anne's father. Unless the man saw reason.

"I promised my daughter you'd have your freedom," he said.

Stephen only raised one eyebrow at that surprising announcement. It effectively rendered the last quarter hour of his planning useless.

"Your men are waiting for you in the courtyard. I'll give you safe passage to the edge of my land. Then you're no longer my concern."

"Very generous of you, Sinclair."

"I love my daughter, Englishman. I'll not go back on my promise."

Stephen stood, brushed himself off with an unhurried movement.

"Where is Anne, Sinclair?"

"She doesn't wish to see you. So you can say your farewells to me and I'll bid her good-bye for you."

"I wouldn't want to trouble you," Stephen said, genuine amusement curving his lips in a smile. "Where is she?"

"A place where you'll not find her." He stepped back, allowed Stephen to leave the cell. The air was no better here, but perhaps it smelled sweeter because he was free.

He mounted the sloping steps after Sinclair. Even now he was not quite sure there was not a trap involved. It was too easy.

"Ian will ride with you. You know him well, I believe."

Stephen didn't comment. He entered the courtyard. Faeren stood saddled and ready for him. His horse eyed a groom with such ferocity that Stephen wondered how many nips he'd taken from the boy's shoulder.

The twelve men who had followed him to Dunniwerth were arrayed in the courtyard. Twelve men who had no relatives at Lange on Terne to worry about or who had set aside their own concerns for seeing him safely here.

He and his regiment were bound, all of them, by bonds not easily understood.

He was going to offer them a choice.

He turned and faced Sinclair. His right hand flexed in case he needed to reach either his sword or his pistol.

"Where is Anne?"

"My daughter isn't here, Englishman." There was a small smile on Robert Sinclair's lips.

"Where is she?"

"Somewhere you'll not find her."

"Where?" He took one step toward the laird of Dunniwerth.

"You're hard of hearing?"

"I'm not leaving until I see her, Sinclair."

"Are you as stubborn as my daughter, Englishman?"

"Even more so."

The two men eyed each other.

"Then you'll find her at the island," Robert Sinclair said. "But," he said, his grin coming out like the sun from behind a cloud, "I hope you can swim, because she's taken the boat."

Anne walked to the edge of the clearing, sat down on a stump of a tree.

The afternoon was overcast. A dreary day to match her mood. The forest behind her was alive with sounds. Squirrels rustled through the layers of dead leaves; the birds relayed a melody of sound and warning. A breeze soughed through the tree-tops, clicking the branches together, creating a whispering melody of new leaves.

The cottage sat as it always had, a plump mushroom upon the landscape. Over the years it had had its share of visitors. Girls in search of their fortunes. Women to procure a syrup for a cough. Everyone at Dunniwerth had known Hannah, even though she rarely ventured from the island. She had been Hannah's most frequent visitor. Here she'd learned to craft the fragrant candles from the honeycombs of bees. She'd dried flowers and cut onions, strung garlic, and a hundred other chores.

"Hannah, look!"

The excitement she felt was like no other. She was ten years old and had crafted her first basket of reeds. It stood on its flat bottom just like the one Hannah had made. Although it had taken her weeks instead of days, her fingers not having the flexibility and dexterity of her friend's, the squat bellied basket looked as well made as any she'd seen at the fair.

"You are truly a maker of fine baskets, Anne."

"Truly?"

"Your skill is enormous. I shall hire you myself."

"Can I take it home, Hannah? I promise I shall return it. But I want Father to see."

"Indeed, he should. Take it home and give it to him if you wish, Anne. He would prize it, I'm sure."

"You do not mind?"

A cool hand cupped her cheek. "Of course not. There will be other days and other baskets."

The woman she'd known had been as motherly

to her as Maggie. She'd truly been blessed to have both of them. But there were signs all along, and she'd known, even as a child, that things were not as they should have been.

"Hannah, why do you look so sad sometimes, as if you want to cry?"

"Do I?"

"Yes. If you want to cry, I'll not tell. Sometimes I cry, too."

"What do you cry about?"

"Pretty things. Sometimes something is so beautiful I cannot help but cry. Ian says that only girls do something so silly."

"Ian is a silly boy. Pay no heed to him."

"All the girls seem to. He has grown to be very tall."

"Do you think him handsome?"

"No. He is still a bully."

"One day he will be grown, and I'm sure be a nicer man."

"Or one like Hamish who struts just like the cock in the henhouse. Why are you smiling?"

"It was just, perhaps, that I was not prepared for your description of Hamish. The years pass so swiftly."

There had been laughter here and a sharing of joy, but had it been enough for Hannah? Would it be enough for her? How odd that mother and daughter had both fallen desperately in love with men who were not destined to stay with them.

She did not have the nature for such sacrifice. She could not see herself staring wistfully off into the distance and wishing things were different. She would prefer to be more like Juliana. To declare herself a leper in order to be with her husband. To choose exile rather than loneliness.

Four hundred years separated her from Juliana. Title, birth, language, time, life itself stood between them. Yet the words she had written were timeless, and the message oddly the same as Anne's thoughts.

Had Juliana ever been angry with Sebastian? She had evidently rejected his concept of honor. It would have demanded of him that he leave her, his home, in order to do what he thought was right.

God protect her from men of honor.

Juliana, at least, had had courage. She had not relied upon Sebastian to change his mind or return to her. All Anne had done was hide on an island and feel sorry for herself.

Shame was as unpalatable a dish as cowardice.

She stood, brushed off her hands, tidied her hair, and straightened her dress. There were things that needed to be said, truths that needed to be spoken before Stephen left Dunniwerth.

She turned and he was there. Not the Stephen she'd known, solemn and somber and only occasionally lit with amusement. This man was the embodiment of exasperation. A storm cloud walking. He was dressed in white shirt and black breeches. He was as sober in his dress as his expression, seeming to study her as the silence between them increased.

He was also dripping wet.

"Did you swim the loch?" she asked in amazement.

"Given that there was no boat, yes."

He wore no boots. Stephen was always dressed

more soberly than his companions, but she'd never seen him looking like this.

"It cannot be good for your arm."

"I doubt a day spent in a dungeon is considered good treatment, either," he said amicably. "You didn't tell me I was entering a hotbed of Covenanters," he said pleasantly. She distrusted that tone of voice. It was at odds with the look on his face.

His irritation did little to cool her own.

"Your men will be expecting you," she said, turning away from him.

"No doubt," he said. "After a while they will either stable their horses or leave for England. It is, after all, their choice."

She turned and stared at him.

"Perhaps I'll tell the king that I was captured," he continued. He came closer with each step. She had the oddest feeling she was being stalked. "Or perhaps," he said, smiling, "I'll simply decline to participate in his war."

Too many questions tumbled through her mind. The main one his reason for following her to the island. To blame her for the day he'd spent in Dunniwerth's dungeons? Fine, she was culpable. Her father had taken it upon himself to imprison an Englishman he'd thought responsible for her disappearance. But she had not known. In fact, the moment she'd entered the red-brick walls of her home, she'd done everything she could *not* to think of him. The result had been a dismal failure. When she'd learned what her father had done, she'd ensured that he'd been released as quickly as possible.

"Did you mean what you say, Stephen? About not going to war?" She held her breath for his reply.

"Perhaps," he said. And that was all. One word.

Did he expect her to beg? If she spoke at this moment, the words might well be tinged with tears, droplets clinging to the tail and to the spire of each one.

"One would think you did not care, Anne," he said, touching her nose with his fingertip. "Except that you've been crying."

"A mistake," she said irritably. "I'll not be like Hannah. Pining away for you."

"Did I ask that of you?" He smiled then, a soft smile that scraped at the edge of her temper.

"You haven't asked anything of me," she said softly, the truth of that statement muting his smile. There had been no declarations between them, no vows of love, no sweetness that comes before a parting or instead of it. Even now they faced each other as adversaries instead of lovers. Angry with each other for the grief they'd each experienced. Afraid, perhaps, because of what might come between them now.

He was a man of isolation, and she had been a woman of cowardice. It would take courage for each of them to step out of their respective roles. Yet he had done so by coming to the island. It was her turn now.

"Stay right there," she said, pointing at the ground at his feet. "Do not move."

One eyebrow arched upwards. "You have a deplorable habit of doing that, Anne Sinclair," he said dryly. "I feel it only fair to warn you that I don't feel particularly well disposed to obeying orders at this moment."

She ignored his scowl, left the clearing, went to her hiding tree. She stood on tiptoe and reached inside the hollow. She retrieved her drawings, wrapped in oilskin. The first of these drawings was a childish rendition. An image of a vision she'd had. He'd been sitting in the bailey, concentrating upon his drawing. His fingers were black with the charcoal he used, but they flew over the page, adding detail to doorways and embrasures, creating the proper angle of a merlon. She'd drawn him sitting there, his gaze on the east tower.

Another drawing had Stephen as the boy she'd first seen, sitting on the bed, Betty kneeling before him. There was a look of such loss on his face that it made her heart ache even now.

She rolled them into a cylinder again, held them close to her chest. Her heart pounded, a clarion bell of anxiety.

In this one thing, she would be as brave as Juliana. And in one other, too. She would tell him how she felt, so that if he chose to ride away from Dunniwerth, he would do so with the knowledge that she loved him. A memory or a regret for him to keep all the days of his life.

Chapter 31

In only moments she returned to the clearing.

Across the grass their gaze met. Her arms were wrapped around a package. Something she considered valuable or precious from the way she carried it.

She was an amalgam of beauty, grace, strength, and anger. Or perhaps it was not anger in her eyes. Another emotion, perhaps, one that made her look away.

Only hours ago his life had been somewhat his own. His body had been loaned to the king for the duration of the war; his arm strengthened to wield a sword and his aim sharpened to fire a pistol. He'd endured what he'd must because it had been there to tolerate. But dominion over his thoughts had always been his. When had that ceased to be?

When he'd realized he did not want to leave her.

"I want to show you something," she said and placed the parcel on the tree stump then stepped back. He unwrapped it, since it was clear this was what she wished.

One by one he spread the drawings out. They

345

were not witty portraits or clever caricatures, but sketches of him in various poses. One showed him standing at Langlinais's east tower. Another bending and placing the brick that gave access to his hiding place back into its groove. Still another standing in front of his father, a look on his face of studied indifference. And one of him as a boy the night his mother had died. Dozens of sketches of him.

He felt his blood heat and then cool.

Questions came to his lips and were dismissed before being given voice.

"I did the first of them when I was ten," she softly said. Her words settled into his mind like stones, each of them separate and distinct, as if she built a fortress with them.

He turned and looked at her.

Her eyes were wide. Was it fear he saw there?

"I've seen you all my life," she said. "In my visions. No other person, Stephen, only you. The first of them happened when I was eight," she said, and began her tale.

One so improbable that it could not happen. But he listened even as his hands shuffled the sketches and saw scenes she could not have otherwise known. A moment atop the east tower, when he'd felt a loneliness so acute that the pain of that moment speared him even now. A picture of him leaning over the Langlinais bridge. How many times had he done that as a boy? As many times as he'd ridden Faeren over the hills and meadows of his home.

It should have angered him, this odd knowledge she had of him. She had, with these visions, invaded his privacy at the deepest level. But he realized that they were not something over which she had any power or control.

And he did not accept the idea of sorcery. Or witchcraft. But he believed in her.

She'd known his name. The hiding place he'd had as a boy. And looked on Langlinais as if she knew the castle as well as he. And he'd heard her call to him in a moment of great danger. Not fever then, but fate.

Silence stretched between them. Not the awkward pause between strangers. They had been too intimate for that. It was an utter stillness, like the one before a storm. He glanced up at the sky, certain that it was to rain again. Another thing he would have to grow accustomed to, the eternal rain of Scotland.

He sucked in his breath, felt the cool air bathe his throat, swirl inside his chest.

"I've seen you all my life," she said again, and the words made him recall another moment. A night when she'd wept on his chest and told him that he'd always been there. She'd spoken the truth, and he'd disregarded it, pushed it behind his own pressing concerns.

It seemed to him that those things he had once cherished, such as loyalty and virtue, honor, nobility, trust, all of them were becoming suspect in this new world riddled by war. It was as if what had been important about his life had disintegrated, crumbled into dust like ancient silk. Harrington Court was no more, his plans for restoring Langlinais nothing but the dreams of youth. His country was at war, his king no doubt incensed with him.

He doubted if he would ever return to London, or that he would ever see the court he'd known restored to its previous power.

But into that emptiness had come another life. One prepared for him even as he was unaware. A woman sent to him to ease his pain. To give him hope again. To frown at him and make him smile. She had a variety of smiles, all suited to her, warm brown eyes, and an endearing laugh. She was stubborn and brave, compassionate and sensual. She had the ability to make him think and the capacity to render him senseless. She had discovered him from beneath the man he'd thought he was.

His earldom was more than land. It was more than Harrington Court. More than even the castle, Langlinais. It was a heritage of men who had persevered despite obstacles and circumstances that might have felled other men. It had pushed him onward even beyond what he'd thought himself capable. Such courage would have to stand him in good stead now.

Only one thing concerned him. She stood silent, her hands clenched in front of her. He wanted to place his hands on her cheeks and purse her mouth, free the words that were entrapped there. *Stay with me.* Not once had she said it. He wanted the words.

But she had given up part of herself and waited for him to ridicule her. He saw the proof of it in her eyes. Fear. Not anger. That and a tear. One from a woman who did not cry easily.

Was love come so easily as that? Yes. But it had happened earlier than this moment, hadn't it? When they'd stood in a dark tower, and she'd shivered against him as lightning split the sky.

She bent forward to gather up the drawings. He reached out and encircled her wrist with his hand. She turned her head and looked up at him.

"I don't understand," he said, offering her the truth.

She pulled away.

"But perhaps there are some things that I don't have to understand. The miracle of Langlinais, for one. These drawings, for another."

She seemed to be made of ice, so still she stood. He wanted, in that instant, to warm her, to hold her tight in his arms. Instead, there were words that must be said first.

"I've no home," he said. "And I do not doubt that the king will offer a reward for my head, to be matched only by the Parliamentarians. Or your father," he said wryly. "But I've dreams enough to occupy me and wealth I've managed to hide away. I come from a long line of men who have always believed in the future."

She straightened.

One step toward him, then another, and her hand was on his chest. A surprisingly capable-looking hand, with long fingers and an imperious thumb. Not unlike the rest of her.

"Anne," he said, and the sound of her name on his lips was like a gentle rain. As he heard her indrawn breath, his lips curved into a smile. She had the power to effortlessly distract him from any task, even that of studying her hand.

She was his to protect and defend and keep safe. To love and need and worship with body and mind and soul. His through all time, as Sebastian had loved Juliana. If the world crumbled about them, he would hold sacrosanct a few sparse clods of earth for her to stand upon. There he would hold her in his arms and find an answering comfort in her embrace.

"Amantes sun amentes," he said with a smile. "Lovers are lunatics," he said, in answer to her frown.

As a declaration of love, it lacked something.

"An té is mó fhosglas a bhéul," she countered. "You talk entirely too much." Her cheeks grew pink. "Loosely translated, that is."

"I think I need to learn Gaelic."

"Not an insurmountable feat for someone with such skill at Latin."

"I could barely understand that old man we met on the road," he said. "Was that Gaelic he was speaking or some sort of gibberish?"

"I think it owed more to a lack of teeth than to an abundance of nationality, Stephen," she said calmly.

"What would your father say if you married an Englishman?"

"I'll tell him you're my Latin tutor." Her cheeks deepened in color as he watched. So she recalled that night as well as he.

"I'm not the sort of genial husband you had in mind," he said, smiling. "But I doubt a man of pleasant disposition would fare well among you Scots."

"You'll stay, then?"

He reached out and touched her cheek. It felt warm beneath his fingertips.

How could he ever part from her?

She turned her head and kissed the tips of his

fingers, then grabbed his hand. Their fingers entwined even as their smiles grew.

It began to rain. Again. But he decided that it didn't matter. He was, after all, already wet.

"We should go back to Dunniwerth," he said.

"Yes," she said, smiling. "But it's dangerous to be on the loch when it storms."

"The cottage, then?"

She stepped closer to him, placed a chaste kiss on his cheek. But her palms rested on his chest, and her smile had an edge of daring to it.

"Here?"

He smiled at her, amused. "You're afraid of storms."

"You'll have to protect me," she said, running her fingers to the laces of his shirt. "Lie with me," she said softly, standing on her tiptoes to whisper the invitation in his ear. As if the squirrels and the birds might hear and pass the news to the rest of the forest court. "The only time we've loved has been in parting, Stephen. I would have this time be in welcome."

"In the rain?" he asked. In snow, in sleet, in dead of winter. In a flood, he thought, or with lightning crackling about him.

She nodded.

Her fingertips on his skin had an odd effect of stilling his mind. There were other objections he should think of, surely. Instead, all he could remember was the vow he'd made to himself to love her once not in parting but in joy.

Above them a canopy of new leaves protected them from the worst of the rain.

He stared at her and she stared back, her eyes

wide. The patter of the raindrops on the canopy of branches above their heads indicated how hard the rain was falling. Droplets clung to the leaves above them, falling heavily to the ground from time to time. A fine mist penetrated this odd bower.

He started at least a hundred sentences in his mind. A hundred approaches, a single one. The words stuttered to a halt, sliced to death by her silence.

He bent and kissed her instead.

His lips coaxed hers open. A gasp and her tongue met his. There, in this matter he was at least adept.

In the shadow of her throat, her blood beat hot and quick. He placed his lips there, heard her sigh. Would he have known her if she had not been sent to him? A thought that pulled him back from the edge of passion.

"Why did you come to England?" He knew the answer before she spoke, but required the confirmation of it.

She smiled then, the warmth in her eyes so deep and full that he felt himself surrounded by it. "To find you."

He should not have been at Langlinais. He should have been at war. Instead, he had been suffused with a disgust so pervasive that he had acted in a way not himself. He had left the battlefield and returned home. In time to meet this woman and rescue her. A chain of coincidences. Except of course, they were not. The drawings proved that.

He kissed her then, welcomed her into his heart with a feeling not unlike humility. And gratitude.

As it was with them, the kiss turned heated.

He should have stayed her hand when she unlaced her dress, carried her into the cottage and protected her from the rain. Garment by garment she removed her clothes even as he argued with himself. She should be veiled from the rain. She should be laced up, draped and tucked and protected from the elements.

Instead, he laid her down in the clearing. He unlaced his shirt, his fingers fevered.

She watched him, her eyes warm and welcoming. The fascination of her gaze made his breath tight and heated his blood. There was no semblance of smile on her face now, only a solemn study as each part of his body was bared as if she were to be judged on her recall.

She glanced up at his face. Her cheeks were pink, her lips open just the slightest bit. There was more to her than curves shadowed by a dismal day. More than arms and legs and secret places. His hand stretched out, and he noted with amusement that it trembled. As well it might, given this moment and this woman.

He was as hard as he had ever been, but as she watched him, he felt himself swell even further. He had the sudden mental image of a pikeman in harness.

He laughed at himself even as he lowered himself over her.

He kissed her, spiraling into the sensation of it. His breath was caught. He needed to breathe, but instead of air there was Anne.

He'd suspected that there was another dimension to love. Another depth. His instinct proved correct, after all. And so did hers. There was a strange rightness to their loving in the rain. It was elemental and almost pagan. Life at its core and its simplest.

He sluiced the rain off her breast, mouthed a droplet trembling upon her nipple, felt himself speared by a sense of tenderness so sharp it was almost pain. Was that love? If it was, he would bandage up his wounds daily and count himself a fortunate man.

The rain found an opening in the bower of leaves and anointed both of them with shuddering drops.

She gripped his shoulders with her nails. Even in this she demanded. Their kiss was transformed by his smile, by her soft laughter as she opened her eyes.

Joy filled him, an odd complement to passion. But he discovered in those moments that it was a better emotion than lust, as gold is more valuable than silver.

She stroked his chest, her fingers threading through the light furring of hair there. Measured his shoulders with hands that made his skin shiver. She raised herself up and kissed his shoulder with soft, warm lips, tasted his flesh with the tip of her tongue.

Her fingers slid gently over the bandage on his arm. "Does it still pain you, Stephen?"

He wanted to tell her that his only discomfort was some distance removed from his arm, but he did not. Instead, he shook his head, then contented himself with his explorations of her. The curve of her underarm led to the plump swell of her breast. Her ankles were fine-boned and sensitive to his touch. The hair between her legs was as fine as down and damp.

One hand lifted her breast to his mouth. He suckled her nipple with a gentle then a more insistent tug.

"I like that," she murmured.

He spoke against the curve of her breast. "So do I."

The rain filtered through the leaves, bathed them in a warm shower. He felt it on his back as he leaned over her, smiled at the thought that they both might drown of love as he entered her, each slow and slipping moment accompanied by her slight gasp.

He entered her slowly, the feeling exquisite in its execution. There was a sense of fullness, but it was aided by the melting warmth inside of her.

One hand held her hips still, the other played with the tendrils of hair at her temple. His mouth settled over hers, his kiss soft and coaxing.

She was him and he was her and she could not tell where one began. Or ended. "More," he murmured, his lips on her throat. Soft, biting kisses traced from her neck to her shoulder.

He eased forward again, moved her legs aside with one hand, rose over her.

"Look at me, Anne." It was a gentle command issued in a harsh voice. "Look at me," he said again when her eyes fluttered shut. "Please."

She blinked them open. His face was shadowed, his smile tender.

The words were accompanied by a slow easing into her. Further than he'd ever been. Harder and yet more gentle. He pushed her knees back, rocked over her. Teasing movements that made her grip his shoulders hard, tear at his flesh. She bit her own lips in the need that tore through her.

He bent and sucked her nipple, his teeth grazing the delicate flesh.

Her ears rang with odd sounds, a rushing noise, or one of deep-throated bells. The sun was inside of her, heat and melting warmth. She felt light and heavy at the same time. Her limbs floated, her hands oddly flailing, her toes curled and flexed.

He kissed her, then rested his open mouth on hers, exchanging breaths. The heat in her body burned higher. She was nothing but sensation. A pulsing, throbbing feeling, an ache that was linked to his movements, to the words he spoke. A cadence of love spoken in a gentle voice.

Now, now, now, now, now. A sound, a movement, a beat.

He smothered her keening cry with a deep kiss.

Anne sat in the curve of his arms, leaning against his chest. He leaned his head against the trunk of a venerable tree, smiling softly. His eyes were closed, evidently too great a temptation for her. She leaned over and dusted a kiss on each eyelid.

His smile grew broader.

"Your feet are very large," she said, as she settled back into position. "But so are mine." He wiggled his toes, and she giggled. It was the first time she'd ever done so, and he was delighted by the sound.

Her touch on his big toe made him squinch it up, curl his foot.

"Are you ticklish?"

He yelped as she dragged one nail across his

arch. He opened his eyes and pulled his foot away, protection against her tickling touch.

Stephen then reached out and trailed fingers along her jaw. He'd thought her lovely but had never considered how beautiful she was, with her eyes shining defiantly and a pink color to her cheeks. Her chin ended in a soft square, as if shielding her stubbornness in beauty.

She sat beside him, tucked and laced, while he had yet to finish dressing. The truth of the matter was that he was so pleasantly weary at the moment that the effort was beyond him.

He closed his eyes again, drifting into a soporific state of relaxation.

"I knew I would love you," she said softly. "But I did not expect to like you so very much."

He opened one eye.

"Why should you not like me?"

"You're occasionally very fierce," she said, smiling at him.

"You've never appeared to be restrained by my ferocity," he said carefully.

"I was being brave," she said. "It's a Sinclair trait. We're exceptionally courageous."

"And unpretentious," he added before shutting his eyes again.

She laughed. "My father has enough pride to fill all of England."

"You might have mentioned that Dunniwerth was so large." He opened his eyes. "Or that he was an earl."

"Did you think me a poor laird's daughter?"

"It might be better that you are an heiress. I've

just purchased land from your father. I think he tried to beggar me."

Her smile grew brighter, and her eyes appeared to sparkle at him.

"You have?"

"For a king's ransom. It is, he assures me, a perfect place to build a fortress."

"My father thinks Dunniwerth is beautiful. I would not let him overly influence you," she said, smiling.

She settled against him.

"Not once did I think you were interested in my fortune," he said.

"It was not chief among my interests," she admitted.

"My mind, perhaps? My ability to translate Latin?"

"Your ability with a sword," she said demurely, but with such a wicked gleam in her eyes that he fell back against the tree laughing.

"I love the way you laugh," she said.

"I've not had much chance to do a lot of it," he confessed. "After my father died, I spent too much time in London, trying to maintain my inheritance."

"Did you?"

He smiled. "I did. Only to find myself nearly taxed to the death for it."

"What will we do with this land of yours?"

"Build our home," he said. "Something to last as long as Langlinais."

"Something even more beautiful," she said.

The words spun a web around them, made the moment perfect in its simplicity.

He brushed her smile away with the edge of a forefinger, bent to kiss her again.

"*Ego te amo*," he said softly. "I love you." He doubted she heard him. Because at the exact moment, Anne Sinclair of Dunniwerth was saying the same words back to him. A coincidence of speech. An accident of timing.

Or perhaps the hand of fate again, opening their hearts.

Epilogue

S *tephen.*
 A call. A cry so loud that it stopped him in midstride.

Stephen scrambled out of the earthworks. It was the beginning of the foundations for their grand castle, Sperare. Even now the name was being transformed into something unintelligible by those who spoke only Gaelic.

The castle would take years to complete, but in his mind he saw it soar to the sky. Only he and Anne knew that it would closely resemble Langlinais. Nor would any casual visitor realize that there was a special strong room, one that contained a treasure of history if nothing else. Juliana's chronicles would rest there, held in trust for generations.

Douglas called out a greeting as Stephen stood and looked toward the island. The boy had been returned to Dunniwerth six months ago. A peddler had taken pity on Douglas and brought him home, but the journey had been delayed by the necessity of avoiding English troops. Now he spent his time in the foundations, doing errands and carrying dirt, as they all did.

While it was true Stephen's father-in-law never lost an opportunity to comment on the lack of fortification of their new home, they had become wary friends. But there was one person who would never come to Sperare. Ian Sinclair did not want to witness any of their new lives here.

Stephen.

They made their home on the island while Sperare was being built. Today Anne had remained behind in order to tidy up the graves in the clearing. The weeds were high and nearly obscured the stones. He'd made a promise to himself to investigate the small, round building when he had time. But other occupations, that of being a husband and a builder, had taken precedence.

Stephen.

He raced down to the shore and into the boat tied there. His land was directly opposite the lake from Dunniwerth and equally distant from the island.

He said a prayer that Anne had not hurt herself, that one of the stones had not toppled onto her. Had an intruder slipped past his own defenses or that of Dunniwerth's and come to the island? Or had Anne burned herself again trying to bake bread? A hundred such fervent questions flew through his mind. He rowed to the island faster than he'd ever made the journey.

He could not dismiss the feeling or think that it was only that he had not seen her all day and she was in his thoughts. He felt her in his mind and knew that she called to him.

He didn't bother tying the boat, only stepped from it and raced to the clearing. Anne stood still in the middle of it. When she saw him, she smiled.

She looked neither injured nor in pain.

Seconds later, he was in front of her, his hands on her waist, then her shoulders. He touched her everywhere, all the while asking questions that she could not answer for the swiftness of them.

She laughed. "I am fine, Stephen," she said. "I wondered if you'd hear me."

"Was this a test, Anne?" He was to be excused, perhaps, for the fact that the question was shouted. He was more than furious. She might have needed him, and a lake had separated them. It had taken too many minutes to reach her. Moments in which he'd felt only a sick dread.

Her soft smile did little to diffuse his anger.

"No, Stephen." She placed her hand on his arm, stood on tiptoe to place a calming kiss on his cheek. "No, my darling Stephen. But only the strangest and most wonderful thing."

She stood back, gripped his hand, and pulled him with her. They entered the ruin of the circular building. There was no roof on the building, and as at Langlinais, the timbers that had once supported it had long ago rotted and fallen to the floor.

Overgrown with weeds and saplings, the building nevertheless maintained an aura of almost holy beauty, especially where the shadows merged to mimic archways, and a tall tree, fully leafed, appeared almost like a roof. Grass sprouted in the mortar between the stones. Flowers grew against the bricks, and vines used the altar as support.

The silence was complete, as if nature wordlessly communed with God in a place mortals had deserted.

"Why did you bring me here, Anne?"

"Even before Hannah lived here," she said, "there were rumors that the island had been a forbidden place. I asked Gordon once why it was so." She put her arm through his. There was a look of excitement on her face. "He said that it was because of the brothers who had lived here."

She smiled at him.

"I'll tell you the story the way Gordon told it to me. Once there was a brave Sinclair," she began, "but then they were all brave. This one fought with Robert the Bruce, and a more tireless fighter was never seen." He wondered if she knew that her voice had settled into a cadence, a soft, enthralling burr. "After the land was settled, he came home to Dunniwerth with his new bride, a sweet lass by the name of Honora. She was a cousin to the great king himself, but there was love between them, all the same.

"One day, the lass took ill, and despite all the healers and the wives of the clan, it looked as if she might die of her fever. The Sinclair was beside himself with grief. He prayed that his young wife might be saved and promised God any gift if He would make it true. That night a man came to the door of Dunniwerth. He told the Sinclair that he could cure his dying wife. The Sinclair watched carefully as the man tended his sweet bride. She was not only cured, but out of her bed a week later."

She began to rub his arm with her hand. She did that often, seek a way to touch him, as if she could not believe he was real. The sunlight filtered through the trees and sought her out, giving her a radiance that was oddly fitting. He wondered if she knew how precious she was to him.

Or how effortlessly she could coax him from anger.

"The man had many brothers, and they were seeking a place where they might live in peace. The Sinclair, mindful of his promise, gave him the island in reward and sent him the stone in order to build a chapel. They never married but lived here in safety until the last of them died in his old age." She glanced up at him. "I thought it a sad story, but I never told Gordon so."

He agreed, still not understanding why she'd called to him. He looked about him. Stone carvings such as these took years, a labor of love and obvious talent. There were four stone pillars in the deserted structure, each of them carved with trailing vines that then led to an inside wall. In each corner was a detailed carving of the face of a young man, his eyes closed as if in reverential prayer.

He turned, and Anne was smiling at him. Her fingers reached out to trace a series of lines cut into the stone. Inset into the walls at spaced intervals were deep cuts, each carving the outline of a sword. Behind the sword was a square, and intersecting the middle of the sword a crossbar, so that it appeared both a sword and cross.

"Stephen, do you remember Juliana's glyphs?"

He nodded.

"I thought I knew the man in one of them." She shook her head. "It's why I drew him over and over. But it wasn't the man I knew, but his shield.

I recognized it. Look." She continued to trace the line of the carvings with her fingers. "They're the same," she said.

"The cross of the Knights Templar," he said softly, recognizing it.

He turned and followed the line of ivy. It stretched along the top of the wall until it ended at the altar. Chiseled into each end of the long stone structure were two figures, each of a winged man bearing an elaborately carved chest on his back.

Anne followed him, her voice a whisper. "The brothers were knights, weren't they?"

"It would fit into your story. It was rumored that Scotland was the one country where they could find refuge."

"And the island would be a perfect hiding place for them," she whispered.

He came to the altar, where the ivy trailed to circle another cross. This one was carved from a square block set into the body of the altar, the raised design of it deeper than the other emblems. But that was not the only difference. There were groove marks outside the cross, equally spaced around it. Like sunbeams might appear. Not unlike the glyph Juliana had drawn.

"Anne, have you ever noticed this cross?" He knelt before it, both hands outstretched to trace the design.

She knelt beside him.

"Is there something special about this one?"

"Look how deeply it's cut." He pressed against the corners of the stone.

She watched him intently.

"Do you think it's a hiding place?"

Just then the stone moved reluctantly below his hand. A plume of dust escaped as Stephen pressed harder on the right corner. The stone turned slowly, grating against its base. A small peg worked as a fulcrum, revealing a hollow space behind the carved stone.

They each looked at the other, the moment silenced by both anticipation and a trickle of fear.

Stephen reached inside. His fingers encountered a gauzy material that he hoped fervently was not the fleshy relic of some obscure saint. As he pulled it from its hiding place, it disintegrated in his hands. Cloth, a tunic, bearing the distinctive red cross of the officers of the Templars. But that was not the only object in the small cavern. He bent and looked inside, his breath halted by what he saw.

He stretched both hands inside and slowly pulled out the coffer. In carving it was the equal of the one that shielded Juliana's codex. But it began to crumble in his hands.

Anne traced her fingers over the rotted wood, their gaze meeting as their hands did.

He raised the lid slowly, realizing that he was not startled by the contents. He heard Anne gasp as he lifted it from the chest. The Langlinais grail. Sebastian's grand ruse. The knights had evidently never learned of the deception, had venerated it as a treasure, carried it to this safe place, where it had lain undiscovered for three hundred years.

To be found by a man of Langlinais.

The coincidence of it was staggering. He saw the same thought in Anne's eyes.

Her hands were trembling as she reached out and

took the grail. He watched her as she studied it, turned it to find the light. It sparkled like a jewel, the damp air that had been so damaging to the cloth and to the wooden coffer had no effect on gold. Or on the small wooden cup that rested inside the reliquary.

Men had been willing to kill for such a relic. They had counted it among their most precious of possessions and built a structure to house it. An act that might well have been viewed by some as steeped in piety.

He stood and pulled Anne up with him. It had not been the structure of Langlinais or Harrington Court that had been important to him, but what the buildings had sheltered. The sounds of laughter, the expressions of life. The emotions of all the generations that had gone before.

He'd not felt the sharp grief over the loss of his heritage that he'd anticipated. A connection to Langlinais was there in Anne's drawings, in her visions, the words of Juliana's chronicle. And now, strangely, in this grail.

Anne smiled up at him, her eyes luminous. Not with tears but with joy. Another bridge between them. That they could love so deeply and so well.

He had the sudden thought that they'd missed it all along. It didn't matter what the treasure of the Cathars had been. Myth, rumor, or magic. It wasn't a grail or a codex. The true treasure existed in two people finding each other in a world not disposed to love. That was the miracle of Langlinais. And he had brought it here with him. A greater legacy than brick or stone.

He placed his hands on her waist and lifted her

above him. He was so filled with happiness at this moment that he wanted the world to know it. Her laughter was full and rich, coaxing forth his own. His hands at her waist were her only support as they twirled in a circle, her arms thrown out, the cloud of her hair shining in the sun. An angel flying in the air.

A dream he'd had once. A foretelling of the future? Or only a promise, to be granted to him in the fullness of time?

The echo of their laughter carried over the lake, borne by the gentle breeze.

Afterword

The *Santa Helena* shipwreck is modeled after an actual occurrence. In this case, a seventeenth-century adventurer plucked great piles of silver from the coral reef where the ship foundered.

The statue of Juliana and Sebastian is fashioned after an effigy considered one of the most romantic in Europe, the Greene Monument at Lowick.

There is a legend that the Knights Templar, so persecuted in the fourteenth century, found sanctuary in Scotland with the Sinclairs. Some interesting archeological evidence exists that leads one to wonder if they really did make their home on a tiny island in a lake bordering Sinclair land.

Dear Reader,

What a wonderful group of books are coming your way next month! First, fans of Sabrina Jeffries are going to be thrilled that *The Dangerous Lord*, her latest Regency-set, full-length historical romance, will be in bookstores the first week of March. Sabrina's known for sexy, sweeping love stories. Her heroes are unforgettable, and her heroines are ripe for love. You won't want to miss this exciting love story from one of historical romance's rising stars.

Rachel Gibson has tongues a-waggin'! She is quickly becoming known as one of the authors to watch in the new millennium, and with *It Must Be Love*, Rachel has once again proven she gets better and better with each book. Here, a ruggedly handsome undercover cop must prove to be his latest suspect's boyfriend—but when he begins to wish that this young woman really *was* his very own, complications ensue . . . and romance is in the air.

Suzanne Enoch's spritely dialogue and delicious romantic tension have captured her many fans and *Reforming a Rake*, the first in her "With This Ring" series, is sure to please anyone looking for a wonderful Regency-set romance.

And lovers of westerns will get all the adventure they crave with Kit Dee's powerfully emotional *Brit's Lady*.

Happy Reading!

Lucia Macro

Lucia Macro
Senior Editor

Avon Romantic Treasures

*Unforgettable, enthralling love stories,
sparkling with passion and adventure
from Romance's bestselling authors*